# E.T. GUNNARSSON

# Abandon Us

*An Apocalyptic Survival Thriller*

BRAGI PRESS

First published by Bragi Press 2022

Second edition

ISBN: 978-1-7363773-6-9

Editing by Susan Malone
Cover art by Zealous"

This book was professionally typeset on Reedsy.
Find out more at reedsy.com

*For my father and mother*

*- and -*

*For the first-edition readers*

*"I fixed it, lol"*

# Acknowledgement

\* \* \*

Firstly, I'd like to thank my mother and father. *Forgive Us*, *Abandon Us*, and the *Odemark* series wouldn't exist without their love and support. They've been there from the first page to the final draft. All the effort behind every page is dedicated to them.

Secondly, I am super grateful to my editor, Susan Malone, who helped turn the disaster of early drafts into a comprehensible telling of a darker world and helped me improve the book for the second edition.

Thirdly, my sincere thanks go out to my beta readers Craig Bowles, Scott Holland, and Robert Ginther. This was the first time I worked with beta readers, and the experience was great. Reading and commenting on a manuscript is difficult; I genuinely appreciate your work.

Fourthly, I'd like to extend my gratitude to Craig Bowles, who delivered an excellent reading of *Forgive Us* and *Abandon Us*.

Finally, I'd like to thank Zealous" who created the cover art after winning a cover competition at https://99designs.com/.

# Prologue

* * *

*Men will never weep for a dying world.*

*Grief is the child of consciousness when the self comes to terms with the truth. It is born from the moment when it's too late. When grief dies, its corpse becomes a memory, and regret manifests as maggots to feed on it. These children of decay stand as reminders that something could've been done.*

*Even now, men do nothing, allowing their machines and greed to defile their only Eden. Nothing is done as the skies darken, and the air strangles all life. Could they be forgiven? Men kill when hungry, and if the parasite called "greed" is never full, how could they be judged?*

# I

# Part One

*"By the rivers of Babylon,*
*there we sat down,*
*yea, we wept,*
*when we remembered Zion." –Psalm 137:1*

# 1

# Old World

*12:07 PM, September 8, 2070*

\* \* \*

Robert swung the trash bag through the store owner's gas mask, spilling garbage everywhere as it tore. With a kick, the man fell and allowed Robert to sprint after his friend William. He caught up to him by a dumpster in an alley two blocks away. From there, they bolted over piles of trash into a street and another alleyway.

Heart throbbing, Robert's limbs felt like spaghetti, and his chest tightened as he hyperventilated. He hadn't meant to hit the man. Casting glances behind them, Robert tried to calm his breathing and maintained a casual gait while they increased distance from the store.

"Shit," Robert growled.

William looked behind them, leading them onto a sidewalk. Robert gripped the hexagonal filters on both sides of his gas mask and readjusted it.

"Shut up. We got away," William said.

"I shouldn't have hit the guy," Robert replied.

William raised a brow, "You hit him?"

"Yeah, with a trash bag. And I kicked him."

William stopped and shook both hands at Robert in disbelief.

Robert raised his hands.

"I-I... okay, I panicked. He was chasing us!"

William shook his head, "Robert, oh my god, you're such an idiot," he scratched his head and groaned, "Well, now they'll be looking for two people who assaulted someone instead of two candy thieves. Too late now. Let's just keep walking. At least we have something to eat for once."

Robert tensely sighed and rubbed the back of his neck. The pair snuck along the streets and alleys. They stepped over piling trash, passed homeless people lying on the ground in herds, and crossed roads peppered with self-driving cars.

Above in the heavy smog, hundreds of drones flew back and forth among buildings covered with neon signs. Some were for businesses or private engagements, though some were personal drones for entertainment, photography, or other hobbies. Drone sizes depended on usage, ranging from small package carriers to large cargo carriers. A few people were riding Aeroboards along the air routes, a sort of drone-like flying skateboard capable of supporting the weight of a human. They were easy to fly thanks to intelligent stabilizers and crash detection.

Robert glanced up. Typically, those with Aeroboards were wealthier people. They flew above the commoners, avoiding the worsening problems of modern life as if they were above the issues everyday people faced. Rich pricks.

"Where are we going?" Robert asked.

"To a homie's hood. We need to get away from all the cameras around here. His gang has destroyed most of the cameras in his area, so we'll be safer there. Plus, I have business over there today."

Robert tilted his head, "Business?"

"Yeah, one of the big players in the local scene wants to set up a deal. We always meet with new customers to ensure they aren't police before setting up drone deliveries."

"Oh, we're doing one of those deals," Robert grunted.

"Get over it. You're eighteen. I'm twenty-two. We need money, and we need to eat. It's not like there are any jobs around here. Have you found anything in the past six months?"

Robert shrugged and rolled his eyes, "Nothing."

"Exactly. Damn corporations are replacing everyone with robots."

Robert shook his head as his jaw tensed, "Screw the rich."

"Screw the rich," William repeated.

He spoke again after a few minutes, "Can't believe that the store owner caught you on the way out. Of course, it had to be on the day we have to do a drug deal."

"Ain't the first time we got caught or the first time we steal to eat. It'll be fine; that's how we screw the rich. We steal from them–greedy bastards."

They walked a few more blocks before William hastily pushed them into an alley. He gazed at the origin of a deep, droning sound mixed with sirens. Three police drones flew through the smog. They carried squads of officers above the city skyline, lights and sirens on. The pair watched them disappear before going back out onto the soot-stained sidewalk.

"Where do you think they're going?" Robert asked.

William shrugged and spoke in a high-pitched voice, "Probably responding to a call about an assault in the same direction we're leaving from."

Robert shook his head, "Right. Stupid question."

The visage of the tall buildings around them changed as they approached gang territory. The pollution-stained buildings were tarnished by graffiti and had bars on their windows. Drug-dazed homeless people stood outside in their shadows. Trash piled everywhere.

William removed his gas mask and began eating the candy they had stolen. He threw each wrapper on the ground, chewing noisily as he downed chocolates and gummies.

He waved a piece of chocolate at Robert, "Want some?"

Robert waved the chocolate away, "No thanks. I'll eat later when we're inside."

"Suit yourself."

"Put your mask on, man. It's not good to have it off out here."

William scoffed, "It's a few minutes with it off. I'll be fine."

"Whatever you say, bro."

They crossed an intersection where sensors registered their presence and stopped cars to let them cross. During the last few decades, manually driven vehicles had been replaced by AI-driven cars, resulting in almost zero traffic fatalities.

As the pair crossed, William glanced at them with a scowl, "Look at those rich pricks."

"Assholes. They think that they're so much better than us," Robert said.

"You said it. They'll eventually join us out here as shit continues falling apart."

Robert adjusted his gas mask again to stop the straps from rubbing his skin, "This new tattoo hurts."

"Ah, get over it. You've been whining about it all day."

"My mask is rubbing on it. Let me see yours. How's it not hurting?"

William turned slightly. Tattooed on his neck was a black serpent coiled in a complex, knotted fashion. The skin around it flushed red from irritation. Robert had the same tattoo, though his skin burned.

"It's hurting. I just don't whine about it. The more you whine, the more you think about it, the more it hurts."

William let out a prolonged, hacking cough while Robert examined the black snake. His whole body quaked as he threw his head forward and spat on the ground.

Robert put a hand on William's back, "You okay?"

William grunted and cleared his throat before spitting again, "I'm fine."

"Put your mask back on. Air's burning your throat."

William waved his hand, dismissing Robert's concern.

"I don't need a mask. I'm fine. I'm not done with my candy."

"Can't walk around so much without it on, bro. At least you don't have to wear it all the time as people in prison do."

"I wear my mask. I just don't like sleeping with it on. I'm breathing fine. I just choked on a bit of chocolate."

Robert shook his head.

William threw the last of his candy wrappers onto the ground.

They arrived at an alley among the never-ending maze of skyscrapers and crowded infrastructure. It separated a laundromat and a general drug store.

Unlike most, this alley stopped halfway between two high-rises. A building rose at the far end, facing the opposite street and presenting a brick wall to the pair.

Parked next to the sidewalk was a luxury car. Robert glanced at it as they passed, unsure of the car's brand.

A woman and two large men waited inside the alley. The woman was dressed in an expensive white dress with golden accents. A white mask with a golden logo covered her face. Wearing black suits and masks, the two men stood with their hands crossed. The dark tint of their visors made it impossible for Robert to read their faces. In stark contrast, Robert and William wore tattered pants and multi-colored, long-sleeved shirts that covered their upper bodies. Sewn into the clothes were small ribs with heating and cooling components. Their dirty and worn gas masks had been bought used. Their shoes barely held together with duct tape and string.

The woman looked at them and wrinkled her nose in contempt. Robert frowned as he saw the wealthy woman's reaction but kept quiet since William waved to her and put on a customer-friendly tone.

"Hey there, are you Mrs. Adamson?" William asked.

Robert glanced at William as he heard the phony tone.

"That is me. Are you two with Mr. Scarpello?" Mrs. Adamson asked.

"Yes, I'm one of his associates. My name is William, and this is my friend Robert. He's here as a witness for Mr. Scarpello."

Robert kept silent.

"Well, I trust Mr. Scarpello. Let's get this underway so I can leave this stinking rat hole."

William smiled and bowed, "As you wish, Mrs. Adamson."

William approached the woman, pulling out a small tablet from his pocket. The woman stretched out her forearm and rolled her sleeve back to reveal a blue, glowing line in her arm. It was an implant, one of the newer technologies replacing portable devices. The tablet read the implant and made a ping sound. It vibrated frantically for a moment before falling silent with a snap. William dropped the tablet and crushed it under his foot so that it couldn't be used as evidence by the police.

"Well. A pleasure doing business with you, Mrs. Adamson."

She followed her bodyguards to the luxury car parked on the street, "A pleasure. Have a wonderful day."

"You too!" William said.

He waited for the trio to drive off before walking out onto the sidewalk, "Rich bitch. Did you hear her tone?" William asked.

"Yeah. What did you do with that tablet thing?" Robert responded.

"It just connected her information to an underground bank account so she can transfer money to it."

Robert gestured behind them as they walked, "Was that really a drug deal? That's it?"

"Well, it's not just drugs. I connected her info to the guy I work for, and now she can buy anything from him. Guns, drugs, stuff like that. She pays, and my boss sends a drone to deliver the goods. Just had to meet her face to face to see if she was real and all that."

Robert tilted his head, "Won't the police catch on?"

"They try. Most drones that people use are unregistered. Each drone is monitored when delivering goods. If the police shoot it down, the pilot just presses a button and destroys all the information the drone has, including its destination and origin."

They walked down another block. William grabbed Robert and ripped him back toward the way they had come.

Robert grunted as he flew around, "What th–?"

"Shut up, shut up, just walk," William hissed quietly.

Robert regained his footing and followed William walking in the opposite direction.

"What's wrong?" Robert whispered.

"Some cops down that way. Just act normal."

Robert glanced behind them. A trio of police officers followed the pair. All three wore gray armored uniforms with blue lights and gas mask helmets whose black visors obscured their features. Each cop wore a belt lined with tools such as tesla batons and guns. They trailed Robert and William at a stark, determined pace, heads locked in the pair's direction.

"They're right on us, bro," Robert whispered.

William walked faster and turned down another street. Robert followed. A pair of officers met them at an intersection.

One raised his hand to stop them, "Hey! You two!"

Robert and William stopped. The other three police officers met up with them and surrounded the pair together with the other two officers. Robert's stomach dropped. His heart beat hard as his breathing halted.

"Is there a problem, officers?" William asked.

"IDs?" one demanded.

"Why are we being stopped, sir?" William insisted.

"We're looking for two suspects whose descriptions match you two. Show us your IDs."

"Oh, one second. It's in my pocket," William said.

William reached into his pocket and gently pushed Robert with his other hand. The push confused Robert as he watched William pull out his ID. One of the officers took the ID and scanned it while the other cops seemed to relax a bit.

The cop read it, "Will—"

William threw a fist through the mask of the officer checking his ID. The man fell to the ground, glass raining from his visor while blood dropped from William's hand. William kicked another officer's leg and turned to run.

"Robert! Run!"

Two of the officers tackled William before he could run. Robert took off. His legs felt weak, and his heart thundered painfully. He went down streets and alleys to escape, jumped over trash piles, and weaved through crowds of pedestrians.

He felt safe after a few blocks and slowed to catch his breath. Homeless people stared at him as he regained his wind.

"There he is!" a police officer shouted in the distance.

Robert gasped. A squad of four officers came out from an alley behind him, pointed at Robert, and chased after him. Robert threw himself over a garbage pile and ran across the road, narrowly missing a self-driving car.

He cut into an alley and disappeared into a maze-like network among the buildings. Robert's fingers clawed off his multi-colored shirt, which he threw into a dumpster before sprinting topless into another alley.

Robert glanced behind him again. The cops were finally out of sight.

"Oh my god. I'm screwed," he whispered.

There was nowhere he could go. If he kept running, the police officers would eventually find him, or a camera would pick him up.

"He went this way!" an officer shouted in the distance.

Robert hyperventilated and ran around the alley as he heard the cops approach. He glanced out into the street before locking onto a dumpster, nearing it like a terrified raccoon, and opening it. Climbing in, he fell into a deep, stinking pile of filth. Raw, rotten food mixed with putrid trash bags grazed his already-irritated skin. The stench of decaying fish enveloped him like a blanket.

Robert let out a shuddering breath as he immersed his body in the filth, covering himself as much as possible. Dozens of boots stomping on concrete passed, each fading. Every sound halted his breath as he tried to hide deeper in the trash. The polluted debris burned his skin, though he dared not move.

Time slowed. Robert lay in the filth for what he thought was an hour and waited until there were no sounds outside. Like a zombie, he rose from the dumpster and ran.

He flicked off the muck and sprinted to another alley full of homeless people.

"Hey! Can I sit with you guys?" he asked.

A woman scowled at him, "Why you bothering us about it? Just sit and shut up."

Robert joined them and faced away from the street.

He had gotten away, though he was alone. Robert had no family or friends to run to, no place to get shelter, and no place to truly hide. But for now, he was free.

Sitting quietly among the dirt-covered derelicts, he contemplated what now?

# 2

# Starving Faithless

*3:27 PM, June 16, 2078*

\* \* \*

Eight years had passed since William's arrest.

Much had changed for Robert since the day he had assaulted that store owner, an event that haunted him. To avoid more run-ins with the law, he had become honest. Instead of running with gangs and thugs, he scraped together money doing odd legal jobs, got an education, and became a service technician. Still, life grew worse even with a reliable job. The economy had tanked in the late 2070s. Robert was one of the few with a job, working for one of the last companies that still hired people.

It was an average day at work. Robert exited the elevator and strolled into the company lobby, mulling over the meeting he had just left. He took in the fresh inside air before putting on his gas mask tightly.

In recent years, the pollution had grown worse. Robert's body was damaged by pollution irritation. Scar tissue covered his chest, neck, and forearms. Luckily, he didn't have a chronic cough as many others had. Gas masks were now a must outside.

A TV played across the lobby. Unlike the TVs of the past, modern ones were thumb-sized projectors. The one in the vestibule was hidden in the ceiling and cast out a display on the wall, presenting picture-perfect renderings. As always, the company TV played the news channel.

*"Breaking news from Texas today. The first American Ark ships left Earth this morning, breaking records as the largest passenger ships ever sent to space. These ships are part of the international Raptured Plan proposed by the United Nations, each ship sending colonists to search for planets with the potential to sustain human life. Other Ark ships from across the world are scheduled to leave Earth within the next twenty-four hours, with Ark stations planned to launch next week. The Ark stations will orbit Earth and monitor atmospheric conditions for space agencies across the planet. We spoke to one of the volunteers scheduled to leave on one of the Ark ships."*

The broadcast switched from a newscaster to a woman with an Ark ship in the distant background.

*"It's amazing. Billions of people have volunteered to leave Earth to do this, and I was among the few selected. I won't live to see my destination, but it's amazing how far technology has come. My ship, the Terminus, will take almost 300 lifetimes to reach its destination. Only a decade ago, it would've taken 900. It's insane. How do I feel about the whole thing? Nervous. I'm leaving everything behind and sacrificing myself to help humanity find a new home. I can't think of a greater honor."*

The broadcast switched back to the newscaster.

*"In related news, protests are happening across the globe against the flight of the Ark ships. Many say that the selection systems were rigged to select wealthier volunteers rather than randomly selecting from the general population. UN officials have denied these claims and are cooperating in investigations examining the selection systems used across the globe."*

Robert didn't care much for the Ark ships. Escaping Earth seemed pointless. To him, the ships were flying coffins with no real destination since there were no known planets like Earth. Only an insignificant portion of the population could go into space, leaving the other fifteen billion behind on Earth.

* * *

Robert entered an airlock room that acted as the entrance to the building. With the press of a button, an alarm sounded as the door behind him sealed shut, and the door ahead opened. A gust of wind blew a flood of polluted air into the airlock, the force causing Robert to shift.

The visual difference between contaminated and clean air was barely noticeable. Robert could only describe it as a blurry film that distorted the invisible. He stepped outside, looking up past the towering high-rise buildings. It was as if a cosmic artist had painted the sky in charcoal. A black layer covered it with streaks of gray cutting across were shards of sunlight broke through.

It was cold. Very cold. The absence of sunlight left the world dreary. Robert couldn't see far before a permanent layer of smog obscured anything distant. Even the buildings seemed dismal. Many were titans of steel, concrete, and glass stained with dark soot. The wind weaved throughout the blackened giants. Gusts cut harshly against Robert's body and picked up dirt, sand, and litter in their chilling path. Dressed from head to toe, Robert was prepared for the cold and polluted air. He had gloves, a long-sleeved shirt, a worn jacket, and pants all sealed around their edges. Circuits and wires filled his clothes, heating or cooling his body as needed. He had his clothes set to warm to keep the cold at bay.

Robert crossed to the employees' parking section and walked toward one of the few vehicles the company could still afford. He had number four, a gray van with company logos decorating both sides. The logo looked like a utility man riding a lightning bolt. Like most people, Robert couldn't afford a car or self-driving taxis. Most vehicles on the road belonged to corporations or the few wealthy that were left. People like Robert had to walk. He was lucky that his job provided him with a van for work. Even so, Robert hated this. They treated him like expendable trash.

Robert opened the van door using an implant on his finger. He sat and put on the seat belt. Like all road-legal vehicles, the van was self-driving with no steering wheel and reliant on an AI to drive. The front was like a couch with space for Robert and a passenger. His tools and supplies were stored behind a wall in the rear.

The van came to life when Robert touched the console with his finger.

*"Hello, Robert Ashton,"* a female voice said.

"Hello, Hypatia," he replied.

*"How may I help you today?"*

"Drive me to my first appointment."

*"Directing to Aunty Shauny's Pancake Stop on 4732 East Oak Road."*

Hypatia's engine, powered by the new-age energy known as Ignium, awoke with a quiet warble. The AI reversed and directed the van onto the roadway. It connected with the road network and seamlessly joined the traffic. Only a faint warbling from the Ignium engine was heard through the car's frame and pounds of sound-dampening material. The warbling increased and decreased as the motor spun, making just enough sound outside to alert pedestrians of the vehicle's presence. Though the van could be entirely silent, it was illegal for Ignium and electric vehicles to be completely noiseless since pedestrians couldn't hear them. By this time, electric cars were typically over thirty years old. They were considered classic and rare—generally, only older people who grew up with electric vehicles owned and cared for them. Akin to the classic-car owners of the twentieth century, communities existed online and in the real world where people gathered and talked about old cars.

At twenty-six, Robert had only seen four or five gas-powered cars in his whole life. Since gas went out of use decades ago, it had to be specially ordered. Only the wealthy and car collectors kept and took care of combustion cars. Gasoline and diesel were rare and made by only a few specialists worldwide. It was still legal to drive combustion cars even though only a limited few were self-driving, and many lacked the technology to sync with the driving network.

Robert reviewed his messages while the van seamlessly navigated through traffic. He had neural-link implants instead of a watch or phone. A phone implant composed of a thin wire lined his forearm, while a smaller implant in his left index finger allowed him to interact with the larger implant. Both were tiny and barely visible, hiding under obscure bumps in his skin. His finger implant provided secure access to everything. It allowed him to open the company car, access his bank account, or enter his apartment. The phone implant gave Robert a neural connection to the Cloud. His mind responded to messages that conveyed information and images rather than text and audio.

Most messages were work-related. His implant translated neural signals, discerned what was essential or unwanted, and then built responses. He sent out replies, telling customers he was on the way, responding to his boss, and agreeing to a meeting later in the day.

Hypatia merged onto the highway cutting across the city, accelerating to 120 miles per hour. Up here, thousands of cars traveled in perfect harmony. Robert gazed at the city through the van's smog-stained windows. The highway stood high above the ground, yet it was dwarfed by the hundreds of skyscrapers lining its flanks. Drones flew among the concrete titans, hundreds going around the city in programmed flight paths. They were the birds of this polluted world. Occasionally, a person on an Aeroboard would fly among the drones, hovering above the trash-ridden streets below.

Robert's arm vibrated while a ringtone played in his head. He accepted the call with a thought after the implant told him who and where the call was from.

"Hi, Zilv!" he answered with a smile.

"Hey, baby!"

Robert crossed his arms.

"What's up?"

"I just wanted to check in on you! What's going on?"

"I'm at work right now. I have to repair a delivery drone on the other side of town. Then I have a few more jobs. I'll be home later tonight... what do you want for dinner?"

"Mmm! I don't know, darling. Whatever you want. Weren't you talking about sushi last night?"

"Can't afford it, you know that. I can pick something up at the store. We still have room on our ration cards for this week."

"That works. Do you want to watch a movie tonight?"

Robert hummed, "Maybe we can watch something. Do you want me to get snacks?"

"We got popcorn at home, darling. Don't waste our rations. Just get dinner."

"All right, love you."

"Love you too, darling! Be safe!"

"Will do. Bye, cutey."

"Bye, love you!"

Flecks of soot hit the windshield as the van approached its destination. This side of the city was the poorest, with the decrepit buildings standing lower. Pollution had stained the structures, and bars covered each window. The streets here were crammed. The unwanted and destitute homeless sat outside, begging for food and gas mask filters to stay alive. Rows of people lay between buildings and along the sidewalk, alone and shivering from sickness and cold. Waste piles rose high everywhere, like snow piles, while the wind blew around trash. A soot-like residue blanketed everything. It stained skyscrapers and could be rubbed off the ground with a finger, blackening the skin.

As Hypatia exited the highway and slowed, nervous butterflies fluttered in Robert's stomach. People on the roadside shot hostile looks at the car. Robert understood. He used to be one of them. With the population at a record fifteen billion, resource consumption was at its highest, and the world economy was struggling. In the United States, massive chunks of the population were unemployed and hungry. Like Robert, the employed struggled to maintain their jobs while barely scraping by. Employment had a high value, and those who had it were hated by those who didn't.

Hypatia entered an empty shopping mall. It was a large, cubic complex that stood as a lonely colossus separated by a parking lot. A closed-down grocery store made up most of the giant structure with lines of smaller buildings flanking it. A greenhouse factory once used to grow and refine food sat at the top, but it had been abandoned due to the store below going bankrupt. Only four active businesses were left: a laundromat, a restaurant, a clothing store, and a fast-food restaurant. Each was located at the base of the massive structure, while all the lots above were empty.

The van parked itself in the vacant lot in front of a restaurant called "Aunty Shauny's Pancake Stop." Graffiti and dark stains covered the rest of the complex, and the concrete walls were chipped from debris carried by harsh wind.

*"We have arrived,"* Hypatia stated.

"Thank you, Hypatia," Robert replied.

The warbling hum of the engine ceased as Robert put his hand on the console. He grabbed his toolbox from the van's rear and walked into the restaurant. The door sensed his implant and opened automatically, closing behind him once he was inside the airlock chamber. A second later, all the polluted air in the airlock chamber was sucked out and replaced with filtered air. Robert kept his mask on, too lazy to take it off. The restaurant's interior was plain, with a black and white tiled floor and drab, beige walls. Every table inside was bare except for condiment racks. A wall with a door and an opening separated the kitchen from the rest of the dining area.

Robert assumed that the business was family-owned. Pictures of the staff, the owners, and one or two awards lined the walls.

The restaurant guests glared at Robert.

This demonstrated an odd divide. On one side, people hated those who worked for large companies and chains. On the other side, family-owned restaurants like this one were respected and loved as providers for the community.

Robert ignored the customers and approached a waitress, "Hello, ma'am, may I speak to the owner? I'm from Nelson's Repairs."

The waitress looked at the logo on his work clothing and nodded, "Yes, sir. Come with me."

She led him through the kitchen. A chef ran back and forth inside, hastily prepping food as he worked with robotic kitchen assistants. Robert followed the waitress into a back storage room and a small office where a woman sat.

"Hey, Shauny? The repairman is here."

"Thank you, Sarah. I'll handle it from here," Shauny said.

Sarah turned and left.

"Hello, Miss Wilson. I'm Robert from Nelson's Repairs. You called about a broken delivery drone?"

"Oh! Just call me Shauny. You're early!"

"Yes, ma'am. We want your drone to be working again as soon as possible."

"Oh? You're sure you didn't stop by early so you could have time to eat some pancakes?" Shauny chuckled and smiled, "I'm just kidding. If you do want some pancakes, feel free to order."

Robert grinned.

She opened a drawer in her desk, pulled out a gas mask, and put it on, "Come with me. The drone's out back."

Robert stood aside as she led him through a small airlock and into a back alley. On the opposite side, a towering skyscraper with a windowless concrete wall made up the first two stories facing the passage. Each business had a dumpster in the back. Even so, trash piled everywhere. Behind the restaurant were five delivery-drone tubes surrounded by metal bars. Shauny unlocked one of the tubes with a finger implant.

"This one is about fifteen years old. It's been holding together pretty well, but one of its rotors isn't working."

Robert crossed his arms, "Any reason why?"

Shauny shrugged, "I think it's just wear-and-tear. We did call your company before because a customer damaged the drone, but that's been fixed."

"I'll see what I can do and see if there's any additional damage."

"All right, I'll be inside. Just come back in when you're done."

Robert nodded and watched her leave. He opened the tube and lifted out the drone, placing it on the ground to examine it. A patch from the previous repair job and a damaged rotor were the two problems he noticed. The rotor could still move but was loose and didn't do anything. He flipped the drone over and opened the bottom to access the inner circuitry. Robert knew the mess of small tubes, wires, and circuits like the back of his hand.

Like most things, Ignium powered the drone. Robert knew much about Ignium since it was a significant part of his job. It was invented around the late 40s and became widely used in the early 50s. Ignium was like an electrical plasma, based on research in electrical and nuclear power. Better than both, easier to manipulate, more efficient, and dirt cheap to create, Ignium opened up a new field of science dedicated to understanding this new energy and its physics.

Like electricity in old technology, Ignium flowed through the circuitry in the drone, powering everything. Robert noticed two issues. The first was the repair patch itself. Small holes covered the mended area, which caused liquid-like blue Ignium to seep through the insulation and shoot out blue sparks. The second issue came from poorly connected wires. Circuits and Ignium wires were always insulated since Ignium got hot and could cause a jolt of energy similar to a strong electrical shock.

Robert grabbed his gloves. Gloves for handling Ignium were clumsy, combining the design of rubber gloves and oven mitts to protect the user from the transfer of energy and heat. He removed the shoddy repair and replaced it with higher-quality metal. He ensured the metal was sealed correctly and hugged the damage so that nothing leaked. Next, he replaced the bad wiring. This involved cutting the wires, putting new ones back in, and soldering them with an Ignium-specific soldering tool. Once the circuits were fixed, he put the bottom panel back on. Finally, he took out the broken rotor and replaced it. After everything was back together, he turned the drone on and tested it. As expected, it rose up in the air perfectly before carefully returning to its storage pod.

Robert smiled. Tools clattered as he packed the toolbox, metal ringing filling the alley. Just as he closed the lid, footsteps replaced the metallic sounds.

Two men ran at him from across the alley. Robert grabbed a wrench and tried to run while the pair sprinted after him and kicked him. He absorbed both kicks and screamed, clumsily swinging the wrench at one of the attacker's masks. The heavy tool went through the man's visor. The other man punched Robert's jaw, knocking him to the ground.

"Fuck! My mask! Take his damn implant!" the first man shouted.

The second man drew a knife and hopped onto Robert. Robert grabbed the knife arm, pushed it away, and hammer-fisted the man in the face with his other hand. Both fell clumsily and kicked each other away. Robert quickly mustered himself onto his feet and engaged with the first man again. The other man came from behind with the knife. Robert threw the first man around, knocking him into the second man and deflecting the blade into his leg. He felt nothing as he blocked and absorbed hits until falling.

"Screw you! Employed bastard!" one man shouted.

"Beat his ass!" the second screamed.

They took turns kicking Robert, hitting his ribs, arms, and legs until they stopped abruptly. He looked up and saw a shape smack both men with a long instrument.

"Are you okay?"

It was the restaurant owner, Shauny.

"What happened?" Robert mumbled.

She put an arm under his armpit and helped him up.

"Those assholes attacked you."

"I think... I think I got stabbed," Robert said.

Blood soaked Robert's leg. It felt like warm water slowly running down his leg. Prickly pain appeared when the adrenaline from the fight dissipated. Robert felt like he was getting stabbed a thousand times by a needle.

Shauny gasped at the sight, "We need to get you to a hospital!"

Robert limped as Shauny led him inside.

"Just take me to my car. I can get to the hospital from there."

"Are you sure?"

"Yeah."

To the customers' horror, Shauny led Robert through the kitchen and the dining area. She took him out to his car and helped him in.

"Thank you, Shauny."

"No problem. Do you need someone with you?"

"No, just take in the toolbox from the back. Call my company to have someone retrieve it later."

"All right," she said, "be safe! Hold your leg and keep pressure on it!"

Robert fell against the van's side, opened the door with a pained grunt, and stumbled onto the seat. As he closed the door, Hypatia greeted him.

*"Hello, Robert Ashton."*

Robert didn't reply and hit the red triangle on the dashboard console. A few options popped up on the screen, each narrated by Hypatia.

*"The emergency mode button has been pressed. If this was unintentional, please press cance–"*

Robert pressed the hospital button.

*"Directing there now. Police have been notified of this vehicle's location."*

Hypatia sped out of the parking lot and merged into traffic seamlessly. In emergency mode, the van had priority in the traffic network. Cars parted as if responding to an ambulance, allowing the van to speed across the city.

Robert tried to control his breathing as each breath became shorter and felt more like a chore. Meanwhile, he clenched his leg. It was warm and sticky, blood drenching his pants and the car seat. He activated his implant to call Zilv. It vibrated with a gentle hum, a ringtone singing in his head.

"Hey, darling! What's up?"

"Zilv, I got stabbed. I'm on my way to the hospital," Robert said calmly.

"Oh, my God! Are you okay? What happened!"

"I'll be fine. Two guys attacked me while I was on the job. I'm beaten up pretty good, but it's nothing too bad."

"Nothing too bad? You got stabbed! Which hospital are you going to?"

"I don't know. I'll send you the location from the car."

"All right! I'll be there immediately."

"You don't have to drop every—"

"Ah! I do! Just send me the location, and I'll be on my way."

"All right. I love you, Zilv."

"I love you too!"

Robert hung up and swiped the digital screen on his forearm to send the location of the hospital to Zilv.

The van went into the emergency lane and pulled up to the entrance. The doors opened automatically to allow Robert out. Drenched in sweat and shaking, he stumbled out and fell. Robert willed himself onto his feet and forward. A doctor, two androids, and two police officers ran out to help him. He fell again and sprawled flat onto the ground. Robert heard the androids assess his condition, the doctor speaking to both while examining him. His vision blurred while the conversation around him faded into mumbles before everything became black.

* * *

Zilv helped Robert outside as they left the hospital. A robotic surgeon had sewn up the wound. Cellular accelerant cream layered the injury, speeding up the healing process so it would heal by the morning.

"How do you feel, baby?" Zilv asked.

Robert leaned on Zilv, "I feel okay. Happy you're here, though."

They hugged one another. Zilv was petite and skinny compared to Robert's tall stature. Unlike Robert, who had a tattoo inked into his neck, Zilv had LED implants in his left forearm that could take any shape or color he wanted. Today, he had purple butterflies wrapped around his forearm, each pulsing ]to the rhythm of his heartbeat. Robert's gaze met Zilv's. Zilv's eyes were purple, glowing from implants that brightened in reaction to his fiery affection.

"I love you, Robert."

"I love you too. Do you want to go get sushi?"

"I thought we couldn't afford it?"

"I'm willing to spend the money. I think we deserve it today. Plus, I might be getting a bonus soon. Hopefully, today didn't ruin that."

# 3

# Hungry Flock

*10:48 AM, June 23, 2078*

\* \* \*

It was a quiet morning in the apartment. Robert was still in his pajamas. He enjoyed the sealed space's filtered air while watching the news projected onto the wall.

*"Washington DC is now the third city to be placed under martial law after riots outside the White House continue for the second consecutive month. These riots are in response to the latest ration laws put into place by President Hudson."*

*"Meanwhile, the death toll from the latest Austin bombings has risen to 300 as first responders continue their search for survivors. The terrorist organization called the People's Militia has claimed responsibility for all three attacks. Their leader, Hans Renning, has stated that these attacks are in response to Governor Kelly ignoring their demands for the condemnation of automated labor.*

*"In other news, hospitals across the country have received an influx of patients with symptoms from a new, undiagnosed pathogen spreading throughout the east and west coasts. The Centers for Disease Control has begun working with these local hospitals to diagnose this pathogen and urges anyone with the following symptoms to seek immediate medical assistance."*

Robert shut off the projector with a swipe of his implant and looked back toward the kitchen.

"Hey Zilv, do we need to go shopping today?"

Zilv turned his head from the dishes and shrugged at Robert, "Yeah, I think so. I was thinking of going after lunch when the lines are shorter."

Robert frowned at the TV, "We can go now if you want. I've had enough of the news."

Zilv crossed his arms, "Are you sure? Is your leg good enough for that kind of walk?"

Robert patted his leg and wiggled it, "Yeah, it's been a week. It's pretty much closed now; the accelerant helped it a lot."

"All right, if you're sure. I'll go get ready."

Robert went to the apartment's front door as Zilv disappeared into the bedroom. Though theirs wasn't a large apartment, it was enough for them with one bedroom, one bath, a kitchen, and a living room. It also had filtered air. The pair stored their shoes, jackets, and masks by the door. Robert put his mask on before grabbing Zilv's mask and purse. Zilv came out after a few minutes, dressed in an old pair of pants and a shirt. Both pieces were older models of smart clothes, each equipped with technology to heat, cool, and dry. Like Robert's and everyone else's, Zilv's clothes protected his skin from irritating pollutants.

He took his purse and mask with a smile, kissing the side of Robert's mask as Robert ran his hand through Zilv's brown, curly hair.

Zilv put on his mask and grabbed some gloves, "Thank you, baby. Put on your gloves. You don't want your skin to get irritated."

Robert half smiled and shook his head, "I'll be fine. My hands are tough."

Zilv poked him sharply in the ribs and made Robert jump.

"Gah! Okay, okay!" he said as he put the gloves on.

"That's what I thought, cutey," Zilv said smugly.

"Meany," Robert remarked in a silly tone.

"Oh, I'm mean? I'm making sure you don't burn your hands!"

Robert opened the door. Zilv went out first. Robert closed the door behind them as they entered the apartment hall and proceeded to the elevator.

"You're still a meany."

Zilv made a baby frown beneath his mask, "Oh, big baby, do you need a band-aid for your feelings?"

"Yes."

Both cracked up while riding the elevator to the ground level. The pair went out into a small parking lot and onto a sidewalk, holding hands. Robert kept Zilv close as he surveyed their surroundings.

Their home sat in an urban hell. Among the claustrophobia of titanic structures, their apartment building was hulking and wide, fitting hundreds of people within its brutalist walls. Air filters were installed in every apartment window. On the street, industrial capitalism bombarded their senses. Neon and video signs tried to push unnecessary materialism onto viewers everywhere. Like everywhere else in the city, all the buildings crowded the roads they surrounded, hills of garbage piling up against them along the sidewalks.

The bitter, shearing wind kicked up trash everywhere. The wind caused the heavy blanket of pollution and dust looming over the city to form a moving wall of toxins that stung unprotected skin. Waves of smog clung to the streets and buildings, leaving black stains over graffiti-marked walls.

"I miss flowers," Robert said.

"That's random. Why are you thinking about that, baby?"

"I just think of it sometimes. Kinda saw the last flowers die when I was a kid, and now we live in this hell. I think my parents planned to take me to a flower zoo before they kicked me out."

"I'm still baffled that they kicked you out for some drugs and failing grades."

Robert frowned, "Well, they had me by mistake and treated me like shit for it. Probably thought I was a drain on them that they couldn't get rid of until I fucked up. At least William helped me."

"William got you into that stuff."

Robert shrugged, "He was there for me. Doesn't matter now, though."

"Yeah. I wish we had known each other when we were younger. I bet you were a cutey back then too. My mom had a flower shop when I was born."

Robert smiled thinly, "I remember you telling me that. I would've loved to see it."

Zilv looked at the ground and mumbled, "I miss her."

Robert pulled Zilv into a hug, "It's okay. Let's not talk about it, darling."

Zilv calmly exhaled and nodded. Robert had talked to Zilv about his parents occasionally, though they avoided talking about their families. Lung cancer had taken Zilv's mother, and depression had taken his father.

They passed unemployed and homeless people while following street after street. Many shivered in corners and alleys, trying to shelter themselves from the toxic air. Some thrashed, their blood full of drugs. Others were sick. They coughed and withered away in dysentery, languishing hopelessly with no options but to keep living. Since Robert and Zilv lived paycheck to paycheck, homelessness crept uncomfortably close.

Recently, the number of sick people on the streets had skyrocketed. Finding a dead body was so common that a government-funded company now used drones to remove bodies. Robert didn't know what they did with the bodies and didn't want to know.

They walked past a homeless man with a cracked gas mask holding up a cardboard sign that read, "The End Is Nigh!" He stared them down. Robert and Zilv avoided the man and turned around another corner, stepping aside as a horde of people rushed past them.

"Whoa, where are they going?" Zilv asked quietly.

"No idea," Robert said.

Sirens filled the streets as police drones raced overhead and disappeared into the distance.

Zilv and Robert walked down another street before arriving at a grocery store. What had been a parking lot full of vehicles a few decades ago was only occupied by the unemployed, trash piles, and a very long line of customers going into the store.

Robert looked at the line and groaned, "Ugh, this is gonna take forever."

Zilv gestured behind them, "Do you want to go back?"

"No, no. Let's just join the line and get our rations. Did you check your card?"

"Of course. I still have some ration slots."

"All right, good."

They stopped a few feet away from the next person in line. Everyone in the queue impatiently crossed their arms, tapped their feet, or leaned against a wall if they were near the store. People were everywhere around the store. Some were going about their daily lives on the street; some sat and waited hopelessly or dug through trash piles looking for a way to survive. The line crept forward. Another group of police drones soared overhead. After an hour, Robert and Zilv reached the front door, where a man in a company uniform greeted them.

"IDs, please," he said.

They both pulled back their sleeves and presented their forearms. The man met both of their forearms with his own to scan their implants. Each time it beeped, verifying their IDs. The man gestured them inside.

"Go on in."

They passed through an airlock before entering the building.

"What's on our cards today? Five items?" Robert asked.

"Yeah, five crates."

The store was massive, filled with rows and rows of shelves that reached all the way to the back of the store. During Robert's childhood, food was displayed for anyone to grab. The meat had once come from animals, vegetables from fields, fish from oceans, and fruits from trees. Now, everything was grown in indoor greenhouses and meat factories. Vegetables were processed into their core nutrients and vitamins before being shipped out in crates. Meat, such as beef and fish, was grown like fruit before undergoing the same processing and shipping.

Robert looked from shelf to shelf, his mouth slightly agape. The store was mostly empty.

"Holy shit," Zilv said.

"Goddammit, there's almost nothing here," Robert responded.

"Come on, baby. Let's grab what we can before anyone else takes the rest."

They approached a wall full of screens, hundreds of pneumatic pipes rising from spaces in between the screens and up into the rest of the warehouse-like grocery store. The last stores with cashiers and walk-through aisles had died out in his youth, succumbing to fully automated stores. Security guards flanked each side of the wall and watched the pair. Zilv and Robert went to one of the screens. Robert inserted his arm into a scanner registering his ID and ration-card information. He was allowed to select five crates. Each of his selections was sent into the store's system. Drones grabbed the items and placed them into a pipe system that delivered the crates next to the screen he was using.

*"Your total is $140.34. Your monthly rations are now expired. Thank you for shopping with us today. Don't forget to take your receipt,"* announced an automated voice.

They grabbed a stack of crates.

"Hey, we have a situation outside!" one of the security guards shouted.

Robert and Zilv watched as a squad of eight security guards ran to the store's entrance.

"What's that all about?" Zilv asked.

"No idea. Let's just grab this stuff and go," Robert replied.

They took their goods and went out through another airlock. Outside, sirens and screaming met them like a storming sea. The line had fallen apart. In its place was a raging mob. Robert grabbed Zilv and sprinted across the parking lot. The crowd split in two. One side clashed with the security guards at the entrance. Using their bodies as shields, the guards tried to form a wall while the mob threw objects at them and tried to push their way in. A mass of hungry people blocked an automated delivery truck at the far end of the lot. The desperate horde bombarded it with rocks and garbage while four people tore at the rear doors.

A squad of police drones came screaming over a skyscraper. Robert pulled Zilv along the store's edge, moving away from the crowd and the store.

"Come on, Zilv!"

"Where are we going?"

"I don't know! We just need to get away from this!"

The police drones landed. Twenty-four policemen rushed out with shields and tesla batons, forming a wall while an announcement echoed over the crowd.

"Attention! This is an unlawful gathering! Please disperse and return to your homes!"

The crowd turned their attention away from the truck to the police, spitting curses and slinging objects.

"Screw you!"

"Kill the pigs!"

"Fuck the fascist pigs!"

"Our right to work! Our right to eat!"

The crowd chanted as they gathered in front of the wall of police officers. Those at the front paced back and forth. Neither side charged. Each side kept shouting as they prepared to battle.

"Our right to work! Our right to eat! Our right to work! Our right to eat!"

Robert and Zilv slinked to the other side of the street.

"Come on! Come on, Zilv!" Robert urged.

A brick flew from the crowd and hit a shield. The mob rushed the shield wall, throwing objects and tearing at the small army. The police swung taser batons and stepped back, holding off the crowd while more police drones flew down from above.

Tear gas, rubber bullets, and tesla bullets rained down on the new arrivals and scattered the crowd. The police spread out, beating and arresting those they caught. The retreating horde threw objects in their flight, tossing whatever they had to keep the police at bay.

Robert and Zilv ran to flee the brutality. Robert crashed into someone and fell to the ground along with his boxes.

"Robert!" Zilv cried.

The man he had crashed into grabbed some of the dropped boxes and kicked Robert before sprinting into the stampeding horde. Robert groaned and held his side. Zilv ran to his aid and helped him pick up their leftover boxes before running away.

Robert retook the lead, shoving another person off their feet while running.

"Keep going, Zilv!"

The chaos faded behind them as they sprinted home.

# 4

# Greedy Mice

7:12 PM, July 5, 2078

\* \* \*

Robert paced as he waited to be taken off hold. The news echoed from the TV behind him.

*"The nation erupted into chaos today as Congress passed new laws banning the hoarding of weekly rations and the redistribution of ration IDs or purchased rations outside a licensed retail distributor. The People's Militia has claimed responsibility for most of the violent riots, stating that these new laws violate the People's Rights."*

*"In other news, President Hudson has officially declared The People's Emancipation Movement, or T-PEM, a terrorist organization. This is in response to a T-PEM member's recent assassination of Congressman Gilston. We spoke to a T-PEM representative to learn his view on the recent events and the new laws."*

The newscast changed from the reporter sitting behind a desk to a hooded man covered in communist patches.

*"Screw President Hudson! Look around you at all the starving people littering the streets like trash. This corrupt government, and the corporations it bends over for, have done nothing for the People! They've never listened! We're the ones out here starving! We're the ones who are sick, dirty, and cold. Not the rich, though! Not the politicians! Oh, no! President Hudson, if you're watching this,*

*your high horse looks mighty plenty for all of us! And for the rest of the rich, y'all look mighty fine for a dessert. It is time for the rule of capitalism and Western government to end. We have nothing to lose but our chains."*

The TV switched back to the newscaster.

*"Overseas, tensions are at an all-time high. Chinese President Xing Huning calls for the removal of US Forces from the Philippines. In Europe, Germany has threatened to leave the EU after receiving no responses to its request for aid during the resource crisis. Here's what officials have to say."*

Robert pressed his finger implant and snapped at the TV, shutting it off. Zilv watched him from the kitchen, lips pursed from worry.

"Sir, my manager told me we can't get you a taxi out of the city," the dispatcher said.

"Look, you have to help us out. My partner and I have to get out of the city as soon as possible. We'll pay any amount," Robert explained.

"I'm sorry, sir. We can't help you."

"The governor will declare martial law here soon, and you're going to trap us here?"

"Sir, you're not the only one asking to get out of the city. Most of our drivers are sick, have been laid off, or have quit."

"And what about the ones that are still working? We will pay you."

"I'm sorry, sir. We cannot help you. Have a good day."

"Wait! We can work out a de−"

The dispatcher hung up.

Robert growled, "Shit! God damnit!"

He inhaled sharply and let out an exasperated groan before flopping onto the couch.

Zilv sat beside him, gently holding and rubbing his head, "It's okay, baby."

"Yeah, I know. I'm trying to get us out of here. We can't just walk out of the city. It's too dangerous."

"You didn't speak with your boss, did you? About taking time off?"

"No, he'd fire me."

"Really?"

"There're hundreds of people that'd be willing to take my position. We need the job to survive, Zilv."

Zilv furrowed his brow, "I know, I know. I just want you to be safe too."

Robert sighed, "Sorry, I'm just tense. I don't mean to be angry at you."

Zilv kissed his forehead, "I understand, baby. I know you don't mean it."

Robert held Zilv for a bit before turning onto his stomach and hugging Zilv around his waist.

"We need a plan in case shit hits the fan," Robert said after a while.

"What do you think we should do?"

"Get a weapon, more food, and water. We should get more gas-mask filters in case the power goes out and the air filter stops working."

"We can't get more food, baby. Hoarding is illegal, and where can we get more rations? We're out for this week."

"No one is gonna find out. William can get us some."

Zilv's lip twitched, "I thought you stopped talking to William?"

"I did, but he got out of prison recently. He's still my friend, Zilv."

"He's not, Robert. Not anymore. He got sent to prison for a reason. Why are you talking to him again?"

"He texted me and wanted to catch up. He's staying away from his old life, but he's not employed either."

"You can't trust him, Robert. He was a thug and a drug dealer when you guys were hanging out."

"Who can we trust, Zilv? No one. Everyone's out for themselves, and we have to do the same. It's business. We won't get caught, trust me."

"Isn't getting caught why he got arrested in the first place?"

"Because we messed up, Zilv. If shit hits the fan, then I don't wanna starve to death."

Zilv pursed his lips, "All right, do what you want, Robert. Just don't get arrested."

"Baby, I won't, don't worry. I'll speak to William and see if he can get us what we need," Robert grabbed Zilv and pulled him down gently to kiss him, "I'll be careful, I promise."

Zilv's tensed brow became flat as he relaxed, parting from the kiss, "All right, fine. Just be safe."

"I will."

* * *

Robert inhaled deeply, listening as he sucked air through his gas-mask filters. It was evening. When Robert was a kid, the sun would still have been shining, only covered by a light pollution haze. Now, the concrete titans and the smog blanket in the sky blocked out the sun. The sun could still be seen when standing on top of a skyscraper, but such a view was reserved for the wealthy. It was already night in the Sodom below.

Only filth-covered people and mutant rats scoured about toward the end of the evening as it became night. The darkness and pollution had cooled the planet. Summer was cold, and winter was unbearable. Even with smart clothes, a worn jacket, and worn pants, Robert still felt cold. He also felt disguised. With the damaged layers of clothes, he looked like the rest of the unemployed.

Most unemployed and homeless had switched their sleep cycles to battle the cold. They slept in the warmth of the day. In the biting cold of the night, they were active and moved around to stay alive.

The recent political climate had turned the night into a cradle for chaos. Robert saw different kinds of people depending on where he went. Some were like him, minding their own business and not bothering anyone. Some sprayed graffiti, while others tried to create more discord. All along the streets, words were written on boarded-up buildings and signs. Robert could see the signs of the People's Militia, T-PEM, anarchists, and those who'd had enough of the world. The markings of the People's Militia consisted mainly of snakes and words of liberty. Those of T-PEM blended hammers and sickles with calls for revolution, while the hopeless anarchists spoke of hate and murder.

Robert read the walls as he walked.

*"Fuck President Hudson!"*

*"Kill the rich!"*

*"I just want to breathe again"*

*"We have no freedom!"*

*"Tired of living in a trash can"*

*"Give me freedom or give me death!"*

*"They're taking everything from us"*

*"I just want to eat"*

*"Nothing to lose but our chains!"*

*"Rebel!"*

*"Rise up!"*

Along with the words came the occasional depiction of police brutality, a raised fist, and images of famous corporation owners, government officials, and the president. The portraits of people often showed them with horns, fanged smiles, and red skin.

Out of the groups, who'd he turn to for protection? Robert was still on the fence. He and Zilv had already decided to try and stay under the radar. Still, they had to consider the future. Civil war. It was going to happen. Then what? He knew he couldn't hide in the apartment with Zilv forever. He was not a fan of communism or the revolutionary ideals of T-PEM. On the other hand, Robert had never considered himself a patriot and was not a fan of the redneck patriotism promoted by the People's Militia. Even so, each side hated corporations and the government, like Robert. People had become more sympathetic toward them with time, allowing the two to gain power. With power, there was surely protection.

He turned down a street. Ahead was a crowd of the homeless and unemployed gathered on the edge of the street corner. The air felt tense. Robert's mind wandered in panic as he expected a night of fires in response to the new laws. A bang echoed in the distance. In its wake, screams and chants filled the street. Slinking into an alleyway, he raised his forearm and swiped his finger over his arm to unlock the implant. He used his thoughts to call William. The sound of a phone ringing filled his head. A few moments later, William's voice appeared in his head.

"Yo, Robert."

"Where are you, William?"

"Robert, I'm literally looking at you. Look at the corner."

"Where?"

"The corner! Look in front of you."

Robert looked around as he moved out of the alley and noticed William waving from a charging station.

"Oh, I see you."

William hung up and walked across the road.

He fist-bumped Robert, "Yo."

"Wassup, bro? It's good to see you."

William wore jeans and a long-sleeved shirt, both of which had holes and tears across their surfaces. His shoes were dirty and stained. He also had a cheap gas mask with a cracked visor, dried-out rubber lining, and discolored plastic. Red bumps and sores caused by the polluted air covered his skin. He shivered, goosebumps sprawling across his skin. Prison had changed his body. He was a man now, built densely with muscle. His left forearm had a scar from an old implant, while a new implant had been put in his right. Tattoos covered his right arm from shoulder to fingertips. A confusing mess of cartoon images, words, animals, and a dragon wrapped up his arm. Unlike most with implant tattoos like Zilv, all of William's were inked into his skin like the snake tattoos he and Robert had on their necks.

"Good to see you too. I'm pretty good. Feels good to be out."

"Sucks that you had to come back into this mess. Are you sure you're good? I got some clothes back at the apartment."

William shook his head, "I'm fine. I'll get some money soon. I'm used to this anyway."

"All right, bro. If you're sure."

"Come on, follow me."

William led him into the alleyway. Robert followed him to a dumpster and leaned on it. He wiped his visor as William eyed both ends of the alley.

"All right, let's get to business, bro. What are you looking for?" William asked.

"A gun, food, water, and gas-mask filters. I have a feeling shit's gonna hit the fan, and when it does, Zilv and I want to be prepared."

"I can get that. How is Zilv, by the way?"

Robert snorted, "He's just been stressed recently because I've been stressed, but he's okay. Still doesn't trust you."

"Well, I don't care what he thinks as long as you two are doing well. I can get everything you need. Food and water are easy, and gas-mask filters too. The gun, on the other hand.... well, it depends on what you're looking for."

"Not really sure what I'm looking for. What can you find?"

"I can find anything. Old, conventional arms are easier. Small stuff like pistols are easy, and shotguns are harder. Rifles are even harder, and stuff like automatic weapons are the hardest. If you're looking for new-age Ignium weaponry, that's more expensive and just as hard to find as rifles. Railguns, plasma rifles, laser guns, whatever you want."

"What do you recommend?"

A huge group walked past the alleyway, shouting and screaming.

William waited for them to pass before he continued, "Well, you can't go wrong with a conventional pistol or a shotgun for self-defense. If you're looking for something easy to use, I recommend plasma. You can get Ignium batteries for them everywhere, and you can put anything in them. You know how they work, right?"

"Kind of...."

"All right, so you don't. Basically, they use Ignium energy to heat up an insulated chamber filled with any material. The material is melted and then spewed out like a flamethrower. They're fun weapons."

Robert's eyes widened, "How much is a plasma weapon?"

"Again, it depends. I recommend a plasma rifle. It's usually around six grand for one, but for you... four grand."

Robert's head recoiled.

"Whoa, that's a bit. How about a conventional pistol?" Robert replied.

"About two grand."

"I can afford that. I'll work on the plasma rifle. How about food, water, and gas-mask filters?"

"Well, I have to do a bit of work to get around the ration systems, but generally double what I pay to get them. Let's say one cereal box is fourteen dollars, so you pay twenty-eight."

"Fair deal. Just message me when you have the stuff, and I'll pay you. We can play it by ear about where to meet. Just gotta make sure no one catches on."

"No one's gonna catch on. Just don't bullshit and tell anyone. I'll start by getting the supplies and move on from there. Sound good?"

Robert's breath faintly quivered as he nodded, "Sound good."

"All right."

"So, now that you're out... have you stayed clean?"

William scoffed, "Of course. I've been in so long that I haven't been able to get anything for a long time. Don't give a shit about it anymore. I'm just focusing on making money and staying under the radar."

"That's good. Stay clean."

"I will."

"I should head home. Zilv's probably worried since I'm not back yet. Wanna get dinner sometime?"

"Maybe, we'll see. I'll probably have the stuff in a week. Peace, bro."

"Cool, see ya."

They slapped hands and fist-bumped. Robert returned the way he came while William left in the opposite direction. Back on the street, Robert met a wall of rioters. Hundreds of people were walking, waving red flags with the communist hammer and sickle. They raised their fists and shouted. Some threw objects at cars and buildings, some vandalized, and a few attacked other people. Overhead, police drones raced across the sky with lights and sirens on.

"Fuck the state!"

"Long live the people's war!"

"Emancipation!"

Robert merged with the crowd, concealing himself. A chant rippled through the crowd.

"Fuck the state! Emancipate! Fuck the state! Emancipate!"

People chanted with their fists up in the air. As they passed burning cars and buildings, people cheered for those who smashed car windows with bricks.

The crowd halted and formed a wall a few yards before Robert. He squinted and looked between people to see a police wall. Police drones hovered over them and shone spotlights into the crowd.

A drone played an announcement drowning out the chanting, shouting, and screaming, *"Return to your homes! This is an illegal gathering and a disturbance of the peace."*

In response, people shouted.

"We don't have homes!"

"Pigs!"

"Screw you, bastards!"

"Fuck the state! Emancipate!"

The mob threw bricks, trash cans, and everything else they could find at the shield wall. Robert gasped. He slinked between people, moving toward the sidewalk and to the edge of the crowd. Bangs echoed as people threw fireworks and firecrackers at the police. Robert felt disoriented between the deafening pops, the shouting, and the chants. He pushed people and scraped through to get an opening. The shouts and turmoil quickly faded as he sprinted down an empty street and ran home.

# 5

# Gumma Pesta

2:24 PM, July 8, 2078

\* \* \*

Robert packed up his tools from the job site and placed them in the back of the company van while listening to the news through his implant.

*"Now to the growing concerns about the new disease spreading across the US. The CDC has dubbed it Fuscus Pestis. Fuscus Pestis, better known as FP-78 or Rabbit Fever, broke out in India in late May and has gradually spread worldwide. The first confirmed instance of an infection in the US was on June 5th in Los Angeles, California. Health officials warn of a possible health crisis and urge government officials to act. We spoke to Dr. Steven Schaffer, who told us about his concerns."*

A man dressed in a hazmat suit standing in a hospital hallway appeared.

*"We have to be careful. I've seen eight FP-78 patients, and only one has recovered. This is unprecedented. We haven't seen an illness like this since the Black Death, the Spanish Flu, COVID-19, or the Wire Flu."*

The newscast switched back to the news reporter.

*"Some states have already begun to shut down airports to combat the spread of Rabbit Fever. Officials are urging people to stay home and to avoid people with these symptoms: coughing, boils, bleeding or blackened skin, intense fever, black mucus and saliva, vomiting, weakness or fatigue, headaches, seizures, and*

*fainting. Officials are yet to determine how FP-78 spreads but believe it transmits through bodily fluids, water, physical contact, and the air. It's recommended to wear a mask at all times in public indoor spaces, to wash your hands, and to maintain distance from others."*

Robert shut off the podcast and went into the van.

*"Hello, Robert Ashton."*

"Hello, Hypatia," he replied.

*"How may I help you today?"*

"9636 Blue Spring Street, Devon's Laundromat. East side of town."

*"Directing there now."*

The van started and directed itself onto the street, the engine warbling as it accelerated. He checked his messages using his implant. He read over the work message from the morning instructing him on necessary precautions due to the pandemic. After, Robert turned off his implant and looked out the window as the van merged onto the highway. Black clouds moved through the sky below the dark pollution haze above. Hopefully, it wouldn't rain. He hated the rain. The charcoal-black water stained everything and caused waste to spread everywhere.

Trash blew all over the streets below. Paper, plastic, and scraps swept through the streets and blew over the homeless lying against buildings and alleyways. Was the rest of the world this dirty? No one cared about cleanliness. Robert was the same. He threw whatever waste he created on the ground. The city didn't clean the streets and rarely came to pick up garbage from neighborhoods since the dumps were already overflowing with litter.

The wilds of the Americas were dead. The vast swaths of the Canadian wilderness had become barren graveyards filled with the skeletons of dead trees. The Amazon was gone as well. The vast regions of the American plains were now a sandy wasteland with weeds few and far between. Black snow covered the Rocky Mountains, leaving them as Stygian titans standing over one of Earth's most significant mass extinctions.

Most pigeons had died from cancer, bleeding lungs from the toxic air, or stomach poisoning. To replace all the dying animal populations, scientists created new "iron lung" species that could survive the failing world. Most "iron lung" animals came from species nearing extinction, though some had been developed from test tubes. These new animals were frowned upon, and many thought their creators were wrongly playing God. Their populations were small, though, and had little presence in the real world. Most were still in labs and zoos.

The van stayed on the highway for ten minutes before exiting to the street level. The graffiti and buildings differed depending on where the van went. Robert saw four allegiances: for the People's Militia, T-PEM, anarchy, and oneself. Hammers and sickles, snakes, anarchy symbols, and words of hatred covered the boarded-up buildings. Homeless people slept between the buildings. Most were sick, coughing from damaged lungs and suffering from searing fevers. Rabbit Fever was spreading rapidly, quicker than what the news said. Those suffering from this new disease were bloody and covered with black stains from bursting boils under their skin. The most obvious were the ones with black vomit, masks off, and faces covered in bleeding boils. All of them were sick and doomed to die. The hospitals were overflowing. Regardless, most couldn't afford the care and were trapped on the streets. They were sitting around just waiting to die.

Robert grimaced and looked away. He had to.

* * *

The car parked and shut off.

"*We have arrived,*" Hypatia stated.

"Thank you, Hypatia," Robert replied.

"Devon's Laundromat" marked the top of the building in black-stained worn letters. Robert grabbed his toolbox from the back and walked through the airlock. The inside of the laundromat was grimy. Dark stains from mud and dirty shoes covered the once-polished tile floor. A few people had been let inside. Most sat to enjoy the warmth and filtered air, while hardly any had the money to wash their clothes. Many of the machines were out of service.

At the front, he rang a bell. Robert sighed as he waited for an employee, ringing it twice more before a fat and unshaven man came out from the back.

He spoke in a deep, grumbling voice, rasping and wheezing between each word, "Yes?"

"Hello, sir. I'm Robert from Nelson's Repairs. We received a call about a few broken washing machines."

The man pointed to a corner, "Right over there. I don't know what's wrong with them. Went out all at once. Just get 'em fixed."

"I'll take a look, sir. Is there anything else I should look at?"

"Nope, not in this economy."

The man disappeared into the back.

Robert scowled and shook his head. He went to the washing machines and fiddled with them, kneeling. He opened the doors, checked the interior, pressed the buttons, and tugged at each device. None responded to any input from the controls. Everything else seemed fine. He fetched a dolly to lift each machine out of the way. The last offered some resistance. Robert gave it a tug causing it to crackle.

"Whoa!" he let out as he shielded himself.

One of the connections had broken and left a gap in the tube-like wires, allowing Ignium to leak out. The blue-colored plasma spewed out, sending sparks and energy crackles from the hole like a volcanic thunderstorm. It had burnt the surrounding area, though none of the damage was severe or visible behind the machine.

"Goddammit."

Robert stood and looked around.

Most buildings had control panels in their main lobbies, backrooms, or backsides in case of fire. Robert ran to the main board and flipped a switch to turn off an entire row of washing machines. He cleaned around the mess of wires, cut the old ones off, and soldered on new ones. Once the cables were together, he turned on the switches at the control panel, went to a washing machine, and turned it on. It came to life, Ignium freely flowing through it.

Robert smiled and turned the power off before moving each washing machine back in place and returning the dolly to the car. Inside, he rang the bell again. A sigh followed the ring.

The man returned from the back and looked at Robert, "Yes?"

"I fixed the washing machines, sir. One of the wires was damaged and leaking into the surrounding area. I fixed the damage and patched the wire up. Everything should be good now. If not, give us a call."

"Good. Thanks for coming out. Hopefully, the damn things will keep working for more than a week this time."

The man disappeared again.

* * *

Robert stepped outside and walked to the back of the van with the toolbox. He paused at the sound of yelling.

"Screw you, communist!"

As he looked over, he watched—along with a few other people—as two men aggressively gestured at each other and shouted. One was a T-PEM member with a hammer-and-sickle pin on his breast, while the other was a People's Militia member with a Gadsden rattlesnake patch on the back of his jacket.

"Your kind has had your run! Look at what you did with the country, fascist!"

"And what will you do with it?"

"We will do better with it than you!"

They were face to face, fists clenched. The T-PEM member threw a fist first. The Militia member shielded himself and kicked back. The two grappled and rolled to the ground, kicking, punching, and screaming. A few people stood with their arms up and palms open, using their implants to record the fight as it went down. The T-PEM member gained the advantage. He got on top and threw his fists into the man's mask until the Militia member railed his knee into the man's back and threw him off. The T-PEM member fell. The Militia member ran and grabbed a trash can. As he turned, the T-PEM member looked up at him.

"Wait! No! Pl–"

"Raaah!!"

The metal trash can crashed down upon the T-PEM member's head. His head bounced off the ground, gas mask and nose cracking loudly. The crowd gasped.

"Is he dead?" a woman cried.

"Someone call the police!" a man shouted.

The Militia member kicked the man one last time before he noticed the crowd around him and took off.

Robert stood back nervously, avoiding the conflict. A few people surrounded the body.

A woman took off the T-PEM member's mask and checked his head, "He's alive!"

"W-Where am I?" the man asked, blinking slowly.

His nose was bent in an unsettling manner, blood gushing from it. The back of his head bled as well from hitting the asphalt so hard. His gas mask lay beside him, entirely destroyed, causing him to cough as polluted air filled his lungs.

The woman held his head up, "You're okay, you're okay. Help is on the way. Does someone have a gas mask?! Anyone?!"

No response came.

"All right, just hold on. Help is coming! Anyone has a gas mask, please?" the woman called out.

After a few minutes, sirens echoed in the distance. Three police drones flew over the skyscraper horizon and descended upon the scene. A squad of police officers rushed out.

"Everyone back away!"

The police made a small wall. As they obscured the view of the scene, Robert retreated into his van and turned it on.

*"Hello, Robert Ashton."*

"Hypatia, get us back to headquarters. Now."

*"Directing there now."*

The crowd had dispersed quickly out of fear and hatred of the police. The van backed out onto the street and headed toward the company headquarters. Robert swiped over his forearm and called Zilv, the ringtone echoing in his head.

"Hello, darling!"

"Hi, baby," Robert said.

"What's up?"

Robert rested his face on his palm.

"I just watched a People's Militia guy smash a T-PEM member's face in with a trash can."

"Holy shit! Are you okay?"

"Yeah, I wasn't involved."

"How did it happen?"

Robert filled him in.

"Not like they'll do much," Zilv scoffed.

"No, probably not. I will be at one more job site today before I come home just so you know."

"Okay, baby, be safe. Seriously. I love you."

"I will. I love you, too."

"Bye-bye, darling."

Robert looked down at his forearm and called William. As he waited, the same ringing filled his head.

"Yo," William said.

"Yo, I wanted to talk."

"Wassup?"

"Do you have the supplies and weapons?"

"I'll have them by tomorrow. The plasma rifle is taking time, but I have the stuff for this month. You have the money?"

"I do. Been working as much as I can."

"All right. We have to be careful where we meet. Lots of cameras across the city, and the police are always ready to pounce."

"All right. Just tell me the place, and I'll meet you there."

"All right. Peace, bro."

"Peace."

# 6

# First Darkness

5:12 PM, July 9, 2078

* * *

Robert sat in the apartment watching the news, jaw clenched tight as he grimaced.

*"With the continued spread of FP-78, airports across the country are shutting down. The death toll continues to rise, and experts fear the worst. In Europe, many countries have initiated quarantine lockdowns to stop the spread of the deadly pathogen. Meanwhile, over thirty million people have died from FP-78 in India. The president of India, Madhava Mahanti, has declared a national crisis."*

*"In other news, tensions between T-PEM and the People's Militia are increasing following multiple incidents across the country where each side is attacking the other. We interviewed a member of the People's Militia who was a victim of one of these attacks."*

The news switched to a man covered head to toe in thick clothing with Militia patches. Unlike most people, his gas-mask visor was tinted dark to hide his face.

*"They came out of nowhere. Three or four hammer-and-sickle-wearing thugs jumped my friend and me while we were walking home. I got a few bruises, but my homie got sent to the hospital. They ran off faster than they came when I pulled out a gun. I'm telling all of you right now, arm yourselves. We'll liberate*

*this country from those China-loving commies."*

\* \* \*

Robert's arm lit up, a ringtone echoing in his head. He sat up and snapped at the TV to shut it off before answering.

"Wassup, William?"

"Yo, I got the plasma rifle. You got the money?"

"Whoa, you got it?"

"No, I was just kidding," William responded mockingly.

"Wh–"

"Yes! I got it. It's still four grand. Do you have the money for all this today?"

"Uh, hold on."

Robert swiped on his forearm implant and directed his thoughts toward his bank account. William sighed as Robert accessed it with one of his finger implants.

"Done?" William asked.

"Hold on, hold on. I'm almost there," Robert opened his savings account, "Yeah, I got enough. It'll be everything I have, though."

"The deal can wait if you need it to."

"No, no, it's better to have the supplies than wait too long. Everything is changing by the day."

"All right, meet me at your local convenience store. I got a place where we can do the deal that I'll take you to."

"All right."

"Peace. I gotta go make some arrangements. Meet me in an hour."

"Peace."

William hung up.

"Zilv! Baby?" Robert called.

Zilv came out from the bedroom, "Yes, darling?"

"I'm gonna go meet William in an hour."

"Can I come with you?"

"I thought you didn't like William?"

"I really don't, but I don't want you to go alone. What are we getting today?"

"Food and water for a month, filters, batteries, a pistol for you, and a plasma rifle."

"Robert... How are we paying?"

Robert looked away and clenched his jaw, "All of our savings."

"What! Robert, what if something happens? We need to talk about these kinds of things, babe!"

"I know, I know. Zilv, please. I know. Look, money barely matters anymore. We need real things. We need food and water, and weapons. What did you want me to do? Save it for the next time we get a few rations that last a week?"

Zilv sighed angrily, his soft face flushing red, "That is not the point, Robert. You need to talk to me about these things before you go ahead and just do them! We still need money, and coding jobs are becoming scarce. I'm not pulling in what I used to."

Robert walked over to Zilv, "Okay... okay, I'm sorry."

Zilv jerked away from him.

"Don't be mad. I did it for us. We have no idea what is going to happen in the future. It changes every day," Robert said.

Zilv put his hands on Robert's shoulders, "Look! Just please promise me to talk about this stuff before you just do it!"

"I will! I will! I promise. I just want to do what is best for us."

"What is best for us is what we agree to."

"You're right. I'm sorry. Please forgive me?"

"Don't try to apologize your way out. You *can't* do this. You can't just do crazy shit without even telling me."

"I won't! I'm listening! I promise I'll talk to you first. I was just trying my best for us."

Zilv sighed, "I know you were. You just get your head up your ass sometimes, you know that?"

"I know. I'm sorry. Please forgive me."

Zilv exhaled and leaned into a hug, "Fine. I forgive you. Just talk to me about this kind of stuff in the future, all right?"

"I promise. No more mad?"

"No more mad. Just don't go ahead and do stuff without talking to me, okay?"

"Okay, that works for me."

They held the hug for a few more minutes and kissed before parting from the embrace.

"Let's get ready in fifteen minutes. I wanna get there a few minutes early," Robert said.

"All right."

Robert returned to the couch and responded to several messages. He also went into his bank account and sent the money to William. A few minutes later, he received a "thank you" message from William.

Zilv came over with Robert's clothes before going for a shower. Robert listened to the water pour before eventually making his way to the bathroom.

Once the water shut off, he spoke, "Hey, Zilv, do you wanna go out soon?"

A gasp came from the shower, "Robert!"

"Sorry, didn't mean to scare you."

Zilv stepped out and wrapped a towel around his waist, "What do you wanna do?"

"Do you wanna go out on a date?"

"On a date?"

"Yeah. It's been a while. Since everything has begun shutting down, it might be our last chance."

"We don't have money... And I'm worried about your job. Are you trying to butter me up?"

"Maybe. We can just stay at home and take some time to ourselves."

"I think you're trying to butter me up, mister."

"Not at all. I would never."

"Well, I might like a date night."

"Is that a deal?"

Zilv sighed and rolled his eyes, "Fine, it's a deal."

Robert smiled, "It's a date, then. Let's get changed."

Outside, they tried their best to stay away from other people. Many of the homeless sleeping on the ground were covered in bleeding boils, which showed the increasing spread of Rabbit Fever. Robert couldn't tell if they were sleeping or dead.

"Holy shit…," Zilv mumbled.

"What?" Robert asked.

"It's getting so bad out here."

"It's worse all around the city. We live in an okay area. Other areas? Not so much. There's chaos every night."

Zilv frowned, "I miss when we could buy all the food we wanted."

"I miss being a kid. At least there were a few trees left back then. You remember flowers?" Robert asked with a thin smile.

"Hah, yeah. Mom's flower shop was full of them all year round. Even when the climate got bad, she still had some. I miss that place," Zilv frowned.

"I think I was nine the last time I saw something outside a greenhouse or a zoo. Hey, that gives me an idea. Maybe we should go to a life museum for our date?"

Zilv wrinkled his brow, "A life museum?"

"Yeah, one of those museums that have animal and plant displays. You know, like stuffed lions from the 50s and dandelions from the 60s. That sort of stuff," Robert explained.

"So, a museum that shows all the species that have died in the past few decades?"

Robert tilted his head left and right, "Yeah, something like that."

"Oh, that sounds like a good idea."

"I'll do some searching when we get home."

The convenience store was a small rectangular building. Outside were a few Ignium chargers resembling early twenty-first-century gas pumps. One of the three chargers was out of service. Bars fortified each window while a massive pile of trash leaned against one side of the building. On the other side was a sleeping homeless man.

"Been a while since I've visited here," Zilv said.

"That trash pile gets bigger every time I come here. In a few weeks, it'll be

saw some cops down there earlier."

"Good to know. Come on, you two," William said as he descended into the hole.

Zilv chuckled nervously and gestured to Robert, "You go first."

Robert snorted, "You chicken? All right."

"Hey! I'm not a... Ugh!"

Zilv went in last. Bryan slid the maintenance hole cover back on, bathing the trio in darkness. Turning on their implants, Robert's and Zilv's arms became flashlights. William picked up an Ignium lantern, switched it on, and raised it in the air.

The underground was enormous. Unlike old sewers, it consisted of more than tunnels and sewer pipes. Among the man-sized tunnels were underground power stations, water-filtration sites, and control areas. An underground tram system dominated most of the city's underworld. The underground was a great unknown. Robert had never had jobs down here and was now somewhat grateful to have avoided the darkness and stench.

William gestured ahead, "Come on, let's go. I have your supplies a few tunnels away. We'll grab them and transport them to your place."

Robert tilted his head, "Oh, why didn't you just put it all over there in the first place?"

"We have a system here—delivery, stealth, all that sort of stuff. We are doing it in the least risky way. Come on."

Walking through the sewer tunnels, their shoes squelched, the sloppy sounds echoing.

Zilv let out a disgusted groan, "Ugh! It's nasty down here!"

"Shh! Not so loud!" William hissed.

Robert hugged Zilv, "It's okay, baby. We're only down here for a bit."

"My shoes are ruined. Let's just hurry up," Zilv whined.

"What's the plan here, William?" Robert whispered.

"We're gonna transport most of the stuff under your place. There's a manhole you can go down where there are no cameras near your apartment. You should take some food and water up every few days. I'm still working on finding a hiding place for you to store most of it. It's hard since there are already many hiding places taken by others."

"What happens if we meet any police officers down here?" Robert asked.

"We run. Like most guys, I got something to buy us time." William dug in his left pant pocket and produced a tennis-ball-sized object with a smiley face on it, "Got this little thing. If I throw it on the ground really hard, it goes bang, and it makes smoke and a siren noise. It's shocking and buys time."

Zilv's purple eyes widened slightly, "Is that dangerous?"

William chuckled, "Yes. If I hold it when it goes off... which I don't intend to do."

He led them through tunnel after tunnel. They passed doors and massive areas where machines worked alone in the subterranean darkness. They were the vital organs of the city. Robert had tried to get a job down here, though no positions in his company and other companies were available.

"All right, we're here," William said.

He stopped in front of a hole in the wall, leaned down, and lifted a grate, "Hold this, Robert?"

Robert held it up. William picked up the Ignium lantern again and hovered it over the hole. Beneath them was a pile of supplies, food boxes, water packs, gas-mask filters, and the guns that Robert had bought.

"Hell yeah," Robert said.

"All right, Robert, you're taking the gun and some filters. Zilv, you get the food. I'm taking the water."

William lifted the gun to Robert and put a hand on the grate as Robert took it. Robert let out a goofy, excited chuckle. He felt like a kid on Christmas. He had only shot a few guns and had never held a monster like this.

It was incredible. The whole thing was long, sleek, and white with a small buttstock and trigger. Most of the gun's center consisted of a large chamber for raw material with a battery pack attached to the side. The chamber—called the Melt Chamber or MC—along with the long barrel, was insulated with a material similar to aerogel and could withstand the weapon's molten projectiles. The gun even had a sling. Robert held it for a moment, then put it over his shoulder.

William heaved two water containers up, gave Zilv some of the food containers, and finally came up with a box of gas-mask filters. He closed the grate after hopping out and grabbed one of the water containers.

"All right. Let's go, guys," William said.

"How do you know where to go, William?" Zilv asked.

"I basically live down here when I work. It sucks, but I can't get work any other way. Better to work in this biohazard hell-maze than starve. You're lucky with your job, Robert. And you, too, with your coding stuff, Zilv."

"I know," Robert said.

"My kind of work has been drying up lately. No one can afford to fix buggy bots and drones anymore," Zilv said.

"That's tough to hear," William replied.

Their breathing and steps echoed through the tunnels. A distant metal bang interrupted the steady pace of their footsteps, causing all of them to halt.

"Shh! Hide!" William hissed.

He took them into a small recess in the wall, looking out and listening.

"What? What is it?" Robert asked.

"Ssh! Shut up!" William hushed.

They all listened and held their breaths. Distant shouting and footsteps approached the trio.

"Run! Run!" someone shouted in the distance.

Robert leaned out and looked down the tunnel toward an intersection. A pair of flashlights came from the right as a man and a woman ran out of a tunnel.

"Go! Go that way!" the man shouted, raising his hand.

In his hand was a device similar to the one William had. He threw it down. Smoke flooded the intersection before a shrieking siren pierced Robert's ears. The pair split up and disappeared in different directions. A few moments later, two police officers ran through the smoke.

"Police! Stop!" they shouted.

The officers went down one of the tunnels opposite the trio. Their forms disappeared in the dark.

William hurriedly walked in the opposite direction, "Come on, let's go, let's go."

They went down a few more tunnels.

"William, why were those people being chased?" Zilv whispered.

William shrugged, "Police are cracking down hard on the underground. They've been taking out drug rings and that sort of crap. Probably because the underground has been profiting from helping T-PEM and the Militia, making matters worse for the government."

"You guys have been helping the Militia and T-PEM?" Zilv asked.

"No. It's just business as usual for us. Money doesn't care who you vote for or who you support. Now be quiet. We're almost there."

They arrived in a vast, dome-like room with a swirling pool in the center. Robert recoiled at the sight of the whirlpool. The vortex sloshed and frothed, and the force of the water threatened to suck him away into the unknown. Between him and inescapable death stood a railing. Water had rusted its edges.

"Egh," Robert let out.

Nine tunnels went out from the dome room. Each one had a number spray-painted at its mouth. William led them down the one with the number seven on it, arriving at a ladder.

William stopped at the ladder. He looked around and then up, "We're here."

# 7

# Date Night

4:43 PM, July 16, 2078

\* \* \*

The apartment was quiet. Robert had wasted most of the day procrastinating. He sat on the couch ad listened to the news through his neural-link implant. The audio played in his head as he relaxed.

*"Outrage across the country today as President Hudson issued an executive order to begin a nationwide quarantine in response to the continued spread of FP-78. Leaders of T-PEM from each state and Hans Renning, leader of the People's Militia, have come forward, stating that the quarantine violates the People's Rights. Renning posted his response to the executive order earlier today, having this to say:"*

The news switched to a rugged man wearing militaristic gear. He was inside, smoking a cigarette with his mask off as he spoke, *"This quarantine, this... tyrannical capture of the People's Rights, is not for love and care of the sick and the poor. It is a demonstration of power! It is a display through which the rich show their control over the poor. They think we will lie down! They think we will bow! They think we will submit!"*

*"I know, my friends, that these are difficult times. Again and again, we have made our plea! We have begged and toiled for change that will never come! The time for groveling is over."*

*"The great time has begun. America is awakening. The People—you and I—can finally see. It is the time to rise up, brothers and sisters! We will not lie down! We will not bow! We will not submit! The most precious thing in this world is our freedom! No one can take it! Our time is now. Power will be returned to the People."*

Robert paused the podcast with a thought when he received a message. His heart skipped a beat upon opening the email, "Shit! Shit! Shit!"

He fell back into the couch, threw his fist into a pillow, and held his face with his hands, "Damnit...."

Zilv ran over, eyes wide and brow raised, "Baby! What's wrong?"

Robert growled and then hyperventilated into a sigh, "I just received an email from my boss. They're putting me on temporary leave."

"Why?"

"The quarantine. I'm basically fired, babe. They're not paying me for this," Robert explained with a clenched jaw as he rolled up his fists.

Zilv's jaw dropped slightly. He pulled Robert into a hug and kissed his forehead as Robert wrapped his arms around him.

"Baby. Baby, it's okay... it's okay. We prepared for this," Zilv said.

Robert sighed, "We need money."

"I know. We'll figure something out. I'll see if I can get some more coding work. We at least have food and water, baby."

"You're right. I'm just scared."

They held each other for a while as Robert calmed down.

"I don't know what we're gonna do, Zilv. No money, quarantine, and the country is falling apart. There's no way out of this damned city."

"Robert, darling... we'll be okay. We have food and water and a place to stay, and William can always help us."

"Food, water, and rent for a month. What happens if I can't pay rent next month? William only helps us if I have money."

"We'll figure something out. We always have."

Robert groaned as increasingly worse scenarios played out in his head.

Zilv grabbed his head, kissed him roughly, and looked into his eyes, "Look at me, you. It'll be okay. Stop it. Okay?"

Robert blinked.

"Okay?" Zilv repeated.

"Okay," Robert mumbled.

"Let's think about something else."

"Okay..."

They quietly sat for a few moments and took comfort in each other's company.

Robert let out a sigh, "Do you want to..."

"To?"

"Do a date night?"

Zilv smiled and nodded, "Sure."

Robert stood and made Zilv sit on the couch.

"All right, I have a plan then. You sit here," Robert said.

"What? I don't wanna sit here! I wanna help," Zilv protested.

"Nope! I'm setting up the date."

Zilv stood, "Excuse me, mister. This is our date! I am helping."

Zilv postured at him, raising his fists, "Yeah, I'm helping."

Robert snorted, "Fine, fine. You can help with... setting the table and choosing a movie for tonight."

"A movie?"

"Yeah. We'll have dinner. Then we'll watch a movie and cuddle."

Zilv tilted his head and smiled, "Daw, you're cute. I like that idea."

Robert shrugged and smirked, "It's 'cause I love you."

"I love you, too."

Robert grabbed food from their small pantry and cooking utensils out of a drawer while Zilv took out the tableware.

"What are we eating?" Zilv asked.

"Something meaty. We don't have any real stuff, just synthesized food. I'll just warm it up and make each plate look pretty."

Zilv set the table while Robert took out pots and pans, opened containers, and mixed up their dinner. After, Zilv sat on the couch and searched for a movie while dinner came together.

"What do you want to watch, babe? TV show? Movie?"

"I said a movie. Something romantic," Robert replied.

"Romantic? Come on. I think we should watch a horror movie."

"You want to watch a horror movie?"

"Yeah! I'll see what I can find."

"All right, suit yourself. But if you get scared from it, I'm gonna laugh."

"I won't get scared! When have I ever gotten scared from a horror movie?"

"You remember that one movie with the witch? Oh, and Elder's Blood. You were scared for a week after that movie."

"Okay, well, shut up! That movie scared you too!"

Robert snorted, "Yeah, once at the best jump scare ever. You were scared the entire time...."

"You were scared the entire time," Zilv said mockingly.

"Ay! Don't you repeat what I say."

"Ay! Don't you repeat what I say."

Robert groaned as Zilv giggled. He shook his head and plated the food. He brought it to the table and pulled Zilv's chair out, "Did you find anything?"

"Yeah, we can watch this. Looks like some cosmic horror."

"That sounds cool. Don't play it yet. Dinner is served."

Robert grabbed a lighter and a candle. He put it on the table and lit it before sitting down. Zilv joined him.

"A candle? You're too cute," Zilv said with a smile.

"Hey, candles are romantic. Do not question my romance abilities."

"I will, and I think they're great."

Robert smiled, "Ah, well, you just think that."

"What! I do not just 'think that.' This is perfect," Zilv said.

"All right, fine, thank you."

"You're welcome, mister."

The two ate slowly, looking across the table at each other. Zilv's purple eyes glowed intensely as he smiled, head propped upon his arm. The implant tattoo in his arm glowed, and its shapes moved as it switched between nebulas and flocks of birds. The glow illuminated his short, brown curly hair and undamaged, soft cheeks, untouched by polluted air.

Robert's eyes were fixated on Zilv's as he watched the purple glow glimmer, going up to the roof. Anyway, William should be here in a few minutes."

They sat down on the sidewalk, Robert wrapping an arm around Zilv as they leaned on one another.

A police drone descended from the smog and landed in front of the store. Two police officers emerged from it and went inside. Robert tried to look like he wasn't staring. As he glanced back, he spotted William approaching them from a distance.

William kept his head down as he walked, holding his hands in his pockets, "Yo, wassup guys."

"Hey, William, how are you?" Zilv asked.

"I'm okay. I see the red, white, and blue are here with us. Come on, let's go."

William led them across the road. The trio walked silently, moving from street to street and eventually into an alleyway. It was full of people and tents. A wall of dumpsters and trash obscured the whole camp from the road. William hopped over the dumpsters, trailed by Robert and Zilv.

A large man with a pipe walked up to William, "Who are these fools?"

"Customers," William responded.

"Why are you bringing them in here?"

"I need to get down there. We got some big merchandise."

"All right, we're watching them, though."

Robert and Zilv looked at each other as they followed William to a maintenance hole.

"Help me out," William said.

Robert and another man walked over to the lid and lifted it.

"Thanks, Bryan," William said.

Bryan was taller than Robert and William. He was dressed in a few layers of tattered clothing from head to toe without a single piece of circuitry on him. Unlike Robert, with his smart clothes, the man simply chose the old-fashioned way of layering to stay warm. His mask concealed his face, two dark eyes hidden beneath a small, goggle-like visor.

He stretched his shoulder and popped it once the maintenance hole cover had been moved, "No problem, good luck down there. Guys on the east side

"Have I told you that you're beautiful?"

"Gah! No, no, don't start you."

"You are beautiful! And I don't just 'think that way.' It's just true."

"I hate compliments!" Zilv said, covering his face.

Robert spoke in a silly voice, "Aw, who has the cutest face? And the best smile? And is the prettiest thing ever?"

"No! Stop it, you! I'll... I'll take this knife and poke you," Zilv said, picking up his dinner knife.

"You're gonna poke me with that blunt little knife?"

"Yeah, so you gotta stop it."

"I'm so scared. I guess I have to stop."

"Good! Yeah, be scared."

"Hard to be scared of something so cute."

"Hey!" Zilv said, raising the knife.

"Aaah! Okay!" Robert shielded his face as if the knife would be thrown at him.

"Thought so."

After a while, they had emptied their plates entirely.

"How was it?" Robert asked.

"It was okay. It tasted pretty good, but I know you can only do so much with this kind of food."

"Yeah... I wish it was a nice, juicy steak. A real steak. Not something cubed from a box."

"Would be awesome if they weren't two hundred a pound."

"Maybe..."

"No."

Robert smirked and brought their plates to the sink for cleaning. Zilv joined him, the two working together as they cleaned, dried, and put away everything. Once finished, they went to the couch.

"Darius' Ship?" Robert read the title of the movie.

"It sounds cool. Group of explorers going deep into some ancient ruins and discovering something on the scale of cosmic horror."

"Let's play it. Can't be too bad. It has four and a half stars..."

Robert and Zilv grabbed blankets and started to cuddle when the movie opening started to play. They watched intently for the movie's first hour, only pausing for popcorn, drinks, and a bathroom break. The film was about a man finding an experienced team to lead an expedition into the underground ruins of an Aztec city. Once they had gathered, they flew to the town nearest the ruins and began their first ventures into the ancient place.

As the second hour passed, Robert held Zilv close and kissed his cheek a few times.

"I like this movie...." Robert whispered.

"Yeah?"

"But I like you more."

Zilv rolled his eyes, "Oh my God. You're so cheesy."

Robert rubbed his hand across Zilv's chest, "I'm just saying you're attractive."

Zilv turned and hugged Robert's chest. His cheeks flushed red, purple eyes flaring brightly as they met Robert's, "Yeah?"

"Yeah," Robert said before he kissed him softly, gently biting his bottom lip.

"Okay, you. We're trying to watch a movie. You can't do that," Zilv said and giggled.

"Do what? I'm doing absolutely nothing," Robert said.

Robert lifted his leg, slid between Zilv's legs, and kissed his neck.

"Oh... yeah? Nothing?" Zilv whispered.

"Nothing. I'm just having fun."

"Mmm. I think you're trying to convince me to not watch the movie."

"Maybe... Maybe we can resume it later."

Robert snapped at the TV, shutting it off.

"Really?" Zilv asked and bit his lip as Robert pulled off his own shirt.

"Really," Robert said, pulling off Zilv's shirt.

He ran his hands across Zilv's soft skin, going between the curves and lengths of his legs and sides. Robert's darkened skin was covered in scars that starkly contrasted with his partner's pale, silky skin. Compared to Robert, Zilv was not only shorter but slimmer. Their breathing became more intense. Robert played with him, lifted him up, and set him on his lap. Robert ran his hands across his chest. Zilv worked against his hands, dancing upon Robert's lap before Robert lifted him and placed him on the floor.

"Get on your knees," Robert commanded.

"Yes, sir," Zilv whispered.

# 8

# The March

\* \* \*

Zilv had fallen asleep. His brown hair was ruffled, and his clothes were on the floor. A blanket was the only thing that kept the pair decent. Robert held Zilv while he slept. In the background, a show played in place of the movie. The backdrop noise from the program helped Robert doze off as the minutes marched into the night.

He released a startled gasp as a ringtone echoed in his head and shocked him wide awake. He fumbled a little as he answered the call, letting out an annoyed sigh.

"Yo, Robert. Wassup? How are you?" William said.

"Oh, wassup, bro. I'm doing meh."

"Meh?"

"I lost my job today," Robert said.

"Oh! God damn, that sucks. Look, I didn't call you for no reason. You have what you need to survive without a job for a while, but I don't think that's the biggest deal right now. I've just sent you a link to a live stream. Pull it up on your implant or something. You have to see this."

"Uh, all right. I'll take a look."

"Call me after. Peace."

"All right. Peace."

Robert opened the link William had sent and broadcasted it to the TV. The live stream was from downtown, filmed from a camera implant in someone's eyes. It wasn't common for people to have implants in sensitive areas like their eyes, though professional photographers and reporters often had them. The man filming the live stream walked with a crowd through the buildings and skyscrapers of downtown. The audio consisted of banging sounds, screaming, chanting, and complete anarchy. Robert lowered the TV volume.

Wherever the cameraman looked, there was destruction. People spray-painted walls, burned cars, broke windows, threw stones, stole things, and shouted. The cameraman seemed to be with a group of People's Militia since many wore the image of the Gadsden rattlesnake. Most had weapons. Some had bricks or metal poles, some had baseball bats, and others even had guns.

As they marched, they chanted.

"No submission! Our volition! No submission! Our volition!"

The cameraman spoke, "This is history in the making, folks. More unemployment, quarantine, a pandemic, starvation, and sickness. For those watching, hold your loved ones close and prepare for the worst. Everywhere across the country is like this. This is not a riot. These aren't violent protests. It's a war."

The wave of Militia members continued into the city center, meeting a police wall that surrounded the front of the Capitol building. The cameraman looked up when police drones raced overhead. The live stream became blurry as he quickly ran for cover. Ear-splitting explosions echoed all around the cameraman, so loud that they woke up Zilv.

"Ah! What's going on!"

Robert grabbed him, "Whoa, whoa! It's okay. It's just the TV."

"What are you watching?"

"A live stream of the riot in downtown. William sent it to me."

Zilv became quiet and joined Robert.

The cameraman looked around. The crowd did not run from the explosions. The police tried flash bangs and long-range taser pellets to scatter people. It did the opposite. People furiously shouted and threw things.

"Grab a brick!"

"Smash the pigs!"

The cameraman moved to a safer spot as the mob hailed trash and rocks onto the police.

"Holy shit! Holy shit!" the cameraman exclaimed as he peeked out from behind a bench, "I'm afraid there might be shooting today. People are out for blood. It's only a matter of time."

A brick found its way into the head of a police officer, knocking him back. In retaliation, the police began shooting into the crowd. People scattered and screamed as bullets hit them.

Zilv let out a horrified gasp.

"They're killing them! Robert! They're killing those people!"

Robert's eyes widened, "Oh my God."

The cameraman dared not move, totally paralyzed with horror. The rioters carrying guns found cover and shot back. Some dared the bullets, throwing Molotov cocktails, homemade explosives, stones, and bricks. Outnumbered, the police fell one by one until they retreated into the capitol building, leaving the Militia outside to move forward in a destructive advance.

"You!"

The cameraman turned and raised his hands as someone pointed a gun at him.

"Are you filming?"

"Y-Yes!"

"Grab his ass. He's coming with us!"

Two men grabbed the cameraman and brought him into view of the Capitol building.

The city was burning behind them. Fires raged as the crowd tore everything apart.

"Look at him!" shouted one of the people.

The cameraman gazed at a Militia member with a gun.

"I don't know how many people are watching your stream, but this is our message to all of you!" the man pointed behind them, "This is the People! The many! The oppressed! The hungry! The sick! The dying! This country was built on the backs of our forefathers, and it's now carried by us! It was built with liberty and equality for all! That is not the country I see today! People like President Hudson call us terrorists for taking back what is ours. It's our right to fight against tyranny. It's our right to burn the foundations of government when it does not serve the People. It's our right to do anything to keep our liberty. For those watching, if you value your freedom, your right to life, liberty, and the pursuit of happiness, do not stand idle. Join us, and fight against those who would hold you as slaves!"

Shouts behind the man caused him to turn around as the cameraman shifted his gaze.

T-PEM members flooded toward the Militia from a different direction and gathered in front of the capitol building. The T-PEM group had similar weapons and carried the hammer and sickle image as opposed to the Gadsden rattlesnake. One woman even held a large red banner with the hammer and sickle. No one exchanged words.

The two groups clashed. They fought with melee weapons and threw objects at one another before those with guns began shooting at the opposite sides. Parts of each group engaged with the police at the Capitol entrance.

While the Militia was distracted, the cameraman turned and ran to flee the battle, "Oh my God, oh my God. I need to get out of here!"

His gaze went back and forth. People were dying left and right. They were being burned alive, shot, or brutally beaten. Standing between the T-PEM and People's Militia members, those relishing in the anarchy took the chance to vent their suffering and hatred. The noise was deafening, so incoherent in the live stream that Robert turned the audio down.

The cameraman did not escape the fighting even as he sprinted away from the capitol building. The frenzy had spread throughout the city. Businesses burned, people stomped and killed each other, and corpses from the sick or murdered littered the street. Ambulance and fire drones soared above, none swooping down to save anyone as people cried out for help.

The cameraman sprinted down an alleyway and onto another street, passing T-PEM members throwing Militia members and police officers onto burning cars. They chanted and danced among the carnage.

"Fuck the state! Emancipate! Fuck the state! Emancipate!"

The cameraman turned and sprinted in the opposite direction.

Zilv grabbed Robert's arm and shook it, "Turn it off! Turn it off!"

Robert snapped his fingers at the TV projector and shut it off. Zilv had tears in his eyes. Robert pulled him into a hug.

"It's okay, it's okay, baby. Don't cry," Robert said.

"Oh my God, Robert, the country is falling apart. They killed each other! They're killing each other right now!"

"It's okay! It's off. The TV is off. What's happening isn't happening here. We're okay."

After a few minutes of leaning on Robert, Zilv calmed down.

"Are you okay?" Robert asked.

"I'm okay, I'm okay...."

"I need to call William. He told me to call him after we finished watching the live stream."

Zilv let go of Robert and laid down, "Okay. Please hug me after."

Robert frowned and swiped on his forearm.

"Yo," William said as he picked up.

"Yo, did you see that shit?" Robert asked.

"I'm still watching it, bro!"

"We had to turn it off. Why did you send me that, dick?"

"To show you what's going on. These aren't just riots. This isn't just a quarantine. It's a civil war. You won't need a job for a while, if ever again."

"Civil war?"

"The Second Civil War. All this is on the news right now, and the leaders of T-PEM and Renning have already claimed responsibility for all the chaos across the country and the chaos that will follow. Both groups are getting armed and organized."

"All right, all right. What are you trying to say here?"

"What I'm trying to say is that the country is falling into war, and we—or you—need a plan. I don't think sitting in your apartment with a month's worth of supplies and just the two of you is gonna work, Robert."

"Where else would we go, William? Trying to get out of the city is dangerous, and I don't have a car."

"I'm staying underground. There's going to be fighting, bombing, and all sorts of shit going on in the city, so it's the safest place, in my opinion."

"Look, we can't just get up and leave into the underground."

"Yes, you can. If you want to stay safe, you'll talk to Zilv about it and consider your options."

Robert sighed, "All right, we will talk about it. It'll be hard to convince him, but it'll probably be safer than here. I'll call you back later."

# 9

# Hide Away

8:27 PM, July 17, 2078

The news broadcast played in the background.

*"Following the nationwide riots across the country last night, the leaders of T-PEM and the People's Militia went live on various social platforms speaking about the violence. Travis Dodds, one of the five leaders of T-PEM, was among the first to go live, having this to say."*

The newscast transitioned to a tall, brown-haired man with a clean-shaven face and a hammer and sickle tattooed on his neck. Behind him stood four men with guns, each wearing gas masks with tinted visors.

*"I've waited my entire life for this to happen. A nationwide awakening, a realization across every state and every city. The proles' eyes have been opened. Now they can see the greed of the rich and feel the government's boot upon their necks. Now they can see what those on top have feared for a long time, the looming specter of communism, ever-present, and awakening from its slumber. The threat of a workers' revolution, so ancient and nearly forgotten, has returned to exact its vengeance upon those who'd enslave the humble worker. Soon the world will be remade for the common people, the honest and the humble, liberated from greed and gluttony."*

The newscast switched back to the reporter.

*"Truly terrifying words. Dodds continued by stating the goals of T-PEM and*

*declared war against the US government and the People's Militia at the end of the live stream. In a live response, Hans Renning took responsibility for the nationwide attacks and riots last night before declaring war on T-PEM and the US government."*

*"As of this morning, President Hudson has declared martial law across the country, and one of his latest interviews states that he is not afraid to take military action against both terrorist groups."*

\* \* \*

"Robert, are you sure?" Zilv asked.

"I'm sure, babe. T-PEM, the Militia, and the government will be bombing the shit out of one another, and we have no idea when all of this will stop. William says that we'll be safer underground and that he'll help us. If we stay here, we can only be here for a month, and we'll be vulnerable. What if the military starts kicking down doors? Or what if either T-PEM or the Militia begins looting to keep up their supplies? Or worse?"

"I don't know, darling, we're giving up a roof over our heads and a locked door."

"It's not gonna matter in the long run, babe. We're not gonna be able to stay here."

Zilv looked down and sighed, "If it's the smartest thing we can do, then let's do it. I can't see us staying here either."

"It might be our only option. I'll call William and have him come over. He can help us take what we need."

"All right. I'll begin packing," Zilv went to the bedroom.

Robert swiped his arm and called William.

"Yo, did you guys decide?" William asked.

"Yeah, we're choosing your option. Are you able to come over and help us move what we need?"

"I can be there in an hour. About to make a deal. Whatever you do, don't go out on the streets. It's fire and hell out there."

"All right, we'll just pack until you come. See ya."

"Peace."

70

Robert went to the bedroom. Zilv had already laid out the only two suitcases they owned, an old backpack and a box they had gotten from a delivery once.

"Clothes first?" Robert asked.

"Yeah. I'm thinking clothes, food, supplies, weapons, mask filters...."

Robert nodded and grabbed the delivery box. He raided their pantry and fridge while Zilv carefully laid out, folded, and packed clothes. Robert took as much as possible, including a few cooking utensils, tools, and an Ignium-powered burner. Miscellaneous objects, like Ignium batteries and extra gas-mask filters, also found their way into the box. Once the box was filled to the brim, he taped it up.

He grabbed their masks and gloves and brought them to Zilv.

"Did you get everything in the kitchen, darling?" Zilv asked.

"Yeah, how's it going here?" Robert asked.

"It's going okay. What do you want to take with us?" Zilv asked.

Robert looked at the pile of clothes Zilv had placed on the bed, scratching his chin, "Only a few smart clothes. The long sleeve stuff. Only the things that keep us warm and safe. We can leave the rest."

Zilv pointed at one part of the pile, "All right, thought those would be the right ones. They're already packed. Anything else?"

"Uh... let's bring two blankets and our pillows," Robert said.

"They're gonna get so dirty down there," Zilv said with a frown.

"Doesn't bother me too much," Robert shrugged.

"Wish we had sleeping bags," Zilv said.

"Me too. I'll roll up the blankets and grab the pillows. Can you get our guns?"

"Yeah."

Robert went into their small closet and grabbed his belts. He took the blankets from the bed, rolled each one up tightly, and tied them with the straps. Once compacted, he stuffed each blanket as tight as he could into their emptiest suitcase. The pillows went in last, barely fitting with the folded blankets.

Zilv returned with Robert's plasma rifle. Robert put the rifle's sling over his shoulder and kissed him.

"I think that's everything?" Robert asked.

"I'm going to go through the apartment one more time. Still need to grab the stuff from the bathroom and put it in your backpack. Help me double-check everything."

Robert nodded. They went through the apartment, grabbed anything they deemed valuable, and packed it. Then they sat in front of the TV and waited for William to arrive.

"Ugh," Robert began, "this sucks. I'm gonna miss the TV. I don't wanna watch stuff on my arm. Ours is probably gonna get stolen," Robert sighed anxiously, leg bouncing up and down.

Zilv kissed his cheek, "It'll be okay, darling. I can see you're stressing out."

"I'm not stressing out."

"Yes... you are," Zilv said as he put a hand on Robert's knee to still his leg.

Robert watched his leg slow to a halt. He inhaled deeply and exhaled slowly as he calmed down, "Sorry."

"No, sorry. I'm stressed too. We'll make it through this."

"You're right. I'm ju–"

A knock came on the door.

"Yo! Masks on, bitches! We're leaving!" William shouted from the other side.

Robert and Zilv stood and put their masks on.

"You get the door. I'll get our stuff," Robert said.

Zilv let William in. Robert entered the bedroom and put his backpack on before rolling the suitcases out to the living room. William had changed his clothes since the pair had last met. Instead of tattered clothes, he had a thick layer of smart clothes and a new jacket. He also had a new black mask similar to the police masks and rugged militaristic boots that clicked with each step.

"How are you guys doing?" William asked as he came in.

"Stressed," Zilv said.

"I just wanna get this over with," Robert added.

William scratched his tattooed arm and shrugged, "I don't blame you guys. I came up with a plan for you two."

"Let's hear it," Robert said.

"All right, I'm gonna take you both into the sewers. There's a huge maze under the city, so there are a lot of places to hide. There are a few hobo camps, a few black-market camps, yadda, yadda. I'm taking you to one of the camps I frequent. Kind of a mix between a hobo and a black market. I'm hoping Robert can find work there, and you guys can find what you need since the camp has a little market and extra space for you guys to live."

"That sounds good. What do you think, Robert?" Zilv asked

Robert nodded, "That does sound like a good place. We'll be safe there, too?"

"For a while. The fighting will be on the surface, though the military might conduct raids in the sewers. We'll see. I'm working with some people to see if we can get you guys smuggled out of the city later. Sounds good?" William asked.

"That sounds wonderful!" Zilv said, bouncing slightly and shaking his hands.

"Sounds good. Come on, let's get out of here. Take the box in the kitchen," Robert said and pointed.

William went to the kitchen and picked up the box. Robert took a suitcase and his backpack, while Zilv took a bag.

William groaned, "This is heavy."

"It's the kitchen stuff. Hold on, set it down. There're handles on the sides."

William set the box down. Robert picked up one side, and William picked up the other. Zilv led them out, keeping the door open as the clumsy pair scraped their way out.

"Go that way," Robert said.

"Which way? That way?" William asked.

"No, that way," Robert told him and pointed.

The suitcase in Robert's hand scraped against the door frame.

Zilv chuckled and shook his head, "You guys are literally carrying one box together and can't go through a doorway."

"Hey, don't you judge us. Unless you want to carry the box by yourself?" William asked.

Zilv snorted and shook his head again, "No, no, I got my hands full."

They carefully exited the apartment and went downstairs to the street level. They left the building and snuck through a crack in the fence. To get the box through, Robert and Zilv had to keep the chain-link hole open as William grappled with the whole thing. The opening led them into a dead thicket of bone-dry bushes and trees with cracked bark. The grove was like a basin; its center led to a sewer hole. All around was refuse, primarily plastic bags and containers caught in the dead bushes and trees. They approached a sewer hole and set their things aside as they opened the sewer lid.

"How is this gonna work?" Zilv gazed into the hole.

"Box looks like it'll just fit. Probably will just scrape down the walls and be easy to bring down," William said.

Zilv went into the hole first, followed by Robert and William. They squeezed into the tight opening, scraping against the sides as they climbed down with the box.

They entered a room full of panels and machinery connected to the apartment building, mainly giant Ignium batteries and water controls. William led the pair into a tunnel. When they reached an intersecting fork, they went down the right. After venturing through a few additional tunnels, they arrived at the ladder leading into the circular room they had visited when getting their merchandise.

Zilv approached the drop and looked down, "Oh, sheesh. This is gonna be a pain. Hey, how about you guys go down, and I can drop the suitcases and box on you guys? Think you two can catch them?"

"That might work," William replied.

Robert and William left their luggage, climbed the ladder to the bottom, and looked up. First, Zilv took the suitcases and dropped them down the hole. It was easy to catch the light bags between the two of them. William placed them aside as they prepared for the heavy box.

"Robert, do you think anything in here will break?" Zilv asked.

"Nah, it's just food and cooking stuff. Just drop it to us."

Zilv pushed the box forward. The weight tipped the box to its side as it fell over the edge. The objects inside clattered around as it fell full speed to the ground. William and Robert grunted as they caught the box and nearly stumbled before setting it down.

"Okay, we're not doing that again," Robert groaned.

William rubbed his forearms where the box had hit him, "Come on, let's go," he said as he picked up the box with Robert.

Zilv descended the ladder and grabbed his suitcase. William led them down the ninth tunnel, the last of the other tunnels in the domed room.

Robert frowned. He didn't like the city underground. Each footstep sounded wet, and everything echoed. The whole place had a rancid smell that stuck to clothes, and there were rats. The smell didn't bother him too much through his gas mask. The rats certainly did. Unlike rats of earlier decades, these were genetically mutilated. Tumors covered their vast bodies. Most had fur missing and extra body parts, and they appeared starved and dying. The chemicals and pollutants in the air and water wreaked havoc on many animal populations. Though rats were some of the last surviving animals on Earth, their proximity to humanity made them suffer.

The rats fled in front of them as the trio walked through the slick and moist sewers. William led them through turns, corners, and every twist and roundabout that Robert could imagine. He became confused after their tenth tunnel and eventually forgot the way back.

Abruptly, William stopped, "Woah!"

At the entrance of one tunnel, a brightly burning flare illuminated the surrounding area.

"What? What's wrong?" Zilv whispered.

"Can't take this way. Something's wrong," William said.

"What's wrong?" Robert repeated Zilv's question.

"I have no idea. We can't use this way, though. I know another one. Come on."

They went back the way they came. They passed through even more tunnels, a few rooms with power stations, batteries, water-control stations, and an old metro station. After thirty minutes, which felt like forever, they arrived at a tunnel with lights at the end.

"All right, we're here. When we get there, I'll do the talking. A lot of people here are armed, so no sudden movements, and don't touch your rifle," William said.

Zilv and Robert nodded.

In front of the camp was a wall built from scrap and rubbish. Barrels, cans, trash bags, rotten plywood, metal sheets, and other junk were all layered into a thick divide. Floodlights shone down upon the tunnel length ahead. Men looked over the wall at the approaching trio.

"Flash!" a voice came from the camp.

"Thunder!" William shouted back.

"Who are you?"

"It's William! William Crawford! I'm a smuggler. I made a deal a while ago with Eric to get two of my friends in here."

"Let them in! It's William! Hurry up!"

The "gates" were just two big metal sheets slid aside to make a gap in the wall. The trio walked forward, entering the camp.

Robert looked around at the encampment, which was more significant than he had imagined. Twenty tents led into a domed room with five tunnels. Inside the domed room, a self-functioning village bustled with people selling merchandise and guards patrolling. An Ignium-powered filter station pulled water from different parts of the sewers. Rows of hydroponic shelves sat in one area, empty of crops. Robert assumed that the chemicals in the air made it impossible to grow anything down here.

A few people approached the newcomers.

A short, middle-aged man walked up to William and shook his hand, "Hey, William, how are you?"

"Yo, Eric, I'm doing good. Brought these two along finally," William said.

"Oh yes, Robert and Zilv?" Eric asked.

"Correct. I'm not gonna waste any time today. I got places to be. Do you have a tent for them as I paid for?" William asked.

"With all the filters and food you got me? A tent and a single favor."

Eric approached Robert and Zilv, "I'm Eric. I'm sort of the leader around here, but not really. I just make sure things stay orderly here."

"Nice to meet you, Eric. I'm Robert, and this is Zilv."

"Good to meet you both. Let me give you guys a little tour. I have them handled from here, William."

"All right, see you guys," William said.

"Where are you going?" Robert asked.

"Business, like usual. Don't worry. You'll be fine."

Robert frowned as William went out the same gates they had entered from. After a moment, he turned and followed Eric with Zilv.

"Yo, Bobby. Help him carry that box," Eric ordered.

"Got you, boss."

A guard helped Robert, walking with them around the camp.

"There's a lot of different people living in this camp. We name each camp down here after the street that it's under, so this place is called Rosewood. It'll be safe for you two. T-PEM and the Militia don't bother us, the police don't know about us, and there's commerce here. One of you can probably get a smuggling job like William or work for anyone here. People come and go, but the business stays the same."

Eric gestured at various parts of the camp, raising his palm or pointing his finger, "Over here, you can get your food and illegal rations from Martha. Over there, weapons and ammo from Chris. Anything you need, someone here has it. Of course, if you need help, just ask one of the locals. Most of us are friendly. Just avoid Mad Mike. He just wants to sleep all day and is prone to stabbing people."

Robert furrowed his brow, doubting the camp's safety.

Eric approached a small tent toward the edge of the camp and stood beside its entrance, "Here, you guys will sleep here. I know it's not much, but it's something."

Robert and the guard put the box down as they arrived.

"Thanks, Bobby. You can go back now," Eric said.

"All right, boss. Call me if you need anything else."

Eric waited for the guard to leave. Then he looked back and forth between the two. As he raised his hand, the friendly smile beneath his visor became flat, and his tone grew more serious, "All right, look. William has entrusted your safety to me, so I need you two to listen. There are a few rules when it comes to living here. Number one rule: don't be a dumbass. Don't bother anyone for no reason, don't argue, and don't pick fights. Most important rule."

He pointed at Robert, "And for all that is good, don't tell anyone that you two had an apartment or employment. Most of these people would kick your asses if they figured that out. The reason y'all are so clean right now is for whatever reason you want. You got lucky and got offered to shower or fell in a lake or something. Here, you're like everyone else. I'll get you guys work as soon as possible, so you don't starve to death. Meanwhile, get comfortable. All right?"

"All right," the pair responded.

"Good. Come to me if you need help or got questions that you don't think you can ask anyone else about."

"Thanks for the hospitality, Eric," Robert said.

"No problem, and do not mention it. Goodbye."

# 10

# Smelly Smuggling

*11:34 AM, August 22, 2078*

*\* \* \**

Robert and William sat on a concrete ledge and listened to a news stream through their implants.

*"Fighting continues for the sixth week across the US as insurgent groups battle the military for control across the country. Leaders of T-PEM and the People's Militia continue to avoid authorities and remain in hiding as they organize more attacks on military and law enforcement. As military forces struggle to maintain law and order, more insurgent groups have emerged independently of T-PEM and the People's Militia."*

*"In other news, the FP-78 pandemic continues to spread across the US, reaping a deadly toll. So far, over two million people have died due to what many call Rabbit Fever. Between the pandemic and terrorist attacks across the country, hospitals are overflowing. Many cannot treat new patients, often turning away people who aren't seriously ill or injured."*

*"In Europe, Germany has withdrawn from the EU, pulled its support from allies, and is threatening war with neighboring countries. This was in response to the silence earlier this year when Germany requested aid with its resource crisis. Following Germany's lead, Poland and Ukraine have also left the EU, leading to European tensions unseen since the Russo-Ukrainian war."*

"Turn it off. Let's keep going," William whispered.

Robert swiped his arm and followed William. As they ventured through the underground, they listened for any sound over their mucky footsteps.

With a month of experience, Robert was finally able to navigate the maze of the sewers. He was now a smuggler. His legs had gotten stronger from weeks of walking and running. He now wore a layer of thick clothing over his smart clothes: a jacket and rough pants that kept him safe from scrapes and cuts. He had new padded gloves, similar to motorcycle gloves, and his gas mask had been outfitted with a flashlight. He carried a small arsenal of items: his plasma rifle, a Smoke-Bang, Ignium batteries, an extra flashlight, and a canteen. Smoke-Bangs, a cross between a smoke bomb and a flash bang, were used by most smugglers to escape situations.

"What time are we supposed to meet them?" Robert asked.

"Like 11:45, so in ten minutes or so," William replied.

Robert looked behind them, "Where are we?"

"North side of the city. We're really far out," William said.

"Feels like we've been at this for quite some time already."

"We've been walking for at least an hour."

"Do the guys over here know we're coming?" Robert asked.

"Yeah, we're not gonna get jumped. They're not gonna be making any enemies during this time."

"All right, let's just get in and out. I wanna get back to our territory."

Traveling through the never-ending tunnels, Robert occasionally noticed sections of the sewers where the air seemed to wiggle. These were pockets of chemicals that sat condensed in one spot, asphyxiating whatever was caught in them. Small piles of dead mutant rats were common around the chemical clouds.

Robert paused as the tunnel rumbled and the water at their feet quivered. They stopped and looked around. Robert furrowed his brow and squinted upward at the rumble while William looked entirely undisturbed. Eventually, the quake passed.

"What the hell was that?" Robert asked.

William smiled, "It's just a metro station. A few tunnels around the city do this. Is this your first shake?"

"Yeah, what the hell? I didn't know that could happen."

"Always shocks new guys. Come on, let's keep going."

Eventually, they reached a fork in the tunnels and a slight drop. They descended and came across an old metro station. The entrance to the surface had been sealed off with cement, and the entire station was stripped barren of anything valuable.

"Yo, look at Benny to the left there," William said.

"Benny?" Robert repeated.

He jumped slightly. A skeletal body sat at the edge of the sealed tunnel to the surface. The body had a broken mask, a down jacket, dirty jeans, and a pair of red shoes. Beside it lay a backpack. The backpack was open, with trash in front of it as if people had ransacked it and thrown it to the ground. The body itself was entirely still, as if frozen in time.

"Holy shit. I didn't even notice him."

"Yeah, Benny's been there a while. Not as long as Larry has, though certainly a year or two."

"What does he mean?"

"Means we're almost there."

Robert glanced back at Benny before he lost sight of the body, shuddering as they carried on.

William chuckled, "Do the bodies still freak you out, bro?"

"Yes! They're just sitting there, dude."

"That's what they do, Robert. They're dead."

"It freaks me out."

"Everything freaks you out."

"Ah, shut up, dude."

Many bodies were left to rot in the sewers. Out of public sight, nobody bothered to call for removal services. Their cause of death varied. Some were sick, some were old, some starved to death, some collapsed from chemical poisoning, and a few had been murdered. Most of them had been looted and served as landmarks to determine one's location in the underground. Smugglers often gave them basic names, such as Larry or Benny, or even names based on their clothing.

After passing through more tunnels, they found a junction guarded by three men. Two sat on the ground playing checkers, while the third sat on a lawn chair.

As Robert and William approached, the man on the lawn chair looked up at them, "What's your business here?"

"Making a deal with Mike and Nicole. You might know them," William responded.

"Barely, just know that they're on this side. What are all y'all dealing?"

"None of your business. Just let us through. We won't make trouble."

"Fine, get going. Don't take a right down there," the man warned.

William nodded. They went down one of the intersecting tunnels, took a left at its end, and continued to a small camp. The whole encampment stood between two platforms on opposite sides of a tunnel. The camp consisted of five tents and a few sleeping bags on the concrete. Each platform had rusted machinery. A barrel fire burned on one side of the encampment. As they approached, a few people gathered around the barrel glanced up at Robert and William.

"Yo, we're looking for Mike and Nicole," William said.

Two people stood.

"That's us," said a tall man.

The four approached one another.

"Yo, this is Robert. I'm William. We're here for the deal."

The taller man was dressed in ragged clothes, wore a cracked visor, and carried a pistol holstered on his hip. The woman was shorter than the man and had no hair. Scars and burns covered her face beneath her visor.

"Nice to meet you both, I'm Mike, and this is my wife, Nicole."

The pair exchanged nods with Nicole.

"Come to my tent over here and let's talk," Mike said.

They went over to the opposite platform.

"You guys can sit anywhere. It doesn't matter. Did you bring the stuff?" Nicole asked.

Robert looked over at William since he generally carried their merchandise.

"Yeah, right here," William said.

He reached into his pocket and pulled out a small container. Neither of them knew what was in the container and didn't ask.

"Do you guys have the money?" Robert asked.

"Of course," Mike replied and pulled back his sleeve.

They exchanged the container and tapped each other's implants, a pling coming from both.

"Was good doing business with you then," William said.

The two people opened the container, leaning away to hide it from the pair and whispering. After a few moments, they nodded to each other and turned back.

"This is perfect," Nicole said.

"We have an offer for you two," Mike said.

Robert glanced back and forth between the pair. This was the first time he had heard anything beyond "goodbye" from a customer once a deal was done.

William's eyes narrowed, "What kind of offer?"

Nicole raised two fingers, "We're looking for two smugglers to do surface runs with merchandise. We got some people up there who want some products, but the civil war keeps most smugglers down here. We'll pay you good."

Robert and William looked at each other.

"Who are we working with?" Robert asked.

Mike shrugged, "Just people. It shouldn't matter to you two. Some people in T-PEM and the Militia also want some of our products. You'll get respect from both sides here in the city as long as you don't tell them that you're working for the other side."

"When would we begin?" William asked.

"September," Nicole said.

William rested his head on his hand, "We'll think about it and message you our decision by tomorrow. How about that?"

"That works," Mike said.

"But decide by tomorrow, or we'll find someone else," Nicole said.

"Will do," Robert replied.

William smiled and waved.

"Well, it was a pleasure doing business with you guys. Be safe. Come on, Robert, it's time to go."

"Peace," Robert said.

"Goodbye," the pair replied.

Robert and William hopped off the platform and went the way they had come, not looking back.

Once they were out of earshot, Robert said, "Do you think it'd be worth the pay to go up there? I haven't been up there since we got here. Might be nice."

"I have. It's just as dark, and now there's fire and rubble everywhere."

"We might get paid more up there, and how hard would it be?" Robert asked.

William tilted his head left and right before answering, "Well, we'd have to avoid three sides of the civil war. If T-PEM or the Militia catches us, we get shot. If the military catches us, we get shot or imprisoned. Probably shot. You should talk to Zilv about it."

"I will. It might be easier to survive down here if we get paid more."

"Of course, it would be easier, but calculate the risk."

Robert nodded.

They passed the three men again as they descended the junction they had come from. Eventually, they walked by Benny. Robert glanced at him as they passed, still unsettled by the corpse's stillness.

"What other jobs do we have today?" Robert asked.

"Well, we're going back to our camp to pick up some food crates that need to be delivered to someone in the east. We got a gun deal on the south side of the city, and we have to deliver some 'special' product to someone near 'Yellow Pants.'"

"Yellow Pants" was the body of a woman with yellow pants on the ground of one of the sewer tunnels southwest of their main base.

"What do you mean by 'special' product?" Robert asked.

William glanced at him, "Drugs, Robert. Probably some nose candy."

"Oh... egh."

"Problem?"

"Not really, just not used to being a drug dealer. You remember what happened. Rubs me the wrong way, but money is money."

"I say let people do what they want, bro. Shit's falling apart. They can go out how they want. Plus, we'll escape if we see police or military down here."

"You're right."

As they ventured back into familiar territory, footsteps clattered in the tunnels.

William glanced back once, "We're being followed."

"How many of them?"

"Three, I think. Do you have your plasma rifle ready?"

"It's loaded. Should we talk to them?"

"Let's see what their pace is first. Let's hurry it up."

They walked faster. A trio of footsteps sped up behind them. Their pace was slightly faster than Robert's and William's. Each time the pair increased speed, the trio behind went somewhat quicker than them. William gestured forward three times and broke into a sprint. Robert readied his plasma pistol.

William prepared his gun, "Go! Go! Go!"

"Get them!" shouted one of the men from behind.

Their footsteps flashed as the two groups sprinted through the maze. Robert ducked as a rock flew past them, making him glance back to see the three men right on their heels.

"Shoot them!" William growled.

The pair turned and opened fire on the three men. William's pistol spat bullets with echoing bangs. The men chasing them recoiled. A bullet pierced the leg of one, causing him to scream and fall as Robert pulled the trigger.

Raw material stuffed into the weapon became heated in the Melt Chamber until it liquefied. As it melted, the gun hummed. A cascade of molten material spewed like a flamethrower, filling the sewer with a burning orange magma. Steam erupted as the liquefied material met water, creating a cloud between the two groups.

The two men ran away, dragging their wounded friend as he screamed in pain. Robert and William ran the opposite way.

They ran until they were far from the scene and almost at their home camp.

As he slowed and looked behind them, William began to laugh, "Holy shit! We showed them. Brings me back."

"Who the hell was those guys?" Robert asked.

"Buncha nobodies who wanted our shit."

Robert frowned, "Bastards. Shows them. Let's get back. Zilv misses me."

# 11

# Blind Run

*1:05 AM, September 9, 2078*

\* \* \*

*"Welcome back to Liberty Talk with your host, Billy Wideman. The world's gone crazy, I tell you. In today's news, the war in Europe continues for a second week as German forces spearhead into Denmark. Tensions have risen all over Europe, prompting many countries to take up policies of self-preservation. With the assault on northern Europe, many countries have begun to secure their borders in fear of German invasion. Rumor has also spread of supposed German plans to invade Poland and establish a forward position to invade other Slavic countries. It sounds like World War II all over again."*

*"Most countries in Eastern Europe have begun negotiations to leave the EU and form a Pan-Slavic union. Meanwhile, the UK has become more isolationist with the downfall of Europe, while France has attempted to become allies with the rest of Western and Southern Europe. Now, to our friends in Moscow. They've shut down travel in and out of Russia and have mobilized their military in anticipation of a Chinese invasion. Why would China invade? Trees, ore, oil, and any other resources it can take. As you know, Russia has some of the last stores of lumber worldwide."*

*"To our listeners, I think this is the end of the world as we know it. Call me crazy, but I think when the big boys like America step up to the ring, there will be*

*fire and brimstone in the sky."*

* * *

The radio broadcast played in Robert's mind as he went about his day. Fire and brimstone. He was still nervous about going to the surface, even if doing so could yield a huge reward. The promise of money encouraged him to talk to Zilv.

"Zilv, it won't be that dangerous," Robert said.

"It won't be *that* dangerous? Robert, it's a hellscape up there. T-PEM, the Militia, and the military have been bombing the hell out of one another for months. You could get killed or hurt at any moment!"

"It won't be! We'll go out at night, William will be with me, and we'll use the sewers most of the way."

Zilv sighed sharply, "Are we really not making enough money already? Is this necessary, Robert?"

"It will be easier for us if I can make more. Maybe we can even buy our way out of the city."

Zilv's face, scrunched and red with frustration, lightened as his brow raised, "You think we can get out?"

"I've been looking for people to help us. I think we can get out, get some transport, all that. We just need the money, and it starts with accepting this deal."

"Okay, fine. If you think it'd be best for us, then do it. But I swear, if you get hurt or killed, I'll beat you up...."

Robert chuckled, "Okay, I promise I won't get hurt."

* * *

Another month passed. Robert's feet still ached after long days, but he had gotten used to the sensation. It was their first day of night runs, and Robert could not get rid of the nervous butterflies in his stomach. He and William had been walking for an hour with small cases hidden in their pockets.

"Where are we going up?" Robert asked.

"Remember where Blue Gloves was?" William replied.

88

"Yeah."

"Ten minutes from her. She marks a forked tunnel where we should go right. You know more than I do when we go up to the surface."

"What do you mean?"

William pointed upward, "You lived and worked up there, so you know the city's surface better than me. We gotta deliver this to someone in the Militia's side of the city."

"Wonder what it looks like up there now?"

"Dirty."

"And probably on fire."

"We'll see."

"Remember what it was like when we were younger, before all this?" Robert asked.

"Dirty. It's always been dirty, especially when my mom and I were out on the street after my dad left."

"Yeah, you're right. There was already so much garbage when my parents kicked me out. Still, I kinda miss it. Sixteen with no real responsibility except for getting money with the homie."

"Kind of still like that. Just gotta take care of Zilv now," William told him.

"Yeah."

After a few minutes of walking, they arrived at "Blue Gloves." Robert knew little about the body other than her features. "Blue Gloves" was the body of a woman with blue gloves, rope, pipes overhead, and no more will for the world. He grimaced.

The smugglers went down the tunnel and turned right, finding a ladder going up a wall and to the surface.

"I'll go first," William said.

William grunted as he pushed the maintenance hole open and allowed the pair to slink their way onto the asphalt above. As they climbed up, he put the lid back on. The looming, dark titans that were so familiar to cities surrounding them. At street level, trash and overfilled dumpsters were everywhere. The pollution haze loomed above, rendering the world pitch black under the shroud of night.

Rubble filled the streets. A fire blazed in the window of a distant skyscraper, a lonely light in the smoggy gloom.

"Let's go before anyone sees us," William said.

Robert led the way. The wreckage was everywhere, with boards covering every entrance and window. Explosions had destroyed many buildings, and remnants from fighting littered among the trash heaps. Sandbags, barbed wire, bullet shells, scorch stains, burnt car shells, and bodies. So many bodies. Waste and rubble covered or obscured many of the corpses. Bullets had blown through some, a few had been stabbed to death, and some were burnt and broken from explosions. There were no birds to devour them, though mutant vermin gorged on the rotting feasts.

Robert gagged as they passed some of the bodies, turning away from the corpses as they walked, "What do we do if we encounter a patrol?"

"Hit the dirt, run, or hide. I think T-PEM controls this area. The military hasn't rolled through here yet. I heard they bombed a few buildings to get the resistance out but failed."

"Hopefully, they don't feel like detonating anything tonight," Robert said.

"Let's just get the delivery done so we can get back below."

They hugged the walls of the buildings to avoid the light of streetlamps and any open spaces. Many of the streetlamps had been destroyed or weren't on. Robert passed them and felt an itch. It was his job to fix Ignium products, and he believed he needed to repair faulty or damaged power lines. He frowned. The fear of getting fired and the anxiety of going to work had all been a waste.

Turning down one street, they stopped in shock. One of the giant skyscrapers in the city that towered dozens of stories above any other stood in the distance. Robert had always seen it from the highways as it stood alone in its immensity. Once, it had been a mighty pillar of glory to industrial power. Now, the war had claimed it. The top twenty stories had broken off, a blast had rendered a massive hole in its side, and the whole building leaned in an unsettling manner.

"Holy shit," Robert said.

They gawked at the tremendous ruin before walking a bit further. No one was in the streets. Sidewalks and alleys that used to be filled with the homeless, sick, and unemployed were vacant except for trash and corpses. Robert assumed the three groups fighting in the city took the population into their fold or left their bodies out where the pair now walked.

They disappeared down an alleyway and onto a street before hiding behind a collection of rubble. Just as they came out, a convoy of military vehicles rolled down the road.

There were five. Each was a black, elegant beast of engineering supported by eight wheels. Their thick, steel bodies were curvy, aerodynamic, and made to deflect missiles. They all had gun nests at their crowns and metallic heads with guns that could rotate in any direction and destroy anything. Soldiers trailed the mechanical beasts. Every man and woman wore black armor made from metal that could absorb bullets like a shock on a spring. Most carried guns that shot bullets, but some had plasma guns like Robert and railguns. Robert feared railguns since they shot metal discs magnetically. They were known and feared for their ability to accelerate projectiles fast enough to destroy concrete walls and penetrate thick steel. Some in the underground had railguns, though they had modified them to shoot any kind of scrap metal.

Robert and William remained as low as possible. The convoy passed without noticing them. They waited for the marching sounds to disappear before continuing.

The scenery changed as they moved across the city. Where communist symbols and propaganda had once stood, patriotic, anti-government propaganda and snakes took over. The Militia controlled this area. Robert noticed an occasional banner on street corners. It was generally a white cloth with a snake painted on it.

They hurried along, jogging past a burnt bus before a beam of light froze them in place.

"Stop! Who the hell are you two?"

The beam of light came from a window a few stories above, along with four guns pointed out from the broken glass.

"We're just passing through!" William said.

"Who are you with?"

"No one but ourselves," William replied.

"You ain't commies or Hudson's sheep?"

"Not at all. We're just out here making a delivery for the Militia. Does Walt Stippick ring a bell?" Robert asked.

William looked at Robert, then up at the light. They couldn't make anyone out behind the light but could faintly hear a discussion.

"We know a Walt Stippick," one said after a moment.

"We're here to deliver a special product to him. You guys know where he's at?" William asked.

"Come in here. Door's down there. No funny business, or we'll fill you two with holes."

They ran across the street and through a heavily barricaded airlock that no longer worked. As they got inside and adjusted to the light, they saw a legion of Militia members. Many were dressed like them, carried guns, and were very dirty. Some had smudged visors or darkly stained clothes, while others had bandages around their limbs. Many looked hungry, beaten, and dispirited. The Militia members eyed down the pair as they were led through the building.

The base was an old office building. It was now a bloodied center of fighting. The windows had been boarded up and blocked with everything that could be used, while the first floor was dimly lit. They were led five stories up before reaching a level with more Militia members. All the windows had been boarded up with only small gaps to shoot out from.

A man sat beside a desk listening to a radio. He looked up as they arrived and kept the radio at the same volume as he spoke, "Who are these two?"

"Some guys saying they have a delivery for you," said one of the Militia members.

"You're Walt?" William asked.

"That's me. You guys have it with you?"

They took the cases out of their pockets and laid them on the desk.

The man leaned forward, examined the containers, looked up, and nodded, "These will be much appreciated. You two can leave now. You'll get paid soon, but not here."

They were escorted out of the building without another word.

# 12

# Found You

*\* \* \**

*"Welcome back to Liberty Talk with your host, Billy Wideman. Breaking news today as Germany has launched an assault on Norway and Sweden from newly annexed Denmark. Refugees are attempting to evacuate to Finland, but all passages to the country are either blocked or jammed. The seaports are overfilled, and the land passages in the north are also overcrowded."*

*"Many countries in Eastern Europe, such as Ukraine, have left the EU in an attempt to form a Pan-Slavic union. In Belarus, revolutionaries have executed President Stafan Lyakh, which is part of the wave of civil unrest following resource shortages caused by a halt in European trade deals. Meanwhile, France, Spain, Portugal, Italy, Belgium, and the Netherlands have begun falling into anarchy as the death toll from Rabbit Fever continues to rise alongside widespread famine."*

*"In the East, Chinese forces have been reported to have begun amassing near the Russian border. President Khabalov Danye has stated that the movement of Chinese forces near the Chinese-Russian border threatens national security and that the Russian military is ready for anything. He also demanded the withdrawal of China's forces but has received nothing in return. In my opinion? Dark days are ahead for both China and Russia."*

*\* \* \**

Robert shut off the radio broadcast from his forearm and shook his head, "Keeps getting worse."

"I don't know why you listen to those broadcasts, bro. Just makes all this harder." William said.

"I like to be informed. Maybe one day they'll say the civil war is over."

"In your dreams. Come on, let's talk about something else."

William checked his bank account on his implant.

"Another day, another stack of cash, huh?" Robert grinned.

"Another day, another stack," William repeated and smiled.

Their most recent smuggling deal had gone well, filling their account with plenty for the next month. The venture had been a lifesaver.

Food was becoming scarce as stores were looted and emptied. Only the military could get supplies now, leaving those under their care lucky and those outside of it hungry. Militia and T-PEM raids were motivated by hunger rather than any military purpose, leaving the leftovers to trickle down to people like Robert and William.

"I think I almost have enough money saved to make some deals to get out of here," Robert said.

"Still trying to get out of the city? We're making so much money with this civil war going on," William said.

"Don't wanna stay here. I wanna go out to the countryside and get away from it all."

William shook his head and gestured ahead as his tone became serious, "There's nothing out there, Robert. Just old farms and sand."

"And soon, there'll only be rubble here. Plus, maybe we can go somewhere better. I was thinking of taking you with Zilv and me if you wanted. I might be able to make money."

William quieted for a minute, "If the money runs dry, I'll consider it. Don't wait around for me, though. If you want to go, go."

"Look, I don't want to get caught in some military raid or by either of the other two idiot groups, you know?"

"Whatever you say."

They approached the edge of their base camp. Lights shone on them, guards peeking over the wall with guns ready.

"Flash?"

"Thunder!" William shouted.

"Come on in!"

The pair entered the camp as the guards greeted them.

"Yo, you guys been careful out there? Heard a rumor of a military raid that was happening today. One of the camps not too far down the south end got cleared out," one of the guards said.

"We've been careful," William said.

"Yeah, haven't seen any T-PEM, Militia, or military," Robert said.

"All right, just be careful if you guys are planning to go to the south end."

"Will do," William said.

They went to the center of the camp and stopped.

"Was good making runs with you today. If you want to come with us when we leave the city, just tell me," Robert said.

William gave him a fist bump and nodded, "All right, I'll think about it. Tell Zilv I said hi."

"Will do."

Robert walked toward his tent at the edge of the camp, looking for Zilv as he passed the tents and tattered market stands. He had become somewhat known in the encampment and the city underground. People waved as he passed, some shouting greetings.

Maybe William was right. Here he had money, a little influence, some allies, and the ability to get what he needed. Then again, how long would it last? What would happen if the civil war ended? Either there'd be a new government, the current government would assume greater control, or everything would simply collapse. Being out in the countryside seemed better, even though many small towns across the nation were ghost towns.

How would they survive? There was a chance he could find a well and some filters, but the food was more complicated. No animals were outside the cities, and no crops could be grown. Everything had been moved to greenhouse skyscrapers, one of the reasons behind the resource shortages most of the world faced. People were starving. When he was younger, he ate three times a day. Now, he only ate once a day.

Robert arrived at the tent and opened the flap.

"Hello, darling," Zilv said.

They hugged, pressing their gas masks together in a sort of kiss.

"Hi, baby, how are you?"

"I'm good! I got us some money trading today. How was your day?"

"It was good. Just made a lot of money today. We might be able to buy our way out of the city soon."

Zilv smiled, "Finally! Did you talk to William about coming along?"

"Yeah, he said he'd consider it. I don't know if he's coming along. I don't think we should wait for him anyway."

Zilv sighed, "He's helped us a lot, I appreciate that, but I agree. If he doesn't wanna come with, then he doesn't wanna come with."

Robert sat beside Zilv, holding his arm around Zilv's shoulder, Zilv cuddling against him. They sat in silence for a minute.

"I hate it here," Robert said.

Zilv chortled, "Me too. It's so icky here. Wish we were on an island, somewhere green. Wish this war wasn't going on so we could go back to the surface."

"Yeah, I wish the sea wasn't gray and brown. An island would probably have plastic everywhere."

Zilv leaned away slightly, tilting his head up at Robert, "You're always so optimistic."

Robert chuckled, "Sorry, I'm just used to seeing plastic everywhere. A green island would be nice. You think anywhere in the world might still be green?"

"I don't know. Maybe somewhere in the middle of the ocean? Probably not."

"Probably not. It's okay. At least you're here with me."

"Oh my god, you're so cheesy."

"It's because you're cute, come o–"

A pop sounded in the distance.

"Oh, stop it!" Zilv said, pausing right after, "What?"

"You hear that?" Robert asked.

"No?"

"Shh. Listen."

The popping sounds echoed through the camp and became louder. Screams followed. Robert and Zilv looked at each other. Gunshots.

"We're under attack?" Zilv asked.

"It must be the military. We need to leave! We need to leave now!"

They grabbed what they had stored in the tent: a bag full of what they needed, bedrolls, and weapons. They rolled up their bedrolls, closed their bags, swung them over their shoulders, and rushed out of the tent.

"Robert! Robert!" William sprinted toward them.

Behind him, other people ran as bullets shredded through the center of the camp. Robert gripped his plasma rifle, heart jumping as he saw people get shot.

"Robert! We gotta go! The military is raiding us!" William said.

"What about the others?" Zilv asked.

"Screw them! We need to leave now!" William said.

A small grenade exploded into a fiery blue-colored ball that decimated a tent. The trio ducked as the blast wave echoed throughout the tunnels. The blue fire from the detonation began to consume other tents, multiplying as people ran. Soldiers flooded in after and gunned down the terrified people.

Robert sprinted in the opposite direction. Zilv followed him, trailed by William. Robert glanced back. The soldiers flooded and destroyed most of the encampment in just two minutes. He had no idea why they were attacking and could only assume that the camp was mistaken for an insurgent outpost or a supply outpost for either side of the civil war.

"Where are we going?" Robert asked.

"Just keep running! We need to get as far away as possible! Just go!" William barked.

They ran down tunnels and turns until the gunshots faded out of earshot, stopping on a platform.

As soon as they were on the concrete, Zilv sat down with an exhausted exhale, sweat coating his face, "Do you think we're good?"

William looked down the tunnel they came from, peering to see if there were any figures.

"I don't think anyone saw or followed us," Robert said.

"Will you guys shut up?" William asked. "I'm trying to listen."

William moved the hood protecting his head slightly, revealing his ear as he listened intently. He stood for two minutes before correctly putting the hood back on, "We're good. Rest up. Did you guys lose anything?

"No," Robert said.

"We have everything in our bags," Zilv said.

"Good. I need to figure out what we need to do now." William said.

"Can we move to another camp?" Zilv asked.

William's face scrunched in thought as he sighed, "I don't know. I don't carry a lot of favor with other people. Plus, it looks like the raids down here are becoming more common. Even T-PEM are beginning to take down camps trying to stay neutral."

"Where do we go then?" Zilv asked.

"The surface?" Robert suggested.

"Right into the arms of the war and the cold? Winter is almost here. We'll freeze our asses off," William said.

"We can't just sit down here. We'll get robbed by someone passing by," Zilv told them.

"Okay, okay! Look, let me make some calls and see what I can do, all right?" William muttered.

Robert frowned before sitting down beside Zilv. William glanced at them and went to the other side of the platform.

"What do you think of going to the surface?" Robert asked.

"I don't know. I think it's a bad idea," Zilv replied.

"We'll get away from the stink down here. We can hide in a bombed-out building for shelter, maybe. Somewhere where no one would care to look," Robert said.

"What would we do for food and water? And where would no one look?" Zilv asked.

"I don't know. Somewhere vacant? We can go back down here to get the food and water we've stored up. William and I can still do runs."

"I don't know, darling, I think it's a bad idea. Let's see what William has to say."

"All right."

They listened to William as he spoke on the phone, his tone getting more frustrated with each call.

After forty minutes of failures, he hung up his last call and growled, "Shit! Shit! Shit!"

"What's wrong?" Robert asked.

William groaned, "Nobody is willing to accept us in. I'm not taking us somewhere dangerous, either. We have no good options."

Zilv tilted his head and gestured outward, "Should we try and leave the city?"

William shook his head, "We don't have the money. We're down to a few thousand and need like four or five runs before we get enough to get out. We need even more money to be able to bring supplies with us out there. It's not safe."

Robert grimaced, "Then we go to the surface. We can find some bombed-out building to take shelter in, somewhere with a basement. We can hide from everything there."

"And get found out by anyone fighting the war? I swear you say the dumbest shit," William said.

"Screw you, William. It's not stupid. You guys are so afraid of everything up there, but we don't have anything down here. No one will take us in, and we'll probably get robbed down here. No one is up there except people fighting the war, and who's gonna go into an abandoned basement? We can find a place to warm up during the winter and ride everything out, and we can still do runs."

William sighed and put his hands on the back of his head, "All right, all right, fine. Where the hell do you want us to go up there, then?"

"You remember that old building we passed during our last night run? We can use that one. No one would go into that. It's completely empty and probably has a place for us to sleep. Plus, a lot of the windows are boarded up, so people won't see us or any light we make."

William's eye twitched as he glared. His fists curled as Robert spoke. He inhaled sharply, then let out his anger, "If you think that'll work, then it's probably our best option."

"I think it is, William."

"All right, I know how to get there. Follow me."

# 13

# Coughing Cold

*4:36 PM, November 14, 2078*

*\* \* \**

*"Welcome back to Liberty Talk with your host, Billy Wideman. The People's Militia and T-PEM have gained multiple victories over the past week across the country. T-PEM now controls most of the western seaboard, while the Militia has gained control of cities such as Austin, Denver, and Washington, DC. As far as I can tell, the military is spread thin, fighting against both sides, and is struggling to maintain control. Rumors have been going around that military forces are being called back to defend vital places such as the Pentagon and Fort Knox. My opinion? They're losing."*

*"For our listeners, I say prepare yourselves for more war. Once the US government has been eliminated, both sides will fight over what's left. In cities already free of military control, T-PEM and the Militia have reportedly been battling over the remaining ruins."*

*"In other news, Germany has annexed Norway and Sweden following the surrender of both countries. Meanwhile, other countries are continuing to collapse with resource shortages at an all-time high combined with the death toll from the FP-78 infection. Civil order in Ukraine and Belarus have reportedly fallen apart, while the rest of Europe struggles to hold on."*

The radio was the only thing that helped the trio keep track of time. Even so, the news often was too depressing for them to listen to for long, so they turned the broadcasts off. The city fell apart around them. Fighting went on throughout the day and only stopped occasionally. The city blocks where the three factions fought consisted of nothing but rubble. From terrorist attacks to bombings, the only thing that remained were corpses and smoke. No one picked up or removed the bodies, leaving the streets filled with corpses and rotting fumes.

The trio huddled in a small concrete room and could only listen as war ravaged the country. Robert could not predict when a bomb would drop or a gun would end someone's life. They were vigilant as they listened to the empty halls of their desolate shelter, waiting for a murmur or a footstep to disturb them. Robert had lost weight since they left the sewers, saving the food they had for Zilv and William. They ate once a day. William always urged him to eat more, though Robert often refused. He could deal with hunger as long as they still had food. To pass the time, they played relentlessly boring games like tic-tac-toe and silly variations of checkers made from pieces of wood and scrap material.

Robert felt tortured. He didn't want to survive like this, to scrape by and wait for fate to take them. He felt grateful that he didn't have to fight, though that was the end of his blessings.

"King me," Robert said.

William sighed, "Damnit."

"How do you suck so bad at checkers?" Robert asked.

"Because it's a stupid game," William snapped.

"You're better than me," Zilv said, letting out a hacking cough.

"Are you doing okay, baby?" Robert asked.

"It's nothing. Just a cough."

"You sure? You don't look so good," William said.

"Yeah... My skin's a little itchy and a little warm, but I'm sure it's nothing."

Robert and William looked at each other in concern. The cough had started yesterday and had not stopped. The pair had considered getting medicine, but Zilv urged them to stay. Robert knew he'd shut down if they didn't return, but they needed the medication.

They kept playing for a while and stopped as they heard a rumble outside. It was a squad of tanks. The spearhead of a convoy rolled through the streets outside. The ground shook slightly as dozens of feet stomped, creating a thunderous unified march as orders were barked over the convoy.

"Oh shit," Robert whispered.

"Damnit, not the military," William said.

They listened intently as the soldiers moved past the building. All of them jumped when a loud bang echoed through the street.

"In the windows!" shouted a soldier.

Gunfire erupted outside and was separated by explosive bangs as people gunned down the soldiers and disabled the tanks. Bullets, burning lasers, and molten plasma shot everywhere. The attack ended as quickly as it had started. A few seconds of silence followed the last gunshot before cheers erupted. Whoever had ambushed the patrol had won.

The three listened silently as people tore armor and guns from the corpses and emptied the tanks. It took only thirty minutes before they disappeared, leaving dead silence behind.

"You think they're gone, William?" Robert asked.

William listened, "Yeah, they know they have to leave before a response arrives to hammer them to smithereens. We don't have to go that way."

"What are you talking about?" Zilv asked.

"You need medicine, and we need more supplies to last here," Robert said.

"You guys are leaving me here?" Zilv asked.

"We will be back, Zilv. Listen to yourself. I can see through your mask that you're sick. You're pale as snow."

"What if you guys get hurt?" Zilv asked.

"What if you get sicker? It's worth the risk, darling," Robert said.

"We need stuff too. We will be fine. I'll keep an eye on this dumbass," William said, gesturing to Robert.

Robert snorted and gestured back, "And I'll keep this dumbass safe."

Zilv blinked and shook his head slightly, his gaze switching between the pair, "A-All right, all right. Just be careful, please. I love you, Robert."

"Love you too."

"Grab your shit, Robert. I'll call a guy who can help us," William said.

Robert grabbed his gear and gun as William left the room. Robert put his mask against Zilv's in a mock kiss, though he was afraid to touch him.

"Be safe, don't get hurt out there," Zilv said.

"I won't. Stay low here."

"I will."

Robert walked out of the room, waving to Zilv one more time. William was already on the phone as Robert went out to him.

"Look, we have a little bit of money. I can pay you for it. We need something to treat it... like the flu," William said.

William responded with "mhm" as the other person spoke, "We're not sick. No! We're not sick. We don't have a cough or rash or boils, nothing. Look, we need the medicine. You need the money. Wait, listen!"

As the call hung up, he let out an angry growl, "Fucker. Fucking war. Man, no one is loyal."

"Who was that?" Robert asked.

"An asshole. We can't buy medicine. What are we gonna do?"

"Find a pharmacy and see if there's anything left," Robert stated.

"There won't be any."

"And then where else are we gonna get medicine?"

William rested his hands on his hips and exhaled, dropping his head back, "All right, all right! We can raid a pharmacy. I know a place. Come on."

* * *

William moved the panel blocking the back door. Robert slinked out first and held it open as William followed. They stood in an alley, bathing in the shadows of looming buildings on either side, stinking piles of trash surrounding them. The November air bit as the temperature plummeted to winter frost. It was already freezing cold. The icy claws of winter were coming. Soon it would freeze the country over. Thanks to their smart suits, the pair weren't shivering, but they still felt uncomfortable.

"Let's go before anyone sees us," William said.

William led Robert down one side of the alley, going out to the street.

Robert stopped. Junk and rubble layered the ground between craters formed by explosions. A small path was carved through the wreckage. The shells of burnt-out cars stuck out in the ruin. In the distance, massive plumes of smoke rose from recent battle sites, flames consuming the toxic air as they burned. Even though the streets had never looked good, the destruction shocked Robert. It would take years to clean up after the war if there was anyone left to do the job.

They snuck along, remaining behind cover as they watched the windows above for gun barrels and people. When they could, they went through buildings, crossing over broken windows and through damaged walls. Occasionally, they'd find abandoned military outposts composed of sandbags, barbed wire, and empty tents. Each was stripped clean. The mere presence of the ruined outposts discouraged the two, causing them to go around the deserted encampments.

"Where are we going?" Robert whispered.

"I know a shopping complex near here with a pharmacy. We could find something there for Zilv if it's not picked clean," William replied.

"What do we do if it is picked clean?"

"We figure something out."

Robert frowned as they kept walking. He held his gun firmly, ready to be ambushed at any second. William pointed his pistol and would occasionally halt abruptly to examine their surroundings. Robert almost ran into him each time he paused.

After twenty minutes, they reached a vast, cube-like building that soared into the sky with the rest of the city. Parking lots on all sides separated the colossus from other structures. The war had torn it apart. Rocket holes and black blemishes from fires covered the entire skyscraper.

Hesitating, William eyed windows and corners, "You think we're good?"

"I don't see or hear anyone," Robert replied.

They observed the area before sprinting across the street and parking lot. Robert followed William through a pair of smashed glass doors and into a broken airlock.

Fifty stories formed the inside of the square mall. Escalators that had stopped working a long ago connected the levels. A massive atrium in the center allowed Robert to see the skylights at the very top. On the opposite side, an elevator had crashed into the ground.

Robert fondly recalled shopping here a long time ago. In the center of the first level, a giant fountain had become black from dirt, dust, and polluted air.

"Which level has the pharmacy?" Robert asked.

"Like level twenty-five or something. You like stairs?" William said with a wry smile.

Robert looked up again, "Not anymore."

William chuckled, "Come on, let's get climbing."

They walked past empty and destroyed stores. Robert looked into each store. Some sold cosmetics, others clothes, a few sold toys, and a lot sold technology like implants and devices. Only a few stores had anything left, typically stuffed toys and cosmetics. Looters had ransacked the rest. The second level was much like the first, destroyed and emptied. After climbing over twenty flights of unpowered escalators, Robert sweated, and his legs ached. The higher they went, the more intact the stores were.

"For fuck's sake, whoever broke the elevator is an asshole," Robert said after another flight of stairs.

"Don't give up now. We're almost there. Plus, it wouldn't work without power even if it was still intact."

"I could fix the power if I had tools. I used to work with Ignium all the time."

"Oh yeah, forgot about that. Been a while. Wasn't your boss an asshole?"

"Yeah, but he paid me okay."

"Wonder what happened to him?"

"Probably dead."

"You think one of your coworkers got him?"

"Definitely. I remember he had a few enemies. People get laid off, ya know."

"Yeah."

After climbing the last flight of stairs and walking across the floor, they arrived at "Goldberg's Pharmacy." Next to the store, Robert approached the railing separating them from the deadly drop that was the atrium. He looked over the barrier and down to the bottom floor.

"Whoa," he said.

He wasn't afraid of heights, but the proximity to such a drop made him uncomfortable. It was as if something was pulling him, making his stomach drop as he felt a gentle push behind him.

"Push!" William said with a laugh.

Robert screamed, swung around, and pushed back.

William stumbled back laughing, "Holy shit, your scream!"

"Why the hell would you do that!" Robert inhaled and exhaled while his heart thundered. As he calmed down, he stumbled to the opposite wall.

William cackled.

"You're such an asshole," Robert said.

"I know. I wouldn't push you. You know that," William said as his laughter died down.

Robert pointed at William, "Never again. Now, let's get what we came for and get the hell out of here."

William smiled and approached the pharmacy entrance, "All right, all right. Help me get it open."

The store had two barriers at the front. The first was a sliding chain link gate, and the second was a roll-up door. They grabbed the bottom of the door and lifted, heaving it up.

"Oh shit, this is heavy. We need something to prop it up, Robert."

"You got it?" Robert asked.

"Yep, just hurry up," William said with a strained voice.

Robert let go of the door and quickly ran out into the hall, where he grabbed a metal trash can to put under the door.

"Perfect," William said.

They ducked under the door, turning on the flashlights on the side of their masks. Most of the shelves were empty. Someone had broken the backroom entrance and cleaned the shelves behind the counter. They investigated the remnants.

"God damnit, where the hell is everything?" Robert groaned.

"Long gone. Hey! There're some cards here! Let's see here...." William said, picking up a card.

"Sorry I gave you an STD," he said in a silly tone.

"It doesn't actually say that, does it?"

"No," William said with a laugh. "There're a few cards over here—nothing about apologizing for giving you Bunny Fever. Ah, maybe they have something for the civil war? Nope."

Robert shook his head, "Let's just see if there's anything left."

They grabbed the remaining medicine, ranging from a small bottle of fungus treatment to stomach medication. Only nine items were left. Once they had emptied the front entirely, they ventured through the door into the back room. They got every box and bottle they could.

"What the hell is this?" Robert held up a bottle.

"Obin.... Nara? I don't know how to pronounce that," William said.

"I'll just take it. Did you find anything for Zilv?"

"No, nothing for the flu or anything," William said.

"I don't even know if it would help if we found anything."

"Do you think he has Bunny Fever?" William asked.

Robert stayed silent while he continued searching the shelves. What if Zilv did have Bunny Fever? Would he survive? A nervous sweat covered Robert as every bad scenario played out in his head.

William put a hand on his shoulder, "Look. He'll be okay. We'll find something."

"Let's just take what we have and get back. Maybe we can call someone or raid a hospital."

"Maybe. I have not seen any hospitals that aren't military bases, but I could make more calls."

They gathered up the remaining goods and left the store. William kicked out the trash can as they exited, causing the security gate to slam down loudly.

Robert jumped as the bang echoed, "Christ!"

William chuckled, "Sorry, I had to."

They went to the stairs and descended fourteen flights before William stopped, "You hear that?"

Robert approached the railing and listened. Footsteps came from below as he saw seven people enter the atrium floor.

"Crap, there's other people down there," Robert stated.

"God damnit, are they coming up here? Any way out?"

"Probably. I can't see who they are. We might be able to get out the back way. There's probably an employee-only area," Robert said.

"Like a warehouse area?"

"Yeah, let's go. There might be a door near the bathrooms."

"There are bathrooms two levels down. Let's go."

They ran down the stairs. The voices rose from below, orders faintly reaching them as they went down.

"Spread out! Search for food and water! Grab anything else that could be useful! Watch out for commies and fascists!"

Inside a hallway with bathrooms, they went through an employee door and into a large dark room filled with shelves.

"What is this?" William whispered.

"Probably storage for all the stores on this level. There's probably an elevator and some stairs here," Robert whispered.

They split up and shone their flashlights in search of an escape route. At the opposite end of the storage room was a giant elevator shaft. Near it, a staircase led down.

"Over here, let's go," Robert whispered.

William followed him. They went down the stairs level by level. Metal shelves loaded with empty boxes, crates, and pallets filled each level. Some of the racks had tipped over. Packing peanuts and trash littered the floor around them.

They paused on the second to last level as voices sounded below. Robert held his plasma gun ready, William trailing with his pistol ready.

"Shit, they're down there, too," Robert whispered.

"Let's shoot them and get the hell out of here. They've probably split up. We can hide, too."

"I don't want to kill them, William. They're hungry, too."

"Why the hell do you care? They'd shoot us as soon as they saw us."

"Shh! They're coming up. Hide!"

The pair jumped behind some shelves and turned off their flashlights. They peeked out to see two Militia members come up the stairs with guns. Robert and William snuck around the racks as the Militia members explored the room.

Slowly, they went down the stairs and into the last storage room. This one was different, with massive garage doors on one side along with the elevator. This room seemed to be the center of the mall's storage system. One half was full of water where the floor slanted slightly, the water pulsing as a wire openly spewed Ignium into it.

They hurried out into the open first level and sprinted toward the entrance.

"Hey! Over there! Who are they?" a voice came.

"They're not with us! Shoot them!"

Gunfire erupted in the mall, bullets hailing toward them from the first and second floors. They crashed through the entrance and out to the parking lot, where a Militia member stood on guard outside. He spun around. The butt end of Robert's plasma rifle crashed straight into his gas mask, crushing its glass and his nose. He flipped off his feet and landed on the ground, completely stunned.

"Go! Go!" William shouted.

They ran across the parking lot and reached the other side of the street. Before their pursuers could shoot, they had run into an alleyway and disappeared among the trash.

# 14

# Communism Awoken

\* \* \*

"*Welcome back to Liberty Talk with your host, Billy Wideman. One hundred thousand are dead today following this morning's attacks by Chinese forces in the Philippines, Hawaii, and Oregon. God help us!*"

"*In response to these attacks, President Hudson has called for peace on US soil between T-PEM and the People's Militia, stating that China now threatens the country's fate. In a live stream an hour ago, Hans Renning said that he'd agree to a truce between military and Militia forces to combat the Chinese menace.*"

"*Things are a little hazier among T-PEM, with some leaders stating that they might agree to a truce if an agreement were made. What scares me is Travis Dodds, whose forces now control most of California. Following the Chinese attacks, he posted that those who died in the attacks were fascists. My opinion? He and California might work with the Chinese in the coming war.*"

"*World's coming to an end, is what I say. We're seeing what might be the end of the Second Civil War and the beginning of World War III.*"

Robert sat beside Zilv in the concrete room and shut off the grim news.

An Ignium-powered portable stove cooked a pot of soup. The burner glowed with a blue color, and the soup simmered. Coming from a can, the soup consisted only of cubed food that had been processed and refined from plants and meat. The broth was closer to water than anything else, and the whole thing was tasteless.

Zilv was pale, sweaty, and covered in painful, bruised boils. An intense fever had made him delirious. They had nothing to soothe the pain, no pill to make the boils disappear, and no medicine to end the fever. Robert did his best to help Zilv feel better by feeding him soup. Robert tried not to touch Zilv and wore an extra pair of gloves while caring for him. They couldn't breathe the same air, kiss, or hug. They only had words.

"Soup's almost ready, baby," Robert said.

"Is it?" Zilv asked softly, like a small child who sounded tired.

"Yes. I'll tell you when you can take off your mask."

Robert and William had stolen a fan and an air filter in an attempt to keep the room free of polluted air, but they could only do so much. The fan pushed toxic air out of the room while the filter cleaned the incoming air. Even so, when Zilv had to vomit or eat, he inhaled enough polluted air to make him cough.

"Thank you. Do you think I'll be better soon? I think I will be," Zilv asked.

"Absolutely. You're doing better than yesterday," Robert lied. He turned off the burner, lifted the pot, and grabbed a spoon, "All right, take off your mask."

Zilv took off his mask. He was sweating with a gray face and features sunken in like on a corpse. Boils covered his face, oozing with black blood and pus. He looked at Robert with a loving purple glow, a curtain of misery behind his eyes as the sickness tormented him.

Robert fed him spoon by spoon. All the while, he frowned with sorrow and tried his best to keep from tearing up. It hurt to see Zilv like this, to watch the pain helplessly, unable to remove it. That's all he wanted, to remove the pain.

"Robert?" Zilv whispered.

"Yes?"

"Does this remind you of when we first met in school?"

Robert tilted his head, "How so?"

"Well, we had just started dating, and I got sick with the flu, so you visited after your classes and took care of me?"

"Oh yeah, I remember that. I was studying Ignium, and you were studying AI programming. I miss those days."

Zilv sniffled and let out a hacking cough, "Me too."

William appeared in the doorway.

Zilv looked up and waved, "Hi."

William nodded, "Robert?"

"What?" Robert asked.

"We need to talk when you're done."

"What is it this time?"

"Just come out here when you're done," William said, leaving before Robert could respond.

"You can go out there," Zilv said.

"You sure?"

"I can eat all by myself. I'll call if I need help," Zilv said.

"Okay, if you say so. Don't push yourself."

He stood and left the room, wishing he could hug Zilv before leaving.

"Is he doing any better?" William asked.

"No. He's getting worse."

"We need to get help, someone like the Militia or the military. Hell, even T-PEM."

"We can't. We should leave," Robert stated.

"Come here, Robert."

Robert followed William to a window and peered down at a war-torn street.

William pointed and grabbed Robert's shoulder, "Look at this. The war with China is coming. We need allies."

"The war with China is already here, William!"

"Where are we going to go, Robert? Where?!"

"We need to leave this damned city. This place is gonna get bombed to hell like every other city in the country. We need to get out; you know this. Somewhere in the countryside. We can figure out our problems there, but I don't wanna get bombed."

William put his palm on his mask and shook his head, "We're not gonna

114

have food and water in the countryside. How the hell are we gonna last more than a month out there? This war could last for years. Our best chances are to stay here and gain allies. The Militia and the military will protect the hell out of cities like these. They already have everything here."

In frustration, Robert threw his hands up, "And how are we gonna get allies? How are we gonna endure here?"

William shrugged, face red with frustration, "I don't fucking know. They'll probably hide people in the metro systems and shit. Plus, if this building gets bombed, we're all the way at the bottom."

"This shit shack of a city won't hold. Stop being so damn stubborn. We're not gonna survive here," Robert said.

William gestured out the window, "We've tried to secure a way out of here, and we can't just run off out of the city. If we get caught, we get shot."

"We can sneak out."

"How about we try my way?"

Robert rolled his eyes, "And what is that?"

"Zilv is sick, Robert. We need to find one of the groups we've been smuggling for and see if they have medicine. They might be able to protect us."

"The civil war would have run them dry. Plus, we can't just walk up and demand that they help us. They don't care who we are."

"We can join them. Tell them that we're willing to join their efforts through this war and in the battles against the government."

Robert's eye twitched. He didn't want to join anyone, and he didn't want to fight, "That'll put us in more danger. The military is probably still arresting and executing Militia members or will do so if we win against China."

"They can't break the truce."

"I don't want to be part of a war. We've avoided the civil war okay as we have."

"Okay? You mean scraping by? Going days without food? Having no medicine or a safe place to sleep? Look at this!" William pulled up his shirt to reveal an emaciated waistline covered in red, irritated patches from pollution burns.

Robert sighed angrily and averted his gaze, "Look, if you think we should go and find help, let's do it. You're right. I'm tired of scraping by."

"I'll go get our shit. You go tell Zilv. We are doing this."

Robert walked over and stopped at the doorway.

Zilv had put his mask back on and lay on a pillow. He turned his head sluggishly as he heard Robert come in, "Hi, baby."

"Hey, cutie," Robert said.

"What's going on?"

"William and I are going out for a while to see if we can get you medicine."

Zilv frowned, "You're gonna leave?"

"It'll be okay. We'll be back soon. Just rest up, okay?"

"Where are you going?"

"To find help for you."

"Okay. Be safe. I love you."

"I love you, too."

* * *

Robert stepped into the street, William following. A few days had passed since they had been out the last time. Little had changed. The roads were empty of life. Only rubble, trash, and bodies remained. This was the United States, ruined by its own people and feebly standing up to communism in the aftermath.

The street was quiet. No explosions, gunshots, screaming, or enormous tanks rolled through the streets. William took the lead as they snuck across the city. They tried their best to stay out of trouble despite the ongoing truce.

It was freezing cold. The air was bitter, and thin layers of ice had formed on the concrete around them. The bodies they passed had frozen and become solid as if stored in a freezer. Even though they wore smart suits, the pair shivered.

"Where are we going?" Robert asked.

"The Militia. The ones we smuggled for a while ago. I'm hoping their base is still there and that they won't shoot us."

Robert raised an eyebrow, "And if they decide to shoot us?"

William shrugged, "I don't know. Dodge?"

Robert sighed, "This is a bad idea."

"I don't wanna hear it. We're doing it."

Robert shook his head and followed him.

Graffiti-covered rubble and military remnants, such as sandbags and barbed wire, were everywhere. Turning down one street, they paused. A few yards ahead were people wearing white clothes with red crosses marking their arms, chests, backs, and masks. The people were moving bodies, picking the frozen corpses off the streets, and placing them on vehicles for transportation.

"They won't bother us if we don't bother them," Robert said.

The pair walked past the group.

The sight was disturbing. The mangled bodies of murderers like the Militia, T-PEM, and the military intermixed with bodies of innocent people caught in the fighting.

The group of people paused their work at the sight of the pair. A few held guns ready as a quiet warning. Robert and William hastened their pace and disappeared down another street, leaving the gruesome sight of stacked bodies behind.

After twenty minutes of walking down turn-after-turn through ruined avenues, they came to a road Robert recognized. Ahead was one of the outposts the pair had visited twice. One side of the building now had a massive hole from which rubble leaked. Along the walls and through the fortified windows were bullet holes, plasma residue, and laser burns. A light beamed down onto them when they approached the doors.

"Stop! Who are you two?"

"We're friends with Walt Stippick!" William shouted.

"We're friendly! We're not commies or Hudson's sheep," Robert added.

A faint discussion was heard.

"We remember you two! Stippick's dead. What the hell do you two want?"

"We're low on supplies. We need medicine and protection," William stated.

"You don't think we're low? We barely have bandages to go around or ammo to spare. Go beg somewhere else."

"Name your price! We'll do anything."

Another faint discussion was heard before a response came, "We need you to make a deal with the Devil."

# 15

# Remember Death

*9:43 PM, December 28, 2078*

* * *

*"Welcome back to Liberty Talk with your host, Billy Wideman. More chaos was seen today across the country as Chinese forces landed on the West Coast, welcomed by the Californian T-PEM leader, Travis Dodds. After these events, T-PEM leaders in Colorado, Wisconsin, and Maine have become divided on who they intend to support in the war effort. Colorado's leader, Chris Wilkinson, has stated that he fully intends to support Travis Dodds in welcoming the Chinese. In contrast, the other leaders have opted to support the US government, Hans Renning, and the People's Militia."*

*"As the Chinese establish a front on the West Coast, the military and the Militia have come together to establish defenses against the invading forces. Despite this, Chinese bomber planes continue to dominate American airspace and rain hell on cities across the nation. In violation of the Geneva Conventions, China has utilized chemical and biological warfare against the US defenders and threatened nuclear attacks if the US does not surrender."*

*"To all those out there listening today fighting against the Chinese, you have my full support. Kick some ass and have a Merry Christmas and a Happy New Year!"*

* * *

Robert shut off the broadcast and touched Zilv's mask.

"How do you feel, baby?" Robert asked.

Zilv inhaled slowly, blinking sluggishly, "I'm okay. The fever is dying down."

"That's good. Have they been good to you?"

"Yeah, the medics gave me some medicine. I'm just hungry, but I can't keep anything down."

"It's okay. We'll get you some food soon. Just relax here, please."

Zilv's body was now covered in boils oozing with black blood and pus. He had constant headaches and could not keep anything down. His fever grew worse every day. Zilv was more like a skeleton than the smiling, loving person Robert once knew. He could not even talk for long without getting exhausted. Robert appreciated and respected those who dealt with Zilv. One of the Militia medics was explicitly assigned to deal with the Bunny Fever victims, while others were told to avoid infected people. Other outpost members disliked Robert and William for bringing someone so sick. The pair were only tolerated because they helped the efforts of the Militia, though they were usually ignored or glared at.

"I'm gonna go, baby. William needs me."

"Okay, I love you," Zilv said softly.

"Love you, too."

Robert left the room. The medic appointed to deal with Zilv grabbed and disinfected him. He had his hands washed, a sanitizing liquid sprayed on his clothes, and his temperature checked.

"You're risking yourself going in there and anywhere near him," the medic said.

"I know. I love him, and he needs my support."

"You're a real idiot, aren't you?"

The medic went into the room. They had already had two or three fights about Robert's visits. Robert scoffed. He didn't care if he was a risk to everyone else. Zilv needed him, and he wasn't going to abandon him.

Militia members sat everywhere on the second floor of the outpost, waiting and listening. For now, all was quiet. Some people looked out the window, some sat and quivered nervously, some smoked, some talked, and some played games to pass the time. William played checkers while a few men watched.

Robert approached the game, "Do you still suck?"

"Yes," William responded.

"You got this," Robert said.

"Don't encourage him!" William's opponent said.

Some of the men were betting on their game. Move by move, they each took each other's pieces. The onlookers went silent in anticipation as they came to their final pieces. The building shook just as William was about to make the winning move. Everyone looked up. The flying hammers of the Chinese had arrived. Winged archangels of death and destruction flew above the city. They attacked weekly at unpredictable times. Their massive Ignium jet engines roared above the fleeing Sodom below. The whole outpost scattered for cover. Sirens echoed across the city, screaming their eerie calls as they signaled the arrival of doom.

"Bombs! Bombs! Take cover!"

Whistling sounds screamed over the rumbling engines. Deafening explosions followed, echoing across the city as the bombs landed. Each blast wave made the ground shake and collapsed buildings.

The explosions died down. Gunfire erupted around the city as the military and the Militia opened fire on the planes with machine guns and anti-air guns. The jets departed, and the defenders shot down one plane only as everyone slowly emerged from cover. Relief filled the outpost. They weren't hit. People went on radios and communication devices, talking to other outposts and groups to see if anyone needed help or was hurt.

Everyone returned to their business. William finished the checkers game with a less enthused victory. As people exchanged their winning bets, he went to Robert.

"What's up?" he asked.

"Zilv's still the same. He's fighting his hardest, but I don't know anymore."

William put his hand on Robert's shoulder, "Shut the hell up. He'll make it, you know it. If you don't give up, he won't give up. Most people die in the first week or so of having it, and he's already made it over a month."

Robert nodded, "You're right. We need to talk to the commander here. This morning I was told that they have a job for us."

"Well, let's go talk to her."

* * *

Guards let them into the commander's office and closed the door behind them. Three other Militia members stood in a line against the wall. The new commander, Vanessa, spoke on the radio as they entered. She had little patience for anyone and had been particularly harsh to Robert and William. Like the other Militia in the room, she wore old clothes and scavenged military armor. A black soldier's gas mask covered her face with a web-like crack across the visor. She had no hair. Instead, irritation from pollution covered her head and skin while bloodied bandages wrapped around her right forearm.

She uttered codes and switched channels for a minute before looking at the pair. She lowered the volume as she spoke, "Good evening, gentlemen. I assume you two are here for my task and haven't caused a mess instead?"

"Yep," William said.

"Good. The military commander in this city, David Kavanaugh, has made a deal with us. We give them something, so they give us something. Our recent deals have gone well. Today, you will retrieve a supply drop on the other side of the city with these three. Do not fail. It has the medicine your sick friend needs."

Robert let out a quiet gasp.

"You are already risking all of us with him here, so if you fail, you'll doom us. Now, this is Ruben, Walt, and Mo. They will be accompanying you today. They have the supply drop location, but I am also sending the location to your implants. Am I understood?"

"Yes, ma'am," the pair responded.

"Good. Get going while it's still dark."

They nodded and left. The three Militia members followed them, climbing down the stairs as they checked their implants.

"It's across the city," William said.

"Shouldn't be too hard. Which way are we taking?" Robert asked.

"We can't take the sewers. T-PEM has been pushed into the sewers since the truce, and I am not looking to get shot. We can hide more easily on the surface," William said.

"Where are we going?" Ruben asked.

Robert glanced back at Ruben, who was the thinnest of the three men and carried an assault rifle. He peered out from his goggle-like gas mask with black eyes.

William spoke, "I'll lead the way, don't worry. I just need you three to make sure our asses don't get swiss cheesed. Speaking of which, Robert, is your plasma rifle charged?"

Robert took his plasma rifle from his back and checked its charge and material chamber, "I'm good."

William gave Robert a thumbs up, then gestured to the men behind them, "Good, let's get going. We're taking the alleyways and streets. You guys know what to do, right? Check the windows, cars, all that sort of stuff."

The tallest and most muscular of the three men, Mo, spoke, "We've been doing it longer than you. Don't worry."

They went onto the street, turned, and disappeared into an alleyway. During the night, everything in the city froze. Even the air was ice cold. All of them had extra layers of clothing, and smart clothes underneath that kept them warm. Still, all of them shivered. The war had slowed with the approach of Christmas and another brutal winter. Infantry fighting had become less frequent, though the Chinese never stopped bombing. There would be no celebrations this year. No one would feast in welcome of the Yuletide or raise a toast for the New Year.

They moved cautiously. At any moment, they could get attacked, so they listened with guns ready. It was pitch black, yet they traveled without flashlights in the open, relying on flickering street signs and neon billboards to make their way around. William checked his implant occasionally as he led the group on a specific path through the city. The city was in ruin. Massive craters had been dug out by the Chinese bombings, leaving many buildings collapsed or severely decimated. Where the bombs had hit the streets were huge holes, some so broad that they could fit a bus and deep enough to stack three cars.

The military and Militia were always on alert, waiting for Chinese or T-PEM soldiers to come out of nowhere and attack. Because of this, William and Robert had to wear Militia marks with Gadsden snakes on their backs and yellow bands around their arms. Robert hated to pick a side. He couldn't care less for any side of the civil war or the ongoing world war, but he needed to survive. Zilv had to live.

They climbed over piles of rubble and trash, wading through the destruction.

Robert spoke hushedly, "I heard the Chinese were dropping chemical weapons?"

Walt, the shortest and broadest of the men, replied, "Every day."

Mo shook his head, "Some of my friends have been killed by gas bombs and something like napalm."

Ruben frowned, his voice quivering faintly, "Yeah. We don't really have a name for it other than Greek fire."

Walt lifted his mask and spat on the ground, snorting as he put it back on, "Chinese bastards. We're trying our hardest to defend our homes, and we're getting burned alive for it. They don't care what lands where. If it kills an American, that's a win for them."

Robert swallowed and spoke, "I'm scared of the future. Who the hell knows what's going to happen? Probably no happy endings. If we win, we'll go back to fighting. If we lose, we'll probably all die."

Walt shrugged, "Dying doesn't matter to me. If I have to die fighting the commies or Hudson's dogs, that's a good way to go."

The other two Militia members nodded.

"Hush down now. We're leaving our territory," William said.

They continued through the streets, cautious of every step. The group checked the windows above and the corners of the road. They peeked down where they were going before continuing. They also listened to the skies.

The Chinese could come at any moment and drop bombs in their wake.

Each climbed down a massive bomb crater along their path, scaling the sides like a cliff. The seared asphalt crumbled under their feet, falling as they got out.

The five of them slinked down an alleyway and hid behind a trash can when they heard a military patrol approach from another street. Clicking footsteps from soldiers and metallic rumbling from tanks and anti-air gun carriers echoed down the road. Despite the truce, they could not trust the patrol. The group watched them pass, then continued onward. All of them were like rats. Concealed by the dark, they slinked and skittered throughout the ruins. It was empty everywhere. No people were in the streets. No one hid in the houses, and everything was vacant. Millions had died from the war and the pandemic, leaving only those who escaped or went under the Militia, T-PEM, or military protection.

They went through the empty buildings. Many appeared as if the people inside had evacuated, leaving their belongings. Trash gathered in the corners, dust layered everything, and furniture was left abandoned in the dormant buildings. If they entered residential buildings, mutant rats scurried away from them into pantries and corners. After ransacking pantries and cabinets, the rats seemed particularly fond of clothes and soft furnishings.

Barbed wire and sandbags became more prominent, along with remains of tents and battles, as they came closer to their destination. An old, destroyed tank sat in the street near a medical tent burnt to cinders. The destruction seemed recent, with the rancid smell of cooked human flesh soaking the air.

"Do you guys hear that?" Robert said.

They paused. The approach of a faint droning sounded in the distance.

Ruben gasped and pointed to a building, "Ah, shit, it might be the Chinese again. We need to find cover."

They kicked down the door to an apartment and ran into a bathroom for cover.

The droning sound got louder and soon drowned out the sound of screaming sirens. A rumble shook the building when the bomber planes flew right over them. Bombs rained from the sky with whistling sounds, landing with thunderous explosions. The building shook with each blast, causing dust around the bathroom to jump with each burst.

Between the explosions were fiery and odd pulse sounds, which were not typical with bombing runs like these. As the explosions stopped, anti-aircraft guns and machine guns lit up the sky. Gunshots echoed and droned in place of the bombers, eventually fading into silence. The group carefully left the apartment and looked up into the smoggy sky as they entered the street.

"What the hell were those sounds?" Robert asked.

"I don't know. Let's just get going," William said.

The unit passed craters from the bombing. They sizzled as the energy from each explosion charred the ground. The ground cracked in a spiderweb fashion, embers lying inside the cracks and producing faint smoke.

They turned down a street. An encampment of white tents sat between ruined buildings, with floodlights lighting up the area, leaving parts in shadows. A large metal object sat in the center of the camp, distorting the air around it.

Robert squinted. People ran around the tents between the light and dark. Medics and injured soldiers were sprinting and attacking one another. They didn't attack with weapons but tackled, punched, and headbutted one another.

Bewildered, Robert turned to William, "Are they...."

"Killing one another," Mo finished.

Robert gasped, his mouth dropping. The people attacked wildly, tearing into one another like animals.

"What the hell is wrong with them?" Robert asked.

Ruben pointed, "I don't know. Do you see that thing in the middle?"

Walt squinted, "Looks like a bomb."

"And the air. It's all distorted," Mo said.

"Let's get the hell out of here. It's a bad idea to stay here," William said.

They could still hear the screams and cries of those in the camp for another street before the sounds faded with distance.

William pulled back his sleeve and looked at his implant, "We're almost there. It's in a grocery store."

A massive grocery store towered in the distance. The top of the building had a dome of glass over it. The parking lot around it sprawled out from the structure, separating it from others. It was empty, a flat nothing of asphalt. One small and one giant crater dented both sides of the building.

They stopped and ensured they were safe before sprinting to the store entrance and breaking through an old airlock. They turned on their flashlights and spread out. The building was eerily quiet and dark. The vast aisles were like a maze, with automated cash registers at the front and shelves going into the back. The store had been emptied over the last few months. There was nothing left except for broken objects.

"Where did they say the supply drop was delivered to? Is it on the next level or what?" Robert asked.

William pointed up, "It should be on the third floor by the deli. They're stored in a backroom."

"Gonna be a pain in the ass to move it down," Mo stated.

"It's worth it," Walt said.

"Let's get up there and leave as fast as possible," William said.

They stayed a few steps apart in the darkness but moved as a unit, shining their flashlights in every dark corner and crevice. It was usual for Robert to be uncomfortable in strange buildings, but this was a different sort of creepy feeling, like a chill that haunted him. He scanned the area, waiting for someone to start shooting at them from the darkness.

After navigating part of the maze, William led them up a set of stairs to the second level. While the first level consisted of shelf after shelf, the second floor was more open with lower shelves and containers. There was also a coffee shop and a restaurant with seating at one end.

"Would be nice to get a cup of coffee right now," Robert said.

"Tasted like shit before everything fell apart. Tastes like shit now," William said with a wry smile.

Walt sighed, "I miss coffee. They don't give us coffee in our rations anymore. I don't care what it tastes like. I just need my caffeine."

Mo raised a hand, pointing his gun around, "Shh! You hear that?"

A steady set of footsteps came from below as if something was walking carefully. All five of them approached the railing, shining their flashlights downward. They heard and saw nothing.

"Must've been an animal," Ruben said.

"An animal that's still alive?" William asked.

"Maybe a giant mutant rat. Nothing that'll bother us. Let's just keep going," Walt said.

On edge, they nervously looked around as they approached the third set of stairs. They gasped as they got onto the third level and shone their flashlights around. All around the deli were the corpses of soldiers with the US flag on their upper sleeves. Their blood was splattered onto the floor, bits of flesh and guts thrown about. A large crate sat between them with a body hunched against it.

Robert put his hands behind his head, eyes wide, "What the hell?"

"Their flashlights are still on," Mo pointed out.

"They must've gotten attacked, and it doesn't look like it happened too long ago," Ruben said.

"We need to get these supplies out of here. Two people stand guard. Three people help get the box ready to move," Walt said.

Robert and William looked at each other and nodded.

"We'll stand watch," William said.

"All right. Let's get going!" Walt said.

The three Militia men worked to get the box free from its restraints. They unlatched and untied it to check its interior for explosives.

Robert shone his flashlight toward one of the holes in the side of the building. It appeared small, and as he squinted, he saw a metal object buried halfway into the floor on the opposite side. He took a few steps forward, squinting at it, "Yo, William?"

"What?"

"Come over here...."

William walked over and stood beside Robert squinting, "That big metal thing?"

"Yeah, and you see the air? It's warbly."

"You guys need to hurry," William stated.

"What?" Walt said.

"What's going on?" Ruben asked.

Robert looked toward the object, then downstairs to the first level, "I don't think we're alone."

"You heard the man! Hurry up!" Mo said.

They crammed everything back into the crate and put the lid on. A scream came from below.

"Incoming!" William shouted and approached the edge of the railing, firing his pistol.

"What the hell are you shooting at?" Robert shouted.

He approached the edge and looked down, plasma rifle ready. Figures raced out from below, crossing their sight lines and heading toward the stairs. Robert aimed and shot. The plasma rifle buzzed as it melted the material stored inside, spewing it like a diabolical flamethrower. He missed as the swarm went around the molten material on the ground.

"Abandon the damned box!" Robert screamed, turning around.

Figures approached from the other side of the building. Robert aimed and shot at the second approaching swarm. The Militia members dropped the box and joined, shooting at both hordes as they approached.

"They're surrounding us! Leave the box! Let's go!" William shouted.

Robert tried to make out the figures in the dark. They looked like ordinary people, though they had torn clothes and were bloody. Most had gas masks, though some were broken. They screamed madly and ran wildly toward the group as if they were utterly fearless of hurting themselves. Someone ran out from the deli and tackled Walt. The pair collided and flew over the railing and down below. As he landed on the floor below, the crazed attackers piled upon him. The rest of the unit ran down the stairs to the second level, shooting whatever jumped out from the dark. Robert couldn't identify anything as he shot at shapes in blind fear.

Mo shot one of the figures down and glanced at the rest of the group, "How the hell are we gonna get out of here? We lost Walt!"

William gestured to the next set of stairs, "We need to get to the first level!"

Robert shot his rifle, coating one of the figures in molten material before shouting, "We're gonna get surrounded, William!"

A flood of attackers came from below at the last set of stairs, erupting like a flight of winged devils. The four changed directions and ran. Bloodied people burst from the shelves on either side, one catching Mo and tripping him by the ankle. A moment later, the horde caught up.

"Mo! No!" Ruben shouted.

Mo was dragged into the frenzied horde, screaming and shooting as he disappeared.

"We have to go! Come on!" Robert grabbed Ruben and ran.

They ran around to the opposite side of the floor and stopped at the other end. The horde approached from both sides. They were trapped.

"William! What the hell do we do?" Robert shouted.

William gazed back and forth between the two hordes, then sprinted toward the railing, "This way! Land on the shelves!"

Both followed, jumping over the barrier before crashing down upon the shelves. Robert was the last to jump and landed on the edge of one with a pained grunt as he smashed into it. With all three of them hitting the same shelf, it tipped and caused the store shelves to domino.

William grabbed Robert and pulled him to his feet. They clumsily took off running. Ruben followed as a hail of crazed fiends came from the railings above. William spearheaded the escape, crashing into one of their attackers. He threw the man aside and stumbled forward with Robert right behind him. Just as the pair got out of harm's way, Ruben fell right into the hands of the man William had pushed. With a panicked scream, he threw his weight and butt of the rifle into the man's face, turned it, and shot five holes into his body.

Robert turned, watching as the horde caught up, "Ruben!"

"Run, dumbass! Run!" Ruben shouted.

Ruben turned and shot into the flock.

"Bring it on, motherfuckers!!"

The horde swarmed and ripped into him. Robert turned and ran after William, sprinting out into the street. Propelled by blind, primal fear, they didn't stop running until the store was far out of sight. They didn't stop until their legs and lungs burned.

"What the hell just happened?" Robert asked, drenched in sweat and shaking.

William stood bent with his hands on his knees, just as shocked as Robert, "I don't fucking know. We need to get back to the base and tell them what happened. Now."

\* \* \*

The city rumbled as the specter of communism returned, manifesting as dozens of planes flew over. People around the city ran for cover, fleeing the red hammer. Over the rumbling of the Ignium engines and air-raid sirens came screaming whistles, followed by explosions as destruction rained from the sky. As the bombs tore the city apart, raging fires rose and consumed everything in their path. Below the chaos, Robert and William ran. They sprinted through ruined streets and alleys, jumping over debris and cars. They came out from a road, and Robert stopped. In front of them, fires raged through a massive skyscraper with craters, consuming it level by level.

"Come on, Robert!" William screamed.

The polluted air filled with smoke and embers while the planes kept dropping bombs. Robert prayed that a bomb would not find itself between their feet. They sprinted into a crumbling building as anti-air and machine guns opened fire in response to the planes.

They listened to planes exploding or crashing down. The attack ended as the aircraft departed, and the sirens became silent, leaving the madness caused by the bombs. They only encountered more death as they ran. Down one street, a cloud of yellow gas followed the winds created by fire, seeping through the ruins as an unstoppable force. They avoided the cloud and went in another direction. Down another street were the remains of a military patrol, consisting of a tank and the bits and pieces of men annihilated by a bomb. Anywhere they went, the reaping sickle of communism had already harvested lives like wheat.

They came onto a Militia camp shrouded in green gas. Inside, people ran around screaming, tearing, and clawing at their own skin. Some people had broken their gas masks and pulled at their faces and eyes, writhing as the gas infiltrated their bodies. T-PEM members stood outside the camp, watching the horror unfold and cheering for their victory.

Robert's lungs and legs burned. He had never had to run like this. It was nearing the bitter morning, and they were still so far off from Zilv. They had to make it back. Robert told himself he had to.

"This way, Robert!"

"This is not the way we came!"

"We can't go the way we came! Listen to me, damnit!"

William led them through an underpass and onto a highway. The highway was full of cars and craters. These cars had probably been sitting here since the civil war.

"Where the hell are we going, William?"

"If we go over the streets on this highway, then jump down a few streets ahead, we should be able to get back faster. Just trust me."

"You don't even know the surface that well!"

"I checked on the map when we were going to the drop. Just. Trust. Me."

They ran through the seemingly endless traffic jam, passing buildings and streets for about a mile.

William turned right abruptly, led them to the edge, and looked down below to the street, "We can make this drop."

"What? We'll break our ankles!"

"We can make it. Just land on both feet flatly at the same time. Follow me."

William jumped over, fell onto both feet, and rolled. Once he recovered from the fall, he looked up, "Come on, Robert! Both feet! Just roll at the bottom!"

Robert shook his head and backed up.

"Come on, dumbass, come on. Zilv needs you. You got this! You got this!"

He ran forward and jumped, flailing his arms as he fell. He landed so hard on both feet that he collapsed flat onto his chest, "Argh! Fucking damnit!"

William came to Robert's side as he rolled onto his back and held his ankle, "Are you okay?"

Robert hissed in pain and looked down at his ankle, moving it slightly, "Why? Why couldn't we have found an off-ramp! Damnit!"

"You're good, you're good. Does it feel broken?"

"No. It's just sprained. Just let me breathe a second and then help me up."

Robert breathed in and out and grasped the throbbing ankle. As the pain died down slowly, he nodded, "Help me up."

William lifted him carefully, gradually letting him put weight on the ankle. "Can you put weight on it?" William asked.

"I can put enough on it. Let's keep going. I'll try to keep up."

William nodded. Robert limped after him, willing his way forward as they went through another trash-filled alley and further into the other side of the city. They were now in a territory they recognized. Militia graffiti and banners surrounded them, covering buildings and street signs. Almost there. As they came out from the shadow of a few buildings, they looked up to see the sun. The sun had barely risen high enough to get over the towering buildings. Only a few rays of light could pierce through the pollution haze. The morning was here. As they kept running, more rumbling engines approached and filled the air with thundering sounds. Air raid sirens sang their ominous warning, sending panic throughout the city.

"Shit! The Chinese are back, Robert!"

"We need to get back to Zilv!" Robert said.

"We need cover! They're right above us!"

"We need to keep running!"

Whistling sounds broke through from high above as more bombs came down. Robert ran, not feeling his ankle or anything else. William ran with him as explosions erupted around them. They ran down another street and then another before they finally arrived. The office building still stood, seemingly empty, as it concealed the hidden Militia inside. Around the building, bombs tore out holes in its neighbors as explosions created devouring fires.

Robert ran ahead, "We're almost there! Come on, William!"

Robert came within a few feet of the building. Just as relief struck his heart, an explosion blasted him from his feet like a truck. The world spun and became black. Robert came around after a few moments, blinking and fixating on a crack across his visor. Ear ringing, he couldn't feel his body. Clumsily, he rolled onto his hands and knees and gazed at the burning office building in front of him. Embers and burning rubble rained from the sky as flames ate the structure.

"Zilv? Zilv?! Zilv!!"

He stood and tried to run into the building. William grabbed him from behind, shouting and holding him back. Robert couldn't hear anything William said as he cried out and pushed against him.

"Let go of me! My baby! Zilv! No!!"

He threw himself forward, thrashing and flailing to free himself. He turned and punched William. William fell to the side and got up as Robert ran toward the flame. William threw himself forward, tackling Robert and dragging him back. Robert cried and screamed, begging to be released. William tried to keep him back as Robert clawed at the ground, struggling until he couldn't. He broke down, hitting the ground in agony.

"No! Zilv! William, he's gone! He's gone. My baby is gone!"

# 16

# Dies Irae

*10:00 AM, January 1, 2079*

\* \* \*

*"We are just getting word of nuclear detonations in Austin, New York, Colorado Springs, Arlington, Washington, DC, and Nevada. We are trying to get confirmation from our neighboring stations but can't seem to get any messages across to them."*

*"This just in. We have confirmation that the news of nuclear detonations across the country is true. We encourage our viewers to seek shelter and avoid going outside. Please wear your masks and avoid contact with outdoor material such as ash and soot that could be potentially radioactive."*

*"Hello? Is anyone out there? Probably not. My name is Matt. I'm one of the few people that survived the Austin blast. I haven't seen a bomber plane in at least a few days. I'm not alone. I'm in a house, and there's things outside and downstairs. I'm upstairs in a locked room, but I don't know how long I'll last. It doesn't matter. No one gonna arrive in time to help me. If anyone is hearing this, hold your loved ones close. Tell them that you love them and that they mean the world to you. I didn't get to do that. Abandon the hope that there's anything left. There isn't. There's no more United States, no more war. It's all over. The end has arrived."*

\* \* \*

The sun rose over the dying city.  Smoke came from the crumbling streets while warplanes droned like bees in the polluted sky above as they disappeared over the horizon.  The war tapered to a slow and brutal end. The continuation of the Second Civil War would not happen. There was no one left to fight in it and nothing left to fight over.  The last significant places of government had been nuked, the cities emptied, and the land shattered. Between the wars, pandemic, pollution, and resource crises, there were no people to walk the streets. The few left hid in the dark recesses of civilization's corpse.

The American nuclear and military response was swift and suicidal. The forces sent to China would never return, and the atomic warheads would destroy any military strength either country had left.  There would be no room for war when nothing was left, especially food for soldiers or steel for machines.

The rest of the world became still. The war in Europe was choked out as each country's population collapsed inward from economic and resource crises, along with pandemic and civil discourse. In its desperation, Germany was the first to fall, followed lastly by countries such as Finland. Russia fell as well, suffering the same fate as America with a swift exchange of nukes with China. In India and Africa, starvation and plague led to anarchy and the collapse of their populations.

Not even animals or forests were left. Humanity's destructive cunning had reaped it all, withering the once-blue Earth into a cancerous dust bowl. Only the horrid mutant animals from zoos, labs and city streets remained. Under the reign of a blackened sky, the new world had been born like a maggot in the festering corpse of the old.

The age of the wasteland had begun.

# II

# Part Two

*"Behold, the day of the Lord [has come],*
*cruel, both with fury and burning anger,*
*to make the land a desolation;*
*and He will exterminate its sinners from it."* – Isaiah 13:9, edited

# 17

# New World

*11:12 AM, January 9, 2079*

\* \* \*

The sun rose over the ruined city. Through his cracked visor, Robert looked out the window as the yellow orb shone behind the black pollution haze. Today was darker than usual. Clouds rained down ash upon the city. It almost looked like a winter wonderland as ash blanketed everything, blanketing the rooftops of black-stained buildings and crater-filled streets. There was no life outside. No bodies, no animals, no people, nothing. Just remnants. The city was a corpse filled with cancerous remnants of trash piles blown about by the toxic wind. Robert turned away from the window and slumped against the wall as he sat on the desk. William sat across from him, staring out into space.

"What are we going to do?" Robert asked.

"Live," William mumbled.

"How? We don't have a lot of food or water left."

"We will figure it out."

Robert frowned at William's shortness. They had spoken little since the end of the war six days ago, keeping their minds closed as they passed the time. The apartment that they took shelter in was empty. The building had been for sale before the Second Civil War, so it was bare except for furniture, a kitchen, and bathrooms. Robert's face flushed red as he pondered about the building. People could have lived here, but the economy didn't permit it, leaving them on the streets. It was an eerie place. Paint peeled off the walls, dust layered everything, and debris gathered in the corners and along the walls. The only noise he ever heard here was the building creaking and moving. He hated it. He hated this world and everything in it.

"We can't just sit here," Robert said.

William sighed, "At least let the sun rise a little. Where do you want to go?"

Robert shrugged and gestured out the window, "I don't know. Anywhere else. We're not alone here. You know that. Those things are still out there."

"I know they're still out there. What are we gonna do? Go out there and risk being found?"

"Well, we can't just sit here."

"I know that. Figure something out. I don't care either way."

Robert frowned. It all seemed hopeless. There was nowhere to go and no place to hide. They were alone and doomed. He turned and looked at the ash storm outside. Hundreds of ruined buildings had been blackened from ash and filled with craters from bombs. Below, destroyed cars, bodies, and military remnants filled the streets. A colossal skyscraper stood in the distance. Taller than most, it loomed over the city like an eternal watcher. It had a massive crater near the top where a bomb had landed, though it mainly seemed unscathed.

"William?"

"How dumb is it this time?" William asked.

"Pretty dumb."

William rolled his eyes and leaned against the wall, "Just tell me."

"Why don't we go up?"

William's head perked up, "What do you mean?"

"Why don't we go up? We can go into a skyscraper, which will take us above the streets. We'll be alone up there and safe from the weather. We can even find explosives, blow the stairs up, and make it so that we need rope to climb up."

William blinked, "Pretty fucking stupid."

"Well, where else do you want to go? Stay here and get shot or eaten? Hide in the sewers and get eaten? Try to escape and get eaten?"

William chuckled, "We can go up and get eaten."

Robert let out a grumble.

William raised his hands slowly, "What? All right, fine. Let's wait for the ash storm to pass first."

* * *

Robert cracked open the airlock door and pointed his plasma rifle into the alley.

"Is it clear?" William asked.

"Shh..."

Ash blanketed the alley. The deep gray color made everything monotone, as if he could only see in black and white. There were no figures, voices, or sounds in the alleyway.

"We're alone," Robert stated.

"Where is the skyscraper?" William asked.

"I think a few dozen streets away. I'll lead."

As Robert stepped forward, ash stained his boots gray. It felt like he was stepping on slippery powder that offered no resistance. The ash blanketed the remnants of the American conflicts, covered corpses, filled craters, and layered on military equipment. The wind was the only sound, carrying the ash storm over the city with a quiet howl. The cold, polluted air felt heavy and raw as it penetrated their clothes.

"Do you see anything?" Robert asked.

"I think we're alone. Let's get going and keep it that way.".

They hopped over burnt-out cars, rubble, and sandbags, leaving gray footprints as they passed through buildings. They stopped and gazed through a hole leading out into the street. The air between the ash storm seemed warped.

"How long do you think the gas bombs from the Chinese will be active?" Robert asked.

"I don't know. Maybe days? Months? Years? I'm just afraid of the radiation from the nukes. What if this ash storm is from a nuclear fire? I guess it wouldn't matter if we got cancer and died."

"Let's try not to."

Robert's leg throbbed. It felt a little better, but he wasn't sure if his leg would ever heal right. The explosion had made him a little deaf, especially in the left ear. He fought back his thoughts about the detonation. Instead of processing what had happened, he suppressed it, trying to nullify the memory. There was no time for tears.

They hurried across a small parking lot overshadowed by buildings. Once across, they broke through a window and went into a house.

"Robert?"

"What?"

"I think we're being followed."

They looked through the window they had come from.

"Where is it?" Robert asked.

"There's something out there... look! Something moved!"

Robert squinted, "I don't see anything, but I believe you. Make sure your gun is ready."

Tingling danced down Robert's spine. He could feel eyes on them as he listened for footsteps and watched the shadows. Robert heard nothing beyond their scared breathing, no matter how quiet they were. They moved out of the house and into another building, stopping when they heard distant chatter.

"What the hell is that?" Robert asked.

"Shh!"

They lifted their guns and moved forward, entering a room. Both gasped. An older cell phone lay on the ground next to a body sitting upright. The phone played a broadcast on repeat.

"*-country has been attacked with nuclear weapons. Please remain in your homes and avoid contact with any outside foreign material. We shall bring you further information as soon as possible. Meanwhile, please stay tuned for further instructions, stay in your homes, and stay safe.*"

Robert grimaced. The body looked like someone unaffiliated with any part of the civil war, like someone trying to live through it all. He was dead now—guts tore out, arm pulled off, and thrown a few feet away.

"Poor guy," Robert said.

William knelt beside the body and went through his pockets. He pulled a knife out of the man's pocket and held it up so Robert could see.

"Ugh, that's terrible. Let's not stick around. I don't wanna meet whatever did this to him," Robert said.

Robert stepped out of the ruin. Opposite them, a few figures ran off into the ash storm, disappearing into the dark upon the mere sight of the pair.

"What the hell?" Robert asked.

"Don't stop," William said.

They hugged the side of the street to avoid the open. The skyscraper was not far away now, its ominous figure looming high above the other buildings. Robert felt watched from everywhere—like eyes pierced him, coming from behind, above, and all around.

"How close are we?" William asked.

"Almost there."

"Hurry up. We're going to die if we stay here."

They jogged down another street and finally arrived at the skyscraper. They bolted toward it, pain ripping through Robert's leg. He collapsed at the entrance and looked behind them. Almost a hundred figures stood in shattered windows and along the streets. Some knelt, some were on all fours, and others stood ominously. They stared. Each was still, watching as the pair looked back.

"Robert."

"What?"

"Let's move very... slowly."

Carefully, they opened the airlock and entered. The first level of the building rose ten stories high. It consisted of a giant lobby of glass plateaus, staircases, and a massive space down the middle. An elevator was on one side of the vestibule, while the ceiling above concealed the second level. William led Robert up the glass stairs, climbing level by level and occasionally looking down. Nothing entered the skyscraper, and they seemed to be alone. Guns ready, they mapped out the place and checked each level and crevice to ensure nothing or no one was inside.

They reached the end of the lobby stairs and got to a door leading to the second level. The office space on the second level split into many different stories. They found an all-access staircase rising upward at one end and walked inside. A square concrete shaft with concrete stairs made up the all-access staircase. It went up and up in a circle, with doors at each turn of the stairs.

"So many fucking stairs. This place is massive, Robert. How is this going to work out? How are we going to make sure all of this is safe?"

"I don't know. We can blow the glass stairs below and have ropes going up."

"That'll be a huge climb."

"We can't go back out anyway for now. This is it."

They went up a few flights of stairs before halting sharply. A body sat against a wall on one of the flights, sprawled out with a gun in his hand.

"What the hell?" Robert let out.

William approached the body to check it out, took the gun and ammo, and looked it over, "Shot himself. Won't bother us."

Robert grimaced.

"Are we going all the way up?" William asked.

"Yes. I think there's an area by a crater on the side of the building."

"Shouldn't we check that out? Ya know? Make sure it hasn't made the building unstable?"

"Later. Let's just get to the top."

They walked up the stairs to the last level and the last few stories of the skyscraper, where they found the executive area. The pair kept heading to the top of the building and walked through the door leading to the roof. They now stood hundreds of stories and thousands of feet above the hell below. Robert had never been this high up before and gawked in awe. Even above the ash storm, the thick pollution haze blocked out the rest of the city from sight. As Robert inched to the edge, he maintained a tense grip on the railing.

His stomach dropped, and his muscles felt weak from nervousness.

He stepped back, slightly nauseous, "This is it."

"What? We're tossing ourselves off?"

Robert snorted, "No, no. I think we can survive here."

"I think we have to now."

"We can make this happen."

William shrugged, "Screw it."

# 18

# The Hospital

\* \* \*

It was a quiet day. The cold winds gently twisted between the maze of skyscrapers below. Robert sat against the office desk and stared at the door leading to the stairs.

"We need to secure this place," Robert said.

William sat flat against a pillar in the center of the floor and quietly snored.

"William!"

William startled awake, "What? What? Are we getting attacked?"

"Wake up, lazy. It's like one in the afternoon. We need to do stuff."

William groaned and stretched, "Fine, what do you want to do?"

"We must secure this place if we're going to live here."

"Ideas?"

"Blow the stairs below and get some ropes so we can go up and down. Those things will get stuck below."

William threw his hands in the air to mimic an explosion, "You want to blow up the downstairs area and possibly kill us or collapse the building?"

Robert rested his head against the office desk behind him, "What are you thinking then?"

William pointed at the office desk Robert sat against, "We can just block it

146

up. Plenty of desks and stuff around here to do that."

"We can do both. I'm sure the military left some explosives around here."

"You think it's safe enough to go out on the street with all those things down there?"

"If we're quiet. They have so many bodies to keep them focused anyway, so they won't bother us."

William gagged, "Ugh, they're so disgusting. What the hell did those commies drop on us?"

"Something from hell."

William waved his hands and then pointed at the desk again, "Look. Look! I think it's easier to block it all off."

"It's a lot of work, and what if they find a way in?"

"They won't find a way in if we block all the doors."

"And how are we gonna go in and out? It'll be a pain in the ass."

William blinked sleepily, dropped his head back, and sighed, "Fine! If you want to risk our asses to go get some big boom stuff, then let's do that. I'm sure we can find some usable supplies at the same time."

"Come on then, let's go."

Robert stood up and put on his backpack. He picked up his plasma rifle and checked its ammo supply and energy. They lived on a floor with a sleeping area for their bedrolls and a spot to relax and play checkers. A shelf held the last of their food, water, gas-mask filters, and medicine. They needed many things but lacked the courage to find them. They moved a desk that barricaded the door into this level and went down the stairs to the first level.

"Is this what you want to blast?" William asked quietly.

Robert nodded.

William examined the glass stairs and gazed down to the bottom of the building, "What if we blow all the glass up? Or what if we weaken it all?"

"It'll be fine. We can blow the bottom stairs and attach ropes somewhere to go up and down."

"Let's just go. I saw a military base in a hospital not too far from here. They might have explosives."

Nothing disturbed them as they went out to the street. Robert felt no chills and found no figures watching them from the ruins. They were alone. William led them along, stepping over rubble and garbage. Everything was empty, desolate, and void of life except for the rats that ate war-born corpses littering the streets. There were no plants or animals beyond rats or people. Robert already missed their sky haven, their quiet abode above the ruins. This place was Purgatory. Devoid of light, love, life, and laughter, it was a hollow place.

They hurried from street to street and through building after building until they arrived at a hospital. Each point of the giant star-shaped building towered over the streets. A metal wall lined with towers and machine-gun nests hidden within them surrounded the building. The war had ravaged the hospital. Bomb holes were everywhere, and fires had blackened a large part of the building. Five soldiers hung from the front gates, roped up, and painted with communist symbols.

The pair stopped and stared at the facility.

"Looks like shit," William said.

"You think there's anything left?"

"Plenty. I haven't seen anyone in weeks. No one gonna be hauling shit with those things around."

"Let's be careful of the burnt areas. I'm sure they're in danger of collapse."

Guns ready, they approached the tall metal walls of the structure. Instead of going through the gate, the two slinked through a destroyed wall section and crept inside. The inside of the walls was even worse. It consisted of tents and vehicles, all consumed by fire. All that was left were the charred remains and the toxic smell of burnt material such as plastic, cloth, and rubber. Robert was thankful that the crack on his visor did not go all the way through the glass.

Among the burnt-up remains and coal-black piles were skeletons, flesh seared off, and bones stained by raging flames. Everything seemed so still. A layer of ash coated it all as if it had snowed. They sifted through the remains, trying to find any supplies that might have survived the fires. The remnants of the tents were hopeless. Anything left was generally plastic that had melted beyond recognition. Destroyed tanks and vehicles offered some ammo and weapons from dead soldiers. The two hid what they could not carry. They stuffed supplies beneath charred remains in out-of-the-way areas and under vehicles.

They cautiously approached the hospital entrance. Robert could only imagine the horror that awaited them. He assumed many dead would be left in the hospital, especially those who had died from gruesome war injuries. They walked through the airlock doors to the hospital. The doors no longer had windows and did not slide open automatically, forcing them to step through the frames. Paper and objects lay everywhere. Parts of the building had collapsed, burned, or been destroyed. Ignium wires and lights dangled like vines from the ceiling, some sparking and charring the ground around them.

The rotten smell blanketed the inside of the building. The burnt-up walls trapped the fumes of the bodies filling the halls and the rooms.

Robert was thankful for his mask as he grimaced at the bodies, "Ugh, this place is horrible."

"Just tough it out. There's plenty of things around here for us to grab. We need to find a storage room or something, see if the military left any weapons in here."

They crept through the halls, flashlights on. Only certain parts of the building had power from backup Ignium generators, leaving the rest of the destruction in darkness. So far, the building was just as empty of life as the streets. Instead of going up to more hospital rooms, craters in the building, and machine gun nests, they tried to find a way down. After passing by a few elevators, they found one that worked. Robert pressed a button on the elevator console and looked up as a light turned on.

"Step back. We don't know if anything is in there," William said.

A ding made them point their guns at the elevator. The doors slid open, revealing nothing within the empty car. Once inside, William pressed a button to take them down to the lowest level. A jerk shook the elevator before it descended, stopped, and opened its doors to reveal a basement. The remnants of the military were everywhere. Boxes of supplies sat against the walls, piled high in every space where they could fit. The pair stepped forth into the darkness. Water pooled in different parts of the basement and made their shoes squelch with every step. Certain areas had ankle-high water, while some had a thin layer.

Robert's breath quivered, "Seems they had flooding down here."

"Probably a broken pipe. Most of this stuff is in boxes, so it should be fine. We need to get food, ammo, and explosives."

The dirty black water stained the walls all over the basement area. They waded from room to room. Shelves stood inside each room, accompanied by empty hospital beds, extra hospital supplies, military boxes, and weapons. Some craters and bins were already empty.

"This place is weird," Robert said.

"What do you mean?"

"This was probably one of the biggest military bases in the city, and there's absolutely no one left. All these supplies are still here too. It feels like there's something here, but we haven't found anything. Not even signs of those things."

William shrugged and pointed above them, "They probably died out to those monsters and T-PEM, along with bombings from China. Whatever fire burnt this place down probably did a number. Who knows, maybe they escaped and left all this behind? It doesn't matter. We just gotta take what we need and leave."

"Yeah. It's just weird."

"Are we just gonna keep calling them things?"

"I don't know what else to call them. Lurkers? They seem to hide and lurk a lot."

"Lurkers works."

They eventually arrived at the hospital's mortuary. A pile of bodies sat in one of the corners while more covered tables and the floor.

"Oh God," Robert groaned.

"Nothing but bodies here. Let's skip this one for now."

They turned back, went through another hall, and glanced into the rooms. At the very end of the hallway, stacks of large green crates filled a vast space. Rifles and pistols lined each wall.

"This must be it. Look for something that looks explosive," William said.

Robert stopped halfway through the room and knelt in front of a few crates.

"William! I found MREs! There're a few boxes over here!"

"Grab a box!"

Robert grunted as he lifted one of the boxes and heaved it onto his shoulder. He walked around as he continued searching.

"Robert! Found something! I think it's C4!" William exclaimed.

The pair met up at the opposite side of the storage room.

"That looks right," Robert said.

"We can lift this one. It has handles."

Robert put the MRE box on top of the C4 crate. Both lifted the container by the handles and walked back to the wall.

"Ugh, this is gonna be a long-ass haul," Robert said.

"It was your idea. Let's just go."

They went to the elevator and pressed a button to go to the first level. The elevator opened and took them to the first level, where they walked out toward the entrance. A metal bar flew out from the front desk, spinning and hitting William in the arm. William screamed in surprise and dropped the box.

"William!" Robert cried.

A figure jumped out from the desk and sprinted through the front entrance. Robert could not distinguish the shape as it disappeared and only spotted a machete-like weapon and a backpack. He chased it out the doors and watched the figure hop onto a car, climb over a wall, and disappear into the streets beyond.

No use giving chase.

"You okay?" Robert asked.

"I'm fine. Who or what the hell was that?" William asked, rubbing his arm.

"No idea. It ran off quicker than anything I've ever seen. Jumped up and disappeared over the wall."

William inhaled sharply, "Let's leave before it comes back. Come on."

# 19

# American Looters

\* \* \*

Robert stared at the hospital from a distance, crouched behind a pile of rubble. His gaze followed the walls outside the building containing ruined tents and military vehicles.

William sat beside him, "Well?"

"Seems like the usual. Nobody's around, as far as I can tell. No Lurkers and no people. What are we here for today?" Robert asked.

"Water. We need to make an air well."

"What's an air well?"

"Like a dew collector. It's like a device that captures moisture from the air and collects it in a bowl. Aren't you the smart one?"

"Shut up. Where are we gonna get stuff to do that?"

"In the hospital. They might have stuff for tents or flags. We just need a layer of cloth and some poles. Probably some filters too."

"How do you even know about this?"

"I read a little bit when in prison. It's what they used in Africa in desert areas to grow food. It's pretty cool. Come on, let's go."

They ran toward the hospital, slinked through a hole in the wall, and crept inside. Parts had collapsed over the weeks as the building crumbled from harsh wind. They avoided deep water, damaged Ignium wires, and structurally weak areas.

"What are we checking out first?" Robert asked.

"Upper floors. We can split up and handle each floor ourselves. Just give a holler if you need help."

"Are you sure we should split up?"

William's gaze shifted between the many halls of the hospital, "Egh, you're right. I don't trust this building. We'll stick to the same floors. Second floor first."

They approached the stairs and went up onto the second floor. This part of the hospital was massive. Hospital beds, equipment, and the putrid odor of death filled every room. They entered a hall. As they passed, Robert looked into rooms on either side, spotting body after body inside each. This must've been where the military kept their wounded.

"Egh, God, why do we come here?" Robert groaned.

"So we can take all this to the Tower before anyone else steals it for themselves."

The main lobby was composed of a circular room with a circular desk in the center, full of computers and papers. Five hospital wings went out from the desk, each lined with more and more rooms.

William looked down each wing, "I'll go down this way. You go that way. Just check the rooms before going in. See if anything is hiding. Shout if you need help."

"All right."

Robert glanced back once before going down. He flashed his light into each room, gazed at the corpses inside, and waited for any movement. Nothing. Nothing moved, hissed, or even blinked as he illuminated each room. Eventually, he reached the end of the hall and the last rooms. They were closed with secure doors that had reinforced windows and digital locks. Robert approached one of the doors and peered through a circular window at the top of the door.

Supplies. Box after box of medicine and medical supplies were stacked up to the ceiling inside the room.

"Yo, William!"

"What!"

"Check this out!"

William jogged across the lobby and looked at the door, "What?"

"Look inside," Robert said.

William approached the window and looked in, moving his flashlight around to see what the room had, "Jackpot. It's locked, though."

"It's a digital lock."

Robert knelt by the door, looked it over, pressed a few buttons, and watched the screen turn red.

"It's in lock-down mode. Doesn't matter when we press. It needs to be reset. I'd pop it open, but we don't have any screwdrivers. We could break the door?" Robert said.

William turned and stared at Robert. He put his hand on his hips before gesturing to the door.

"What?" Robert asked.

"You have a plasma rifle. Just melt it."

"Oh!"

Robert stood back and shot the plasma rifle at the door. The gun heated the material in its melt chamber in two seconds and spewed it onto the door. The glowing orange liquid melted the door, causing a large hole. Robert shot again. The gun spewed out more of its liquid venom onto the hinges.

William kicked the door down before the molten material cooled, "And that's how we handle business. I'll check out what's in here. You check out the rest of the building."

Robert nodded and turned before moving back down the hall. In the lobby, a figure darted out of a room, ran up the stairs, and disappeared. Robert gasped. He pursued it up a flight of stairs to the third floor.

The figure was gone. It didn't seem to be in any of the rooms or down the first hall. He approached the lobby, glancing down the three other aisles in confusion. A click sounded. He whipped around and pulled the trigger as the figure bolted toward him. The gun spewed out its molten venom a second too late. The figure pushed the gun's barrel upward, kicked Robert in the stomach, and sent him to the floor. It ripped the gun out of his hands and gently laid the blade of a long weapon on his neck.

"Stay down."

Robert's jaw dropped. A woman. She held a wicked weapon. Its blade was like a thick scythe, long with a slight curve, while the rest of the weapon was composed of a wooden handle wrapped in cloth and tipped with a hook. The hook seemed to be from a snow pick. The edge of the blade was bloody.

"Whoa! Whoa! Don't hurt me!" Robert said.

"Stay on your ass," she ordered.

The despicable blade slowly parted from his neck as she put his rifle far away on a lobby desk. She turned and stared down at him. A smart suit covered her from head to toe with worn jeans and a dirty hoodie layered on top of it. She had a mask with goggles, visors, and small filters. A belt with a holstered pistol wrapped around her waist and a hiking bag hung from her back. She also wore soldier boots. Her eyes were a deep shade of brown. Dreads rested on the sides of her neck, most of them bundled up inside the hoodie. She lacked gloves, which left her dark skin exposed and covered by burns from polluted air.

"I'm staying, I'm staying," Robert said, holding his hands above his waist.

"I knew you would try to shoot at me. Too bad you weren't smart about it. Plasma weapons take a moment."

"Why didn't you kill me?"

"Because you wouldn't have shot me if you had known I wasn't one of the monsters. You're not a murderer, not yet. I can hear it in your voice and see it in your eyes."

Robert blinked, "What?"

She raised her hand, "Look, I'll admit. I'm a little selfish. I'm keeping you and your friend alive simply because there's plenty of loot here for all of us, and your visits keep the monsters away from here."

"Wait, have you been watching us?"

"No, we've just come across each other three or four times. You just never saw me."

"Wait, you threw that metal bar at William?"

"Yeah, sorry about that. I thought it was only him and he'd attack me. Should've just run away."

"What's your name?"

"Ruth. I guess you're Robert?"

"Yeah, heard our conversations?"

"You two are loud. Are you two with the Militia?"

"No, we just stole these clothes."

Robert glanced behind Ruth. William inched toward her, gun ready, and pointed at the woman.

"Wait! William, don't!" Robert shouted, raising his hand.

Ruth turned and raised her hands slightly.

"Who the hell are you? What did you do to Robert?"

"Calm down, buddy! I didn't do anything and don't mean any harm."

"She's good, William! She's good. Lower the gun!"

William looked at Robert, then at her, "What are you talking about? I heard you shoot. What the hell were you shooting at?"

"She scared me. We're good now!" Robert said.

William glanced at him again, then lowered his pistol, "Who the hell are you?"

"My name is Ruth. I used to live around here before everything fell apart. I'm just looking to survive, just like both of you are. We can help each other."

"Help us? How?" William asked.

"Look, you two have elephant feet. You're keeping the monsters scared off, and I'm sure both of you have the muscle power to keep anyone else at bay. There's plenty of loot here for all of us. If you two share, I can maybe help you. I'll owe you a few favors."

William shook his head, "How can you help us?"

"Well, I know my way around. Let's just say I'm not afraid to climb. I watch the streets all the time, and I know where things are. I can tell you guys about what's going on around the local area and deliver goodies to you. We can make a sort of deal."

"Look, can I stand up? Let William and I talk it out before we agree to anything," Robert said.

"You can stand. Hell, I'll even give you privacy if you need it."

Robert stood and urged William to the other side of the lobby, where Ruth could not hear their whispers.

"Look, William, we're not going to be able to take everything here before other people, or things figure this place out. Shit, I don't know if we can get everything to the Tower. She could help us, and if she doesn't keep her word, we know how to handle her."

"We don't know who the hell this is, Robert."

"I don't think she's the type to do anything," Robert said.

William covered his visor with his palm and groaned, "How do you know that? How does someone like her get through all the shit that's happened alone? What if she has friends? What if we go outside right now and get swiss cheesed by her friends?"

"I haven't seen anyone in a while, William. This is the first person we've seen in days that isn't a Lurker. We can handle it. I think we should make the deal to see if it benefits us."

"Fine, fine. We're trusting strangers now. Next time a van with the word 'candy' on the side of it pulls up, I'm going in. Maybe I'll get something."

"Shut up. We'll be fine."

The pair went over to Ruth.

"Okay, we have a deal. We share the loot here, and in exchange, you help us when we need it. Sounds good?" Robert asked.

"Sounds good. Do you have an implant? We can add each other and call when we need help," Ruth suggested.

"Oh yeah, network balloons are still working, aren't they?"

"Yep."

They rolled back their sleeves and exchanged contacts using their forearm implants. When they were done, Robert rolled his sleeve back down and rubbed it slightly as the toxic air irritated his skin.

William pointed to the room with supplies, "All right, now that we know each other a little, let's start this deal. We've just opened a room full of medical supplies. You can have some stuff from in there."

"In exchange for?" Ruth asked.

"Pipes. I need pipes, specifically PVC. Know where we can get some?"

Ruth crossed her arms, "Yeah, I can go get you that. I'll take some stuff with me and go get some pipes. Where should I deliver them?"

Robert waved his hands, "Wait, hold on. How do we know you're not just gonna run off with the stuff we give you?"

"Does it matter? I'll only take the surplus. Not like you'll run short on anything here in a while. It can be a trust exercise. I promise I'll deliver some pipes. Just tell me where to drop them off."

William and Robert looked at each other, then at her.

"I'll send you the street address. Get us as much as you can," William said.

"How big? What are they for?" Ruth asked.

"They're for our business. I'll send you some specific measurements. Just message me when you are getting them."

"All right, I'll get going now. Bye," Ruth said.

"Peace," Robert replied.

Once she was gone, William turned to Robert, "We're stupid for doing this."

"Have faith. Us keeping our guns down is what is allowing her to get what she needs to live. Let's just keep exploring."

* * *

After a few hours, they left the safety of the Tower. Moving loot from the hospital had taken multiple trips in one day, and Robert's legs and ankle injury now ached. They would have to keep making more trips for a while but had given up for the day.

"Where is this?" Robert asked.

"A few blocks away. Far away enough that she won't be able to tell where we live. We're going around a bit so that we come from a different direction."

"Ugh, today is going to kill us. So tired of lifting things. Wish we had more hands."

William pointed at a ruin, "Maybe Ruth can help us, or maybe you should ask the Lurkers if they'd like to help."

"Hah, I haven't seen any in two days. Have you?"

"No, the streets are quiet. Too quiet, but I appreciate the peace."

"When are we blowing the stairs?" Robert asked.

"Soon. We need to make an escape route out of the Tower in case anything goes wrong. Maybe a few."

"How about a zipline to another skyscraper?"

"Sounds crazy. We'll see."

The titans of the old world stood alone and empty. Knowing that Ruth was out there gave him some hope that other people were alive. Where were they?

Hopefully, people would come together to endure rather than fight. Despite many places being empty of anything useful, pockets like the hospital gave hope that people didn't have to scrape by to survive. So few were left that there was plenty for everyone.

They went down a few streets before they turned and went through long alleyways and over rubble. Eventually, they were going straight again. Robert looked at corpses as they passed by. Many were not decaying since the air was too inhospitable for decay. Instead, they were being eaten by mutant rats and Lurker. The pair never went out at night since the bitter darkness was when the monsters came out.

"We're here," William said.

They stood in the middle of an intersection, surrounded by cars and a destroyed tank.

"Where are the pipes?" Robert asked.

"Obviously, they're not here because she just fucked us, Robert."

"They have to be here, William. Don't say that."

"Oh, look at that! We trusted a stranger and got screwed! Good goddamn job, Robert!"

"You know, if you'd shut the hell up, maybe you won't get your head eaten off," Ruth said from a window above. She sat and stared at the pair.

"Where are the pipes?" William asked.

"In this building. You'll find them in a room on the first floor. Just do me a favor and shut the hell up. I like you two, and I don't want you guys getting shot or eaten because you were loud."

Robert frowned before entering the building through a window. William followed closely. They looked around for a few moments before they found a room with a large stack of white PVC pipes.

"See?" Robert said.

# 20

# Speak Not

*2:13 PM, February 5, 2079*

* * *

*"The nation has been attacked by nuclear weapons. Communications have been disrupted, and the extent of the damage is unknown. Please stay tuned to this wavelength for instructions."*

William shut off the emergency radio, "I'm tired of hearing that same old warning broadcast."

"I don't blame you. We're probably the last people left sitting around a radio. Come on. It's your turn."

William pondered his next move before moving a piece across the board.

Robert looked up and smiled under his gas mask. He picked up his piece, moved it, and placed it confidently, "Checkmate."

William sighed extremely long, "I hate this game."

"You'll get better. Again?"

"Later. I wanna keep tinkering with the radio. Take a look at our air wells."

They had built the air wells in a crater in the Tower. The hole spanned over four levels of office spaces and was stained with dark burns. The air wells stood at the bottom, on the least affected level, with a sturdy floor below. Each air well had a large cloth net held up by a tripod of pipes. Each net made a bowl that led to a tube and into metal pans or plastic jugs. Robert approached the center air well, whose net came from an American flag. He knelt beside it. A plastic jar sat beneath the center, filled up a quarter way. Water dripped in slowly.

"How are they?" William asked.

"They're filling up. If we wait long enough and filter them, we should be set for water," Robert said as he checked the rest.

"The problem is we don't have a lot of water filters."

"Yeah. The one here in the right corner is not as full as the others. Might be the net."

William's gaze drifted from the chessboard to Robert and the air wells, his brow furrowing, "Maybe, we can find a new one if we have to. Any ideas on how to get water filters?"

"None."

"We'll think of something," William continued changing channels on the radio.

Robert approached the edge of the floor where there was no wall and looked down. The sense of inevitable death pulled at Robert as he gazed down a straight drop to the streets below. It was strangely seductive to be so close to something so dangerous. He had been trying to overcome his fear of the edge, but every time he stood near it, his heart throbbed, and his stomach dropped. A ringing sound filled his head. He yelped and fell backward before coming to his senses and answering the call.

"My fucking god, Ruth! You scared me."

"Sorry, what?" Ruth asked.

"Nothing, nothing, was just being stupid. What's up?"

"I was just calling to see if those air doohickey things were working. I need some water."

"See, I think we're in a position for trade. We need water filters."

"I can get water filters if you can get me water."

"That sounds like something we can do. Where are we meeting?"

"I'll send you the address and the time."

"All right, I'll tell William."

"Peace, I gotta go find some filters."

"Peace."

"Well, I answered our air filter problem," he said.

"Ruth's got us?" William asked.

"Yeah. I'll tell you when we have to leave."

* * *

Robert opened the door as William walked out. He had a water jug attached to his back like a backpack. He grunted and stepped carefully out into the street.

"We're taking turns," William said.

"I already agreed that we are. We'll be fine. It's still day, and it's been quiet."

William squinted at the polluted sky, "As much 'day' as there can be. You know, we have to drop this thing if we get attacked."

"We'll be fine. No one's out here."

The wind caused garbage and ash to blow all over the place. Recently, cars and tanks had begun rusting as the wind and weather scraped up their paint. The stench of rats filled the air as the mutant pests burrowed inside thousands of bodies left from the war in anticipation of winter. With the toxic air and pollution, the decay was slow. There were no flies and maggots to eat flesh and so many bodies that the rats had overfed. Even the Lurkers, wherever they were in the shadows, were gorged. Only a few kinds of bacteria could survive the pollution, and they slowly decayed the rat-filled bodies. Descending into the stench in the streets was always shocking, but eventually, the pair grew used to it. The gas masks prevented them from smelling the long decay, and for that, they were grateful.

"Do you think a lot of people survived?" Robert asked.

"Probably out in the country or in remote places. Doomsday preppers are probably doing fine right now."

"Oh, are you telling me that being in the city was a bad idea?" Robert asked.

"Shut up."

They grew silent for a while as they walked in quiet frustration.

"How do you feel lately?" William asked.

"Like shit."

"Still thinking about what happened?"

"Yeah, I still miss him. I'm just glad he doesn't have to go through this hell."

"You can talk to me about it if you want."

"I'd rather talk about other things."

They walked in silence before Robert spoke, "Do you think the planet will become green again?"

William looked up at the sky and then around at the trash massed around them, "Maybe? We'll probably be as dead as everyone else by then. If people rebuild, they hopefully won't use Ignium, or there just won't be enough people using it to cause any issues. The pollution haze will fade until the skies are clear, plants might come back, and who knows, maybe some animals will take over. But my opinion? Unlikely. Who can survive this?"

"Don't sound so defeated. We're succeeding at surviving."

"You know what we're really succeeding at?" William said.

"What?"

William placed the water on the ground, "Switching who carries the water."

"Ugh, all right."

Robert grabbed the water with a grunt, heaved it onto his back, and moved forward. At first, the water felt relatively light since his legs and body had become strong from months of running and climbing. It became heavier as time passed. Eventually, he had to give it back to William. They kept taking turns, stopping for a five-minute break and continuing on.

"We should build a few ways to escape the Tower," Robert said.

"I was thinking about that. A zipline or two from a few levels might work in case anything hits the fan like you suggested."

"Ziplines and maybe some ropes to get up and down when we blow the stairs. We can also find parachutes to jump off the top of the Tower if we need to."

William shrugged and smirked, "Well, may the day never come when we have to jump off the Tower."

"Yeah, may it never."

They avoided craters and cars. It was slower, but neither was eager to climb or even haul the water. Robert occasionally checked his implant for directions. Ash began falling from the sky. A black, cloud-like wall loomed in the sky and crept in ominously. An ash storm rose above them, enveloping buildings and cars as its black mass moved with the wind.

"Aw, damnit," William said.

"Wonderful."

The ash storm howled as it enveloped them like a snowstorm, gradually blanketing the ground with ash as a wind carried the gray and sooty material around.

William stopped, "Do you hear that?"

"Hear what?"

They both paused.

"I hear crying," William said.

"I don't hear anything."

"There's crying. Trust me."

"Should we check it out?"

William frowned and shrugged, "I don't know."

"Is it really our business? Ruth expects us."

"It's not, but what if it's a kid?"

"Fine, fine. Let's go see."

Robert put down the water jug and readied his plasma rifle. He checked its ammunition capacity and grabbed random trash to stuff into the weapon. William checked how many bullets he had as he prepared his pistol.

"Lead the way," Robert said.

William nodded. They moved toward a skyscraper. They entered through an airlock and looked around the first level. It was dark and dusty, with shattered glass everywhere. Robert heard the crying. It sounded like a little girl weeping loudly and saying something he couldn't make out.

"Do you hear it now?" William whispered.

"Yes. Is that a little girl?"

"It sounds like it."

The crying became louder. They marched into the darkness with their flashlights on. The first level had nothing but a lobby resembling a hotel. It was a mess. Footprints and dust covered the floor alongside trash and turned over furniture. Scrapes covered the walls, and the building had a peculiar musk. They found the stairwell and ascended slowly. The pair stepped carefully and listened as they got closer and closer to the crying until they could hear what the voice was saying.

"Daddy! Daddy, where are you, Daddy? I'm scared!"

"What the hell?" Robert whispered.

"I'm scared! Hello! Anybody?"

They got onto the level the voice came from and jogged past room after room before William flinched, "Did you just see that?"

"See what?"

"Something just ran past there."

"Probably a rat. Come on."

The voice came from the end of the hotel hall. As they got closer to the end, they saw bodies. At first, they didn't flinch at the sight as they went past the bodies without fear. Then Robert noticed the bodies were fresh and equipped with supplies. They got to the end and looked into the last room.

"William... We should run."

"Daddy?"

William shone the light into the room. Bodies covered the floor. A figure knelt next to a carcass and dug its hands into the corpse's stomach. As the light shone on it, it froze. Slowly, the thing turned around. The pair gasped. It was a man with horrid, twisted eyes growing on his cheek. Extra fingers and tiny stubby limbs grew from his body. Nails, tumors, and teeth layered his skin between torn clothes, and a larger arm-like limb came from his stomach.

He turned and screamed in the girl's voice, "Daddy!"

William aimed and shot his pistol. The creature darted out of sight and ran further into the room while cries and screams erupted from other rooms. Robert snapped around. Human mutants came from the other rooms, all horrid and twisted with fused body parts and wretched growths. They cried out and launched toward them. He aimed and shot his plasma rifle. The material inside spewed out in a string of fiery liquid. One of the mutants was bathed in the hellish venom of the gun, wriggling and crying as it was cooked alive. The other mutants retreated in fear while more came out further down the hall.

"William! William! We need to run!"

"Where? We're blocked in!"

Robert looked at the window behind them.

"We're only two stories up!"

Robert dashed to the window. A gigantic pile of trash sat beneath the window, lining the whole alley out to the street. Robert broke the window with his gun, William shooting behind him at the approaching Lurkers.

"Come on, William!"

Robert grabbed him and jumped. They flailed and wiggled in the air. Robert's heart dropped. What felt like a long drop ended sharply when they landed on the plastic bags. They got up and ran, Lurkers jumping out after them.

"The water! The water!" William shouted.

William ran to the front, grabbed the water jug they had left on the street, and sprinted. The mutants pursued. The pair zig-zagged in and out of buildings, running and making confusing turns to lose their pursuers. Only a few mutants managed to chase them until the pair's legs burned. They ran down an alley. Robert turned abruptly and shot. His gun spewed molten onto two mutants, melting them alive and scaring off the others. The mutants screeched and thrashed before falling over and dying. Robert lowered the gun, listening as the others disappeared into the ash storm.

"Let's go," William urged.

They followed the corners and edges of buildings as the ash storm limited their vision. Robert's heart pounded, and they both gasped at every noise.

"Where the hell did those Lurkers go?" William asked.

"Somewhere. Let's hope they don't come back."

They slowly shuffled through the soot-coated rubbish piles for twenty minutes before finally arriving at an alleyway that Ruth had marked on Robert's map. The pair slowly entered and turned around as footsteps clattered toward them.

"Shit, they're back!" William exclaimed.

Robert lifted the gun and pointed it at three figures approaching from the storm. Another figure ran into the three. The sound of screeching and whipping echoed as a blade fell each. As the last of them was reaped and fell dead, Ruth's voice came from the ash.

"That you two or more monsters?" she asked.

"It's us!" Robert said.

Ruth walked toward them, lowering her blade. She guided them into one of the buildings on the opposite side of the street and led them out of the ash storm.

"Did you guys bring the water?" Ruth asked.

William put the water down, "Right here."

"Are you guys okay?" she asked.

"No," William replied.

"What happened?" she asked.

Robert described what had happened in a shaky tone, "We heard a little girl crying on the way here and investigated. It wasn't a little girl. It was some kind of Lurker that could sound like one."

Ruth's gaze fell to the floor as her head dropped, "I've seen that one. Those things are smart. I don't know what that one is, but it can mimic voices. It usually chooses the voice of its prey to attract loved ones or people that care for whatever it happens to eat. Did you guys kill it?"

"No," William said.

"Dammit. It needs to be killed, or it'll keep killing. Doesn't matter right now. I have the water filters."

She led them into a back room with two small pallets of cardboard boxes wrapped with plastic. They were from an American manufacturer and seemed to have come from the warehouse or a store.

"These will do. Do you have any yourself?" William asked.

"Yeah, I have some. I appreciate the water. You two need to be more careful out there. Mind your own business and move away from noise. You're both noisy enough as it is."

"We will," Robert said.

"Good. Stay here for a bit and wait until the storm passes."

# 21

# Hungry Cruelty

*12:44 PM, August 12, 2080*

\* \* \*

A year had passed. The bitter winter approached again, harsher than the last. Food and water had become rare between the Lurkers and the last survivors of the old world. Survival grew more difficult with each day. Ash and pollution stained the city, and trash still blew through the streets. The cancerous remnants of mankind never seemed to disappear. Piles of trash bags were unchanging, and some bodies from the old world still decayed a year later. The raging fires from the wars had slowly burned out, and wrathful sandstorms now replaced the ash storms the fires had produced. These sandstorms rose hundreds of feet in the air and shredded paint, though the skyscrapers of the old world absorbed most of their wrath.

\* \* \*

Robert walked behind William at the edge of the street. He held his plasma rifle ready, eyeing their surroundings as they moved. They were on edge. The Lurkers had gotten braver and more dangerous in recent weeks as winter approached and food became scarce. The pair had plenty hoarded up, though they still dared the streets to find more.

"Hear anything?" Robert whispered.

"No, nothing seems to be out here."

"They're getting worse. Ruth says she avoids walking the streets nowadays," Robert said.

"Well, I'm kinda fat, and I can't climb like her."

Robert snorted and rolled his eyes, Yeah, you're so fat."

"Hey, I haven't lost that much weight. Anyway, where the hell are they coming from?"

Robert sighed, "Somewhere. Maybe the sewer and metro systems? Or do they live in buildings?"

"Any idea how we can get rid of them?"

"Hiding and letting them starve out?"

"Or blowing them up. We still have some leftover explosives after clearing out the first floor of the Tower."

"That's if we find a nest, get far enough inside, and then get out."

"You're right. There might not even be a nest."

They slinked down another street, occasionally hiding and observing their surroundings before continuing.

Robert's stomach growled, "I wish we hadn't skipped breakfast."

"It's easier to sleep if we save our daily meals for dinner."

"I know. I just miss when we ate three times a day."

"That's before we realized we need to eat to live, not eat to be comfortable."

"I wonder how Ruth is doing?" Robert asked.

"Probably hungrier than us and hiding somewhere. She's a weird one. She told me she prefers sleeping in wardrobes and closets."

"So weird. She's probably safer than we are, even out here. I was hoping she'd join us and help us through," Robert said.

"If you can convince her. Other people don't seem keen on joining groups, though. Remember those twins?"

"Yeah. Wonder where they are now?"

"They said that they were leaving the city. Maybe they made it out," William said.

"Probably not. Who knows what's out there?"

"Death. It's everywhere. You know that."

"You're depressing."

The pair turned down a street and approached a giant grocery store looming beside a parking lot lined with skyscrapers.

Robert paused and stared at the store, "Oh shit," he whispered.

"What?" William asked, looking back.

Robert was paralyzed. William approached him, his face wrinkling, "Are you okay, Robert?"

"I'm fine. It's just... this is the grocery store Zilv, and I used to shop at. We must be where I used to live."

"Oh... It's okay, Robert. We'll be in and out."

Robert's eyes teared. He sniffled and held his tears back, face red as he took a breath and nodded to William. They crossed the parking lot and ran in through the airlock. Broken glass crunched under their boots. The store was massive, with shelf after shelf lining the place, creating a maze. The building itself was dark except for an employee entrance across the store. A flickering flashlight sat on the floor and shone in. Who left that? The interior looked as if a horde of toddlers had hurricaned through it. Shelves had been tipped over, and boxes were strewn about everywhere. It was deathly silent. No figures sprinted away from the light in the darkness, and no eyes gleamed back at them.

"We need to find food. Let's not grab anything that isn't super useful," William whispered.

Robert nodded.

They snuck down aisle after aisle. All the goods the store once had were gone, leaving nothing but scraps and the odd gem among the garbage. William or Robert would occasionally grab a leftover can or a box stuffing it in a backpack before carrying on. Robert's heart throbbed. The darkness was unsettling, and his mind tricked him by forming figures from nothing. Eventually, they had scoured most of the store with little to show for it. Each of them checked their backpacks, shaking the little that they had.

"Think there's anything more here?" Robert asked.

"Probably a little bit? Or nothing at all."

Robert pointed, "Hey, look over there."

William looked to where he pointed, eyeing the employee door with the flickering flashlight next to it.

"What about it?" William asked.

"Might be to the back storerooms. Who knows? They might have more there," Robert said.

"Let's go check it out."

The relatively large door was made up of two swinging panels. Each had glass windows at head level. Robert peeked inside. The outlines of a warehouse full of heavy crates ranged the length of the store. As he shone his flashlight in, he saw bins and boxes on the ground surrounded by dozens of kneeling Lurkers that ate and tore at the containers they could open.

He gasped and ducked out of sight, "Go, go, go! Lights off," he hissed.

They snuck back into the darkness and turned off their lights. The doors pushed open. One of the Lurkers, ghastly and twisted, stumbled out into the store. The flickering flashlight left on the floor illuminated its body. An extra head, composed of random teeth and odd skull structures bulking out of it, was half fused into its own. It could barely walk and was held up by a single foot on the left and a gnarled, twisted abomination of many feet on the right.

"Damnit, there's a lot of food back there, but there's dozens of those things," Robert whispered.

"Luckily, they didn't see us," William whispered.

The Lurker stumbled, looking around for what had disturbed it.

"We should leave," William whispered.

The shrill shriek of a woman caused both of them to jump. A flashlight illuminated the other end of the store. A woman stumbled down a broken escalator leading to the second level and screamed as Lurkers pursued her.

"No! Go away! Help me!" she screamed.

"What the hell is that?" William whispered.

"It's a woman. She needs our help," Robert replied.

One of the pursuing Lurkers lunged at the woman, tackling her off the escalator's railing to the floor below. A crack came from her gas mask as she landed, followed by another bloodcurdling scream as she tried to crawl away. The beasts went after her, clawing and biting at her. A horde of Lurkers poured from the backroom. They clawed and pulled against each other and crashed forth as a monstrous, hungry wall.

"She's dead already, Robert. This is our chance. We can go get the stuff in that room and run!"

Robert stuttered, unable to form a sentence as he watched the Lurkers pile on the woman.

"Do you want to starve to death? Let's go!"

William grabbed Robert and led him into the back room. Robert didn't look back as the Lurkers left their precious hordes of stored food for something fresh. The pair turned on their flashlights and desperately stuffed their backpacks with everything they could.

"Go away! No! Please!" came the screams outside.

"This one, grab this one!" William said as they hurried.

Robert stuffed his backpack full, grabbed everything he could put in his pockets, and hold in his hands. The woman's screaming intensified. Growling and roaring were heard as the Lurkers pulled her apart. She fell silent a minute after.

"Time's up. Let's go!" William said.

Robert ran after William as he sprinted toward a door at the back, fidgeted with the handle, and found it locked.

"Damnit, blast the lock!" William said.

Robert aimed and blasted the door with molten material, melting away the lock and parts of the door until he ran out of ammo.

"God damnit, I'm out!" Robert swore.

"The hinges, idiot!"

Robert looked around, grabbed whatever he could, and put it into the Melt Chamber of his gun. Lurkers poured in through the door to the storeroom and ran toward them. William raised his pistol, nailed one in the head, and took out another with two shots to the chest.

"Robert! The door!"

Robert lifted his gun and spewed more molten material onto the door hinges before kicking the door down.

"Come on, William!"

William shot off the last of his ammo as he ran out with Robert. Robert turned and shot more molten material on the edges of the door, coating it in the hot goo to buy time. Lurkers came to the door, hissing as the goo's heat repulsed them. The pair ran out into the street and didn't look back as they abandoned the gruesome site.

# 22

# The Others

\* \* \*

Robert turned the radio's knob, going through frequency after frequency. Static was all that he found. William slept beside the desk on a dirty mattress they had carried from an apartment. The rough winds howled as they pushed against the Tower, cutting through the city like whiplashes. Robert was bored and sad. Most days they spent up in the Tower came with nothing to do. The bottom levels of the structure had been blown up or reinforced, and they had what they needed to survive. Currently, their primary concern was food. They had plenty of water, medicine, and weapons but not enough food for the year.

All Robert could do was think and switch channels. Usually, he thought about Zilv, sniffling quietly as he recalled all their memories. The pain had not left since the explosion, though Robert bottled it up as much as possible. He crawled his fingers under his mask and wiped away his tears before grabbing the microphone attached to the radio.

"Hello? Anyone on here?"

Nothing. Robert listened to another frequency and heard nothing but static. William slowly rolled over. He grunted, pushed his hands under his mask, and rubbed his face.

"Good morning," Robert said.

"Ugh, morning. Everything good?"

"Yeah, just listening to the radio. Haven't heard anything so far."

"Have we ever heard anything on that radio? I swear, it's broken."

"Well, I have nothing better to do. I checked the air wells, the first levels, supplies, and everything else."

"We need more games," William yawned.

"I'm afraid we're running out of board games that exist."

"Maybe books. Maybe we can learn something."

"Maybe."

William sat up, grumbled, stretched, and stood, "I'm going to go pee."

"All right, what are we doing today?"

"Being bored."

Robert snorted a little as William disappeared down the stairs to the level where they had the air wells. They had a handle mounted where the crater carved a hole in the Tower, which they used whenever they needed to go. It allowed their waste to fall into the streets below.

Robert spoke into the radio's microphone in a bored tone, "Hello, anyone here? Hello, I am Robert. Hello, I am Zord, destroyer of pencils."

Robert switched to another frequency, "Hello, hello. I am Spiggybop, the paper muncher."

"Uh... hello, Spiggybop?" came a deep male voice from the radio.

Robert's stomach dropped as his eyes widened. He gripped the microphone intensely and spoke, "Hello, can you hear me?"

"I can hear you. Can you hear me?"

"Yes, yes, I can! Oh, thank God, finally!"

"How are you doing today, Spiggybop?"

"I'm doing good. I'm just relieved to hear someone else's voice. My name's Robert."

"That's great to hear. My name is Dan. How are you faring in the Land of the Free?"

"Scraping by and trying not to die. You?"

"Same thing here."

William came up from the bathroom and raised one brow, "Who are you talking to?"

Robert gestured to him to be quiet, "I have a question."

"Go ahead."

"Are there others? Or are we alone?"

"Do you happen to be in Albert City?" Dan asked.

"North of it," Robert replied.

"You're the first I've met on the radio in my local area. There are some people left, but they're spread throughout the city. I'm with a group of sixteen, and we've been trading with a few other groups and getting people into our group. Makes it easier to survive against the Devourers."

Robert let out a relieved sigh and closed his eyes, "That's great to hear. By the way, is that what you call them? W– I call them Lurkers."

"Yeah, we call them Devourers since all we've ever seen them doing is eating up the dead. Lurkers is pretty accurate too. I have a proposition for you."

"What's that?"

"You doing good on food?"

"Kind of. Why?"

"If you're willing, my group would be willing to trade with you if you have anything to give in return. We got lots of food."

"I have water. Like a gallon, if you think that's good?"

"That's plenty! Where would you like to meet?"

"Do you know the destroyed bakery on Ellis and Gattis?"

"Yeah, that works perfectly. What time?"

"Three works."

"Perfect, see you then. Over and out."

"Uh, over and out?"

He turned off the radio and faced William, "There's people out there!"

"What? Really?"

"That was some guy named Dan. He said that there were some people in the city. I organized a deal for water."

"Did you tell them about us and the Tower?"

"No, no, I didn't trust him that much. Come on, let's at least be a little optimistic."

William sighed, "Let's be careful. Let's get Ruth to help us. Call and tell her where and when to meet us. I'll go get some water ready."

\* \* \*

Robert walked beside William. Ruth followed as they navigated the streets. A gallon of water hung from Robert's back in a backpack they had made for carrying water.

"I still feel bad about not saving that woman. Wish we could've at least put her out of her misery," Robert grunted.

"There was no way. The food was worth it, and who knows? She could've killed us," William said.

Ruth shook her head, dreads swinging back and forth, "It's just fucked up. From what you guys told me, it was a lose-lose situation. Food and she dies, she lives, and you two die. Fucked-up world. Can't imagine listening to it. You eventually become numb to this, but when?"

"It doesn't leave. You just react less every time," William said.

Robert grimaced, "Let's talk about something else."

Ruth rubbed the back of her neck, "Sorry."

William looked back and forth between the two and then gestured toward Robert, "What's the plan with these people we're meeting?"

"Well, we're trading water for food. They expect only me, but I want to appear with you. Ruth needs to go up in a window or something so she can observe the area. Message me if anything is wrong or come in and save our asses. Hopefully, everything goes right, and we get food," Robert explained.

William rested his visor on his palm, "We're idiots. How can we trust these people?"

Ruth spoke, "We can't, but it's worth a shot. Plus, there's three of us, and we're armed with guns."

"We'll be fine. Everyone's desperate for water, so why would they chase us off and lose a water source?" Robert asked.

"So they can shoot us in the head and take it? Whatever. I'll listen to you

179

two," William said.

"Relax, William. I'll protect you guys," Ruth said.

Robert checked his implant. They had come upon a shopping mall, one of the few buildings that stood three stories high. The three levels consisted of rows of empty businesses. One of them was a bakery with sets of fake pastries displayed on shelves behind broken windows.

Robert set down the water jug and stretched, "We're here. Ruth, go up in that building and check out the streets from there. Message me if anything seems wrong or if you meet any company up there."

"I'm on it. Good luck, boys. Stand and smile and watch out for guns."

"Keep us safe, Ruth!" William said.

Ruth disappeared into the structure before reappearing for a second, waving at them from a window. Robert waved back, then assumed an inconspicuous stance.

William went over and sat on the curb, "Well, now what?"

"We wait. They're coming, hopefully."

"You think they have any frozen pastries in there?"

"Yep, all thawed out. Wet, soppy, and rotten. And probably tasteless."

William laughed and shrugged, "Yep. Hey, the really expensive stuff from Switzerland had taste."

"They totally did not have Swiss stuff before the shit hit the fan."

"Did so," William joked.

"Did not!"

"Did so!"

"Did not! I'll go in there and check myself if anything is left."

Robert received a text and opened it, "I guess we're being told that we are too loud and should shut up."

"Damn, just because she's quiet as a mouse," William said.

Robert looked down as another text came, "Someone's here. Have your gun ready, but don't show it."

Robert checked his gun's charge and capacity before gently setting it down like a cane. Four people approached them from an alleyway. They stood apart, each of a different height, gender, and build. They wore ill-fitting or tattered clothes and had different kinds of masks. Only one carried a plasma pistol openly, while the other three had a bat, pipe, and a metal pole with a spike on it. Each had red marks and symbols on some of their clothes and masks that Robert couldn't make out from a distance. The man with the pistol waved, then stopped as he noticed William. He said something to his companions before approaching.

"Are you Robert?" the man asked.

"Yeah, are you Dan?" Robert responded.

The man was taller than William and Robert, with pollution scars covering his dark-toned skin. His hair was black, and his eyes were different colors: amber and red. He wore a long-sleeve shirt, a leather vest, military pants, and a hooded jacket. Around his neck was a red bandana. Hammer and sickles decorated his clothes. One was marked on an armband on his right arm, one on the back of his vest, one on his gas mask, and one was tattooed on his hand.

"That's me. This is part of my group. Didn't know you had a friend. What's your name?"

"William. Nice to meet you."

"Nice to meet you, too. How did you guys do on the way here? Any uh... Lurkers?" Dan asked.

"No Lurkers, just trash and wind. Where is the food?" Robert asked.

"Oh, we got it," Dan said.

William walked to Robert and whispered, "Cover the Militia patch on your shirt. These are T-PEM. We probably should leave. Now."

They all looked at each other as Robert discreetly covered his shirt with his jacket. He gestured to the water with one hand, "Well, here's one gallon as promised."

Dan nodded to one of his comrades.

The woman walked forward, reaching behind her back. Robert heard a notification sound in his head. A gunshot echoed from above, and the woman dropped dead.

William grabbed Robert and ripped him into the bakery.

"Run!" William shouted.

"Shoot them! Kill those fascist pigs!" Dan shouted.

They dove behind the cover of the bakery counter. The group outside shot at them. Robert gasped as bullets flew in and wood splinters spewed everywhere.

"Shit, shit, shit! How are we getting out of this?" Robert asked.

"We're idiots. Should've taken off as soon as we saw red or at least removed our old clothes. God damnit. Where's Ruth?"

"Upstairs still."

Robert shot out the window with his rifle, plasma cascading everywhere. The people behind the windows ducked. Robert dropped again just as a hail of bullets hit the counter. A scream echoed outside as Ruth flew out from the stairwell and shot one of their attackers.

As they fell back, Ruth opened the backdoor, "Let's go! Come on!"

Robert and William ran after her, shooting behind them.

Dan spoke as they ran, "Are you okay? You're good. Come on, Steven!"

The trio ran out of earshot of Dan and into the streets. William pointed toward where they had come from.

"We need to get back to the Tower! Who knows if they have more friends!"

"Go! Go!" Robert said.

They ran to the other side of the street behind the shopping complex and took off toward the Tower. They didn't stop until they were far away from the bakery and only slowed down to catch their breaths and check their backs.

"What happened?" Robert asked.

Ruth crossed her arms, "I saw that they were T-PEM as soon as they appeared. I noticed one of them said something and had a weird look under his visor. When the woman approached you, she was about to pull a gun and shoot you."

Robert shook his head, "Why would they even bother attacking us? It doesn't matter anymore."

Ruth shrugged, "They are T-PEM, and you guys are wearing Militia clothes. A lot of them lost family and friends to the Militia, so it's just rage."

William groaned angrily, "This was dumb. We can't trust anyone."

Robert shook his head, "It was not dumb. It was unlucky. Who could've known that these were commies? You two need a new set of clothes."

They ran until the Tower was in sight, came to the entrance, and stopped.

"So, this is the Tower?" Ruth said.

"Yeah, this is home sweet home," Robert said.

William pointed at Robert, "Robert, you're an idiot."

"William, shut up! I was trying to get us food."

"And we could've gotten shot if Ruth hadn't surprised them."

"Boys, boys! Both of you shut up! This was a lesson for you two. Don't get into a fight over it."

William began, "What if we've be—"

He lurched forward and pushed Ruth off her feet as a gunshot echoed. A bullet whizzed straight between them. Robert turned and aimed his plasma rifle. One of the T-PEM survivors had followed them, taking off before Robert could fire.

"Are you guys okay?" Robert asked.

William aimed toward the man and shot his pistol. He missed each shot.

"Dammit! He knows where the Tower is now! After him!"

"It's too late. He's gone," Ruth said as she stood and rubbed her thigh, "Ow... thanks for saving me, William."

William's dark face became red with anger, "Don't mention it."

"No, really. My head could've been gone by now."

"That's the least of our worries now," William said.

# 23

# Here's Danny

*3:02 PM, August 30, 2080*

\* \* \*

The trio observed the hospital from afar. It had been a while since their last visit, though little seemed to have changed. Enveloped by the eternal polluted overcast, the streets were empty. Lurkers hid in ruins, sleeping the daylight away and waiting for the night. This left the trio the freedom to move in the day.

"Do you guys see anything?" Ruth asked.

The wall between the hospital and the rest of the city still stood, and the dead soldiers still hung from the gates. Each body was missing legs, and the rest of their bodies were almost bare bones, stained a grimy gray from the pollution.

"Nothing but the dead," William said.

"Wonder if Dan's group hung those guys?" Robert asked.

"Probably..." Ruth said.

William approached one of the bodies, studying it up and down, "I imagine they go here too for supplies. Would explain why a lot of stuff was missing last time."

"Let's be careful. Never know what's out here," Ruth said.

They crossed the street and moved toward the hole in the wall. As they approached, a gust of wind picked up a pile of trash and blew it at Robert.

"Gah!" he let out as he swiped at the trash.

Ruth snickered at Robert as he fussed.

"Damnit, it's windy today," Robert said.

"It's not that windy. The trash just doesn't like you," William said.

They snuck in one by one through a hole in the wall and entered the hospital. They turned on their flashlights but found no one inside. No Lurkers, no survivors.

William pointed upward, "Let's go to the third floor today and see what we can find."

Robert looked toward one of the elevators, "Sucks that we didn't get everything in the basement."

Ruth shrugged and made a swimming motion with her hands, "Would be awesome if we had scuba suits."

"Can you imagine if someone found all three of us walking around in scuba suits?" Robert asked with a grin.

"They'd probably call us idiots. I don't think I've ever seen a scuba diver in my life," Ruth said.

"I don't think anyone has scuba-dived in a long time. Oceans and lakes are too dangerous to swim in. Can you imagine the rashes?" William asked.

They walked up a stairwell to the third floor.

"You're right. Have you guys ever seen the fish that people had to eat in some places of the world?" Robert asked.

Ruth raised a brow and shook her head, "No?"

"Plastic and gunk. I saw a video of them opening some kind of fish, and its stomach was full of plastic and brown muck. Fish was all messed up too. Had multiple eyes, its flippers were messed up, and it was white," Robert explained.

"Mmm, yummy. Plastic bits," William said.

"Yummy. I feel really lucky now. All our food is processed and gross, but at least it's not full of plastic," Ruth said.

"It's not full of anything. Grown in a factory farm, broken down to nothing, then put back together. It doesn't really do the food any good," William said.

"At least we have food," Robert said.

They stopped at the mouth of the first hallway on the third floor and checked their surroundings. William stepped forward and slammed his fist on a wall multiple times, whistling loudly and waiting for a reaction. Nothing.

"We should be fine," William said.

"I'll take the right wing. Ruth, can you take the left?" Robert asked.

"I'm on it," Ruth said.

"I'll take the north wing," William added.

They went into each wing individually and took whatever they thought was worthwhile. Robert felt calm in the dark ruins. Experience in survival had made him level-headed in the face of the shadowy unknown. Though sometimes still jumpy, he listened more intently for the sounds of hungry beasts or desperate people. He was aware of his surroundings and in tune with the risks ruins posed. He didn't touch anything that didn't need to be touched, avoided areas that might collapse, and moved delicately and slowly, taking time to observe. The right wing on the third level was full of machinery and devices. None of them were usable since the trio had no medical experience. Though Robert knew his way around Ignium-powered items, he couldn't pick apart the complicated machinery. He could not even get the batteries since almost everything was connected to a central power system in the flooded basement. He took what he could: pills, bandages, syringes, and anything else they could use.

At the end of the wing, the wind warbled and howled against the building, intensifying as the minutes passed. As Robert cleared the last room, he approached the window. A wall of sand ran through the streets, carrying trash with it as violent winds raged through the city. It grew in its wrath, picking up larger objects, like garbage cans, and flinging them down roads. Robert's heart skipped as he saw eight figures approaching the hospital, each shielding themselves as they struggled against the wind. They slid and crawled to reach the hole in the hall down below. Then they sprinted into the hospital to escape the storm.

Robert took off to the center of the third floor, "We have company! Guys, we have company!"

"What!" William yelled.

Robert winced. Ruth came from the left wing, and William came from the north shortly after.

"What is it, Robert?" Ruth asked.

"We have company! Eight people down below," Robert said.

"Is it Dan's group?" William asked.

"I don't know, maybe. They have an injured person, remember?" Robert said.

William pointed to the stairs.

"We need to leave then. We can't risk being boxed in by eight other people."

Ruth tilted her head, "How? If they're all downstairs, they'll surely come up here."

"We have to risk going down. I'm not willing to jump out a window for this," Robert said.

"Let's just go before they even get to the stairs. Guns ready, guys," William said.

They prepared their guns. Robert scooped a handful of random material into the Melt Chamber, closed it, and turned off the safety. They ran downstairs. On the second level, they slowed and turned off their flashlights on the way down to the first level. The other group whispered in the distant halls. As they arrived, the trio snuck out from the stairs, slinked through the lobby, and hid in a room. Robert looked out of the door. He withdrew as a flashlight shone toward him and gasped quietly as the light passed him.

"Shh, they're coming," Robert whispered.

The trio pressed against one another as a group of four approached. Robert's stomach dropped as four pairs of footsteps came closer and closer and then passed. A light shone into the room for a moment, then disappeared. The group went straight up the stairs, leaving an open chance for escape.

"Now, come on," Robert whispered.

They ran down the hall and entered the main lobby. A bullet whizzed past them and hit a wall behind them.

"They're not with us! Get them!" someone shouted.

Robert dove over the central desk area of the lobby. William and Ruth scattered. Ruth took cover behind a pillar while William hid behind a wall. The other four group members shot at the trio, shouting for their comrades to come back downstairs. Robert waited for the perfect moment. He pulled the trigger and popped up as the bullets stopped and spewed molten material all over the opposite hall. The four people cowered from the glowing molten spew. William shot one of them in the chest. Ruth blindly fired and missed. The opposing group pulled into a room as the trio fought back, the fourth injured person crying out. The trio ran to the doors. The other half of the group came running down the stairs and shot at them as the trio fled into the storm. The storm battered them with ferocious power. The winds almost picked all of them up and slammed them with random objects.

Robert grunted as he slid along the street, failing to get traction. A large metal can tumbled toward him and hit him. The world spun as the can knocked him over and allowed the storm to pick him up. He flew a few feet and landed with a pained yell. All went black. As he opened his eyes, everything was blurry.

"Robert!" William shouted.

Robert focused on a new crack going across his visor. He slowly covered it with his hand, unsure if polluted air and sand were getting in. He gasped as a pair of hands grabbed him and pulled him along into a ruin.

Robert's gaze fixated on William.

"Robert! Are you okay?" William asked.

"We need to go! Those assholes might follow us!" Ruth said.

"Shut up!" William shouted.

"I'm okay! I'm okay! What happened?" Robert said.

"Something knocked you over. Your visor is cracked," William observed.

"Uh... I'm okay, I think. My head hurts, but I think I just hit it on the ground. Are we okay?"

"No! We need to leave now. Can you walk?" William asked.

"Yeah, help me up," Robert said.

Ruth pulled him to his feet. Robert stumbled slightly and regained his balance. Ruth helped him along, navigating the building behind William.

"Where are we going?" Ruth asked.

"I don't know! Anywhere but here!"

"We can go up! Let's go up! We can cross the alleys if we break windows and jump!" Ruth said.

# 24

# I Spy

\* \* \*

Ruth pushed the hook of her weapon into the ledge, ascending into the office and crossing over to a window. With a grunt, she kicked the window. Glass rained down to the ground below as she pulled out an air-powered BB gun and fired at another window across the street. Three pellets exploded the window, and more glass rained down. She holstered the weapon and pressed a button on her clothes, opening her outfit into a wingsuit.

She leaped and flew across to the other window, landing with a roll and a loud grunt. She put the suit back together with a string. The room ahead was empty except for torn furniture and clutter. No life in the rubbish, nothing in the shadows. She crossed to another window and looked down.

Below she could make out hundreds of cars and a destroyed tank. Lurkers walked among them lazily and slowly. She stepped back and looked at her implant for directions before breaking another window. The gap between this building and the next was an alley, which allowed her to jump across. Ruth pulled out her pellet gun and pumped the lever before shooting the window across from her and leaping over.

The inside was similar to the last building. A Lurker stood at the opposite side, growling as the window broke. Ruth bolted through the darkness, hopped over a desk, and drop-kicked the Lurker out of a window. The monster screamed as it flew out the window and died far below on the pavement.

Ruth carried on kicking and blasting windows down as she moved above the streets. Occasionally, her darting figure would startle Lurkers. She was a phantom, unseen footsteps gone before anyone realized they had been there. She blasted a window across another street and leaped from her window. She glided in with her wingsuit and landed with a roll. As she got up, Ruth gasped quietly. A few dozen Lurkers surrounded her in a ruined hair salon. Some were gathered around a pile of hair supplies, drinking and eating hair products. As Ruth landed on the floor, they paused in surprise before turning to attack.

Ruth pulled out her bladed weapon while her heart thundered in fear. She held her composure as she ran forward and sliced the first mutant she reached. She hooked the next one and slammed it into another. As they stumbled out of her way, Ruth made a break for the stairs on one side of the building. She ran up, slammed through a door, and closed it before breaking another window. The Lurkers from below flooded after her, running into the door and attempting to knock it down. Their combined masses broke it off the hinges, and they clawed their way inside. Ruth had already disappeared into another building when the Lurkers finally got through.

* * *

Ruth climbed onto the windowsill ledge to look down at the street below her. This was where she had lost the scouts sent from Dan's group the last time she followed them.

"Watch the first floors! Shoot any Devourer you see!" came a voice from below.

She climbed around the edge of the window to a corner of the building and looked down again. Twelve people walked below. Most had guns and flashlights, while a group of three in the middle had nothing. The group of three was tied together in a line and moved reluctantly with the group.

They walked to an intersection of the road. Underneath a traffic light, a table with three nooses hanging from it awaited the trio. The group gathered around the table, forcing their prisoners on top of it. They put the nooses around their necks. Ruth could hear them protest yet couldn't quite make out what they said. There would be no speech, no Christian words, and no farewells. She gasped as four people kicked out the table, and the three prisoners dropped. She looked away and covered her visor with her hands as the prisoners writhed. Once the bodies stopped moving, the group began retreating to where they had come from.

Ruth looked down, glancing at the dead prisoners before following the group. She quickly climbed down from the building, jumped onto a light post, and slid down. Ruth moved like a predator under cover of darkness. Not a noise, not a breath, nothing as she tailed the nine people from only a few dozen feet away. She could hear them converse quietly yet couldn't make out who spoke.

"What do you think we're eating when we get back?" one of them asked.

"I don't know. Probably some canned fruit," another one responded.

"Egh, I hate that stuff. It's like stale candy," a third stated.

"Better than the refined meat. What was that stuff last night?" the first asked.

"Pork something. Looked like cat food," the third replied.

"Shut it," a fourth said.

No one spoke about the prisoners. It was as if it hadn't happened. Ruth wondered who the prisoners were and why they were executed.

The group turned down a street and approached an opening on the side of a skyscraper. It led to an underground parking garage blocked by several fortifications and flipped cars. Each person in the group approached the barricade and squeezed through a crack. The last person closed the opening as they went inside. Ruth didn't follow them. Instead, she found her way into the building above the garage.

She entered quietly and searched the first floor, where she found two doors to a set of stairs going up and down. One was blocked off with furniture on either side, while the other was closed. She could see light and a single set of feet through the crack at the bottom of the right door. Returning to the street, Ruth ascended a pole onto a building ledge. She climbed up the side, stopped at a window, and called Robert.

"Ruth? What's up?"

"I decided to pay a visit to your friend Dan."

"What? Really?"

"Well, I didn't meet him, but I found where he and his T-PEM buddies live. They're in a parking garage under some company building. They have it blocked off, and I assume the stairwell up to the building is closed off too."

"Anything else?"

"Yeah. They just executed three people in the middle of an intersection. It was quick, and I don't know why they did it."

"Weird. Is that all? How many of them are there?"

"I don't know. Nine people were along for the execution, and they were the ones who I followed to the parking garage. I assume there's twenty more people in that parking garage. It would take a lot of hands to make the fortifications they have and to keep the Lurkers out."

"This is good, but not enough. We need to find weaknesses, something we can use against them. We can't have them attacking us or launching an assault on the Tower."

"That's the problem, Robert. I can only think of one weakness, and that would be Lurkers."

# 25

# Come Out

*  *  *

Ruth, Robert, and William sat at the table and dug into cans full of processed and refined food. Polluted air had flooded each floor, forcing them to adapt. They lifted their masks to eat, ate what they could, then secured their masks back on when they needed to breathe. It was tedious but kept them healthy. They finished their last bites.

William put his mask back on and spoke, "We need a plan."

"Time to plan for the demise of Dan as soon as we can?" Ruth said.

Robert snickered.

William shook his head and sighed, "Come on, guys. This is serious."

Ruth raised her hands, "Let's make a plan then."

"We still have some leftover explosives from blowing the stairs on the first level. Ruth, you said the entrance to their base is barricaded?" Robert asked.

She nodded, "Yeah, I was thinking about that. The problem is numbers. There's three of us and over thirty of them. Maybe even forty. Who knows? I had an idea on how to level out the playing field."

William's brow raised, "What would that be?"

Ruth pointed outside, "Lurkers. I told Robert when I discovered where Dan's group was that Lurkers could be the answer. I was thinking we could lure a horde of them to Dan's base when we blow it."

"Yeah, but they're smart too. Are you sure they'll just chase us?" Robert frowned.

Ruth tilted her head and puckered her lips, "No."

"What makes them attack people?" William asked.

"Weakness, I think. If someone were alone and appeared injured, maybe calling for help, that might bring them out," Ruth said.

Robert shrugged and gestured between them, "Well, who will be bait?"

Both Robert and William looked at Ruth.

She recoiled, "What?"

"Neither of us can get out if we need to. We're both slow and clumsy, and you can handle yourself," William said.

Ruth sighed, "Fuckers, fine. I'll be bait."

Robert pointed at his foot with a grin, "I mean, with my hurt foot...."

William groaned, "Your foot has been healed for over a year."

"Well, it still hurts a little...."

William shook his head as he spoke mockingly, "Oh, William, my foot still hurts. Can you carry up the water? Oh, William, can you do this? My foot hurts."

Robert and Ruth laughed.

William shook his head and grumped, "So funny. Not."

"Well, my head still hurts," Robert said.

"You'll be fine," William stated.

Ruth put her hands together, making walking motions with her fingers as she spoke, "So, I lure the Lurkers out with my cries for help. Meanwhile, you two sneak to Dan's base, take out any guards, and blow the barricades on my signal."

Robert tilted his head, "What's the signal?"

William began, "Boom. Big Boom. Bada Big Boom. Pop. Poppity p–"

Ruth made a bird with her hands, "No, no, it'll be like... let 'em fly!"

* * *

Robert and William snuck past a few Lurkers gathered around a body in the street. Even though they were as quiet as their boots allowed, the pair moved along like elephants compared to Ruth's finesse. They went ahead of Ruth, sneaking across the city in the darkness. The only sound heard above the wind was the shrill cries from the various mutant packs gathered around the ruins. Shivers ran down Robert's spine. There were many mutants compared to the number of humans left. Their twisted forms were never the same. Many had tumors and extra deformed limbs. Some moved quickly, some slowly, some could climb, and others leaped. There seemed no end to the perversion of the human form in the aberrations. Many Lurkers were starving. Ruth had told Robert and William that many Lurkers had gathered into packs, though feral and broken mutants wandered alone. They frequently snuck past groups feeding on corpses, ravenously tearing them apart to satiate their starvation. It was sickening.

"Down that way," William whispered.

Remnants of T-PEM propaganda littered the street. Hammers and sickles, communist propaganda, and depictions of T-PEM leaders were graffitied onto surrounding buildings. Hammer and sickle flags occasionally dotted the streets, hanging above the remains of sandbags, tanks, barbed wire, and rubble. The specter of communism loomed in places like this. It was no better than the ghosts of patriotism and loyalism who haunted the ruins controlled by the military and Militia. The spirits of the old world faded slowly, dying with those who held the dead beliefs of the past.

Eventually, they arrived at a towering business building. They went to the parking garage entrance, blocked by an array of cars and metal pieces. A hint of light came from a crack in the barricade. No guards stood outside.

William took off his backpack, put it down, reached in, and grabbed a rectangular bomb. One side of it was covered in a black adhesive that stuck to their hands annoyingly, "Well, this backpack is ruined."

He gave one bomb to Robert, then grabbed one for himself and put the backpack back on.

"What's the idea here?" Robert asked.

"One bomb on either side, wire 'em up, and blow them up. Let's be fast."

\* \* \*

Ruth went out into the street. Lurkers roamed in the dark, ruined streets. The twisted creatures were starving and desperate. To survive, they ate whatever garbage they could find. They tore at rotten food and broke the bones of the dead to eat as much as they could. They drank from where they could, even polluted water from broken pipes and blackened puddles in the ground. Many were intensely sick or in anguish; their twisted figures rendered pale as they slowly died inside. They screamed and groaned in pain, writhing as they wandered.

She carefully snuck out into the center of the street, climbed onto a car, and turned on a flashlight secured to her mask. With a deep inhale, Ruth uttered a cry echoing across the ruins. The scream was met by silence as the shocked Lurkers turned toward her and began to chase her. Some shuffled, and some sprinted.

Ruth leaped off the car and raced down the street. Her heart thundered as she heard a horde erupt toward her from all directions. The monsters came from buildings, under cars, behind cars, from alleys, and dumpsters. Within a minute, over thirty were chasing her. She gracefully navigated the streets, cleaving and kicking through Lurkers that got in the way and vaulting over some. To keep the beasts interested, she swore at them. The sound of her voice lured them forward, following in her footsteps.

"Come on, you fuckers! Chase me! I dare you!"

After a while, the horde grew to over fifty Lurkers. Ruth bolted down another street, leaped up onto a car, and climbed on top of a bus. The height gave her a moment's break. She called Robert by pushing her implant a few times before taking off again. As the phone's ringtone echoed in her head, she jumped off the bus and led the horde into ruins once occupied by T-PEM sympathizers.

"You okay?" Robert asked as he picked up Ruth's call.

"I'm peachy! Totally don't have a horde of Lurkers on my ass!"

"Holy shit, how many are there?" Robert asked as he heard the Lurkers scream.

"Dozens! Enough! Are you guys ready to blow the barricades?"

"We've got the explosives wired up. Just tell us when and it'll be gone."

Ruth ducked as a Lurker came up from a car beside her and pounced at her. She cut straight through the neck of another Lurker and ran over its body as the horde closed in. She turned down another street and passed a set of bodies hanging from an intersection light. This was the final street with the parking garage in sight at the other end. With the horde right on her trail, she ran past it with all the speed she could muster.

"Guys! Let 'em fly!" she shouted.

An ear-piercing explosion tore through the barricades blocking off Dan's base and took out a few Lurkers. The shockwave almost knocked Ruth off her feet as she ran. Ruth escaped into a building as the smoke settled while the Lurkers morphed into a chaotic mess. Some ran away, terrified of the explosion, while some stood in shocked confusion. Many looked around, their eyes drawn to the gaping hole of light coming from the once-barricaded parking garage. Those who were not shocked or terrified went toward the light and flooded into the base.

Ruth ran in were William and Robert sat huddled on the fourth floor near a window.

"Holy hell! I hate you two," Ruth said.

All three broke out into confused laughter. The plan had been a success. As their laughing diminished, they could hear screaming, gunshots, and mutant cries. It was anarchy.

The horde flowed into the hole they had just made. People screamed, gunshots echoing as the horde ravaged the people inside. The gunshots and screaming faded into silence as the flock finished off the survivors.

After a few minutes, Ruth pointed to the floor above the garage, "Look! Do you see that?"

"What?" Robert asked.

A muzzle flash briefly appeared below, attracting the mutants still on the street. A group of four ran out from the first floor and fled into the streets.

"Shit! They're getting away!" Robert said.

"Shut up! We need to be quiet. There's nothing we can do," Ruth said.

# 26

# Settled Folk

*2:01 PM, October 25, 2081*

\* \* \*

Winter arrived on time, ready to consume the next half-year in its frigid maw. Just as it barely ever rained, it barely ever snowed. Instead, the world plunged into a frozen hellscape. The summer was already chilly due to the pollution haze blocking the sun. Winter was unbearable.

This winter would be harsher than the last as the remaining humans hoarded what little they could. The Lurker threat, ever-looming as it was, would subside in the bitter months. Many Lurkers would hide away in large, warm groups, huddling against one another like penguins. Many would die. Those that perish would be too broken or unlucky to survive. Some endured and became predatory monsters that kept warm by hunting and feasting on flesh.

\* \* \*

Robert sat against the corner and stared out at the air wells. Each was frozen solid, leaving them with a finite amount of water for winter. Robert felt comfortable as he sat wrapped up in multiple blankets with his smart suit's temperature on the highest setting. He sat for hours, quietly thinking about Zilv as the winds blew through the crater in the Tower. He thought of the first time they were in school and all the time they spent taking apart Ignium machines and working on walls of code. They fit together, Zilv with software and Robert with hardware. The pain had faded. Robert had finally begun to accept Zilv's passing, that he could not have saved him, and that being alive now would be hell. Zilv would've been miserable in the new world.

He went up to use the bathroom at the Tower's edge, enduring the biting wind. As he returned and wrapped himself back up in a blanket, footsteps echoed down the stairs before the door to the floor swung open.

"Robert?" William called out.

"Right here," Robert replied from the corner.

"Get up. We're getting ready to leave."

"Are we meeting with that Ken guy?"

"Yeah. We need some more food, and his group needs some water, so we're going to meet up and trade. Plus, we get to hang out with them. Supposedly, they have some sodas, so we'll have a little celebration."

Robert tilted his head, "Celebration for what?"

William shrugged, "Celebration that we're not dead. Come on, get up."

Robert groaned, stood, stretched, and let out an even louder groan, "I'm going, I'm going. Just meet me down below."

"All right. Hurry up, though."

"I'm on it."

William grabbed a water jug and went downstairs. Ruth went down the stairs a moment after, her feet tapping rapidly as she zipped past. Robert reached his hands under his gas mask and rubbed his face as he walked over to the ledge where the air wells stood. Once he secured his mask, he grabbed a water jug, attached it to his backpack, and grabbed his plasma rifle before slinging both around his shoulders. The water inside the container was frozen solid.

Much had changed outside since they had moved in. The majority of the first level of the skyscraper was destroyed. The once beautiful glass stairs and floors that divided the first part into sections had been blown to bits. Only the very top section remained. From it, they had made a series of rope contraptions powered by Ignium machines. One was a sort of elevator with a rope attached to the four ends of a metal piece. This elevator was used to transport supplies. William stood next to it, heaving a water jug onto it while Ruth held it, stopping it from swinging. Robert did the same. Once the two jugs were on, they allowed the elevator to descend. Then they went to a similar contraption that was smaller and scarier. Instead of having a large platform to hold supplies, this one was just a rope put through a smaller wooden plank and knotted so that the plank wouldn't slip down the rope. William got on it, gripped the rope, and stood on the plank. As he got on, it swung back and forth.

None of them liked the contraption, but it was easier than making a larger version of the first elevator that could support them. They went down one by one. Once Robert was on, and it stopped swinging, he pulled a lever attached to the rest of the construct. He held his breath. It jerked slightly before the Ignium machinery lowered him slowly to the floor below. His knuckles were white as he held onto the rope nervously, and his heartbeat quickened before he got to the bottom. Down below, they had a system that would pull the elevator back up and lock it. Unlocking it was complicated. Robert and William still struggled despite being the creators of the entire process.

They grabbed the water jugs from the first elevator and watched it ascend before leaving. The very bottom floor of the Tower was unsettling. It was dark, dirty, and wide open. Destroyed furniture lay around everywhere. They had begun reinforcing the first floor, barricading all the windows they could, and moving furniture against windows and doors. They had also installed lights on the balcony above to illuminate intruders. They still planned to reinforce the balcony with sandbags, which sat haphazardly in the middle of the bottom floor.

A gust of cold, polluted air swept through them as they went out.

"Holy! It's freezing out here," Robert said.

William gestured to the battery pack on his left hip. It was a small, flat case that melded into the rest of the fabric, "Let's get moving. It'll keep us warm. Did you guys check the batteries of your smart suits before leaving?"

"Yeah, I'm good for a few hours," Ruth said.

Robert looked down at his battery pack and tapped it, "I should be good as long as we don't stay out for too long. I've been using the batteries in mine for an hour or so."

William nodded, "Good, it'll be a cold one tonight."

Ruth tilted her head, "How do you know?"

Robert pointed at William's hands, "His fingers hurt when it's gonna be cold or when it's gonna rain."

Ruth's head recoiled slightly, "What? Why?"

"Just damaged my fingers a lot when I was younger. My joints are all swollen now, and they hurt when the humidity and temperature change. Not like it rains a lot anyway."

Ruth wrinkled her nose and moved her ankles, "Weird. Don't think I've ever hurt myself beyond twisting my ankles once or twice."

"Oh, don't say ankles!" William said.

Robert grinned widely, "Yeah, I hurt my ankle one time. Really aches sometimes. Hey, I think it hurts right now."

"No! Nope. You're carrying that water by yourself," William said.

"Oh, fine," Robert said.

* * *

Ahead of them was a towering warehouse that stood thirty stories tall. Each level was made of metal and stained black. Peeling paint and rust spread over parts of the building, and the structure had scars from enduring the harsh weather. The weather had blown in a few windows. A small parking lot extended around the building. Robert squinted. Once they were sure the outside was clear, they approached the store entrance. Robert went to the right, and Ruth and William to the left. While Ruth watched their rear, Robert and William gazed into the store. After a moment, they turned their flashlights on and entered together. Ruth followed.

Robert moved his flashlight over hundreds of towering shelves connected to multiple floors above. He followed their lofty heights to the levels above. Pillars held up each story and connected to each side of the shelves. Each shelf had rails going up to the ceiling level.

He shone his flashlight around to see if any Lurkers hid in the darkness.

Instead, he only saw orange robots. The warehouse robots had wheels that would lock onto the rails of the shelves so they could climb and grab items from every shelf. All of them lay unpowered and crowded around offline charging ports.

"See any Lurkers?" Robert asked.

"No, but I see some light over there," Ruth said.

A mutagenic bomb the size of a car sat in a small crater next to a tipped-over shelf in the far corner. Light shone from a hole above where the bomb had pierced the roof. It had gone through some shelves and landed on the bottom floor.

Robert squinted.

"It's a bomb."

"Undetonated," William said.

"Let's be careful. That's not a normal bomb," Ruth said.

They jumped at the sound of voices, switched their flashlights off, and crouched.

"Where do you think they are?" a voice said.

"Probably still on the way. Patience. Not like the sodas are gonna get warm."

Robert looked at William, "Those the guys?"

"Worth the risk to ask?" William responded.

Robert stood and shouted, "Yo!"

A few surprised gasps sounded.

"Who are you? Are you with William?" one of them asked.

"Yeah, are you with Ken?" Robert asked in response.

"Yeah! Come over! We brought the sodas!"

They approached the bomb and met five people sitting on warehouse boxes. All five shivered.

A tall man stood and walked over to them, raised a soda bottle, and gave it to William, "Hey, guys! How was the walk?"

"Hey, Ken. It was good," William said.

"Come on, sit down with us. I'll get everyone a drink," Ken said.

Robert and William placed the water jugs in the middle of the group. The trio sat down together on boxes drawn out from the shelves. Ken gave them an open soda can each. Robert shook his can a little. After sitting for so long, the sodas were no longer carbonated and were only cold because the warehouse was freezing. Robert lifted his mask slightly, drank the soda carefully, and swallowed. It didn't taste like a sweet soda but rather sweetened water with a somewhat unsettling hint of carbonation.

Ken was taller than the rest of the group. He had a full-visor gas mask on that showed his whole face. His face had gray facial hair and dark, wrinkly skin from pollution damage. His brow hung low over a brown pair of eyes.

He gestured to everyone with a gloved hand, "So, I brought some more people today. Guys, meet Robert, Ruth, and William. You guys meet Sarah, Andrew, Stephen, and Amy," Ken said.

"Nice to meet you guys," William said.

A short and thin man, Andrew, waved at them, "A pleasure."

Ken put a hand on the water jug, "Damn, this is a lot of water."

William shrugged and tilted his head, "Same as last time."

Lisa, a woman similar in size to Robert with bandages around the left side of her head, spoke, "You've been keeping us alive with this water."

Robert leaned forward with the soda can, shaking it slightly, "Where did you guys get these?"

Stephen, a man wearing a gas mask with a goggle visor, explained quietly, "We raided a grocery store in a rich part of town a month ago or so. Lots of natural food that was really expensive and stuff like this. I swear you couldn't believe what they had. They had real steaks, fruit, and all sorts of stuff. It was rotten, though."

Robert took a sip of the soda and secured his gas mask, "Well, I appreciate this. Never liked soda, but it's a treat."

William gestured to the water jug, "You guys brought your stuff?"

Amy, a frail woman wearing a gas mask with a shattered visor, moved a bag forward, "Right here."

William nodded in thanks and sifted through the bag.

Ken spoke, "How have the ruins treated you guys?"

William pursed his lips, "Shitty as usual."

"Lurkers have been calmer than usual. Think a lot of them are hiding in preparation for winter," Ken said.

Ruth leaned forward, "Yeah, some hibernate. Many of them hide in basements and parking garages and huddle together during winter storms."

Lisa tilted her head, "How did you know that?"

"Oh, I watch them a lot when I'm doing runs in the city," Ruth replied.

"Have you guys seen any T-PEM remnants?" Robert asked.

Ken shook his head, "None. After you guys dismantled that one group, we haven't seen the likes of them in a long while."

Robert frowned, "Chris said that some people in his group saw a few people wearing T-PEM jackets, but they weren't sure. They're on the other side of town anyway."

Ken shrugged, "Well, they've always been oddballs. They refused to join up with us a while back, something along the lines of spreading out the survivors around the city, so we don't eat up everything in one area and starve."

Ruth leaned forward, "It's reasonable. Lots of people in one area leads to over consumption."

Ken looked at Ruth, "You guys seem to have taken that to heart. Only three of y'all."

The trio looked at one another. None of them had told anyone from Ken's group where they lived.

"Yeah, we try to keep it just us," Robert said.

"Easier that way," William said.

They all took sips of their soda when a bang echoed a few levels above them. Each of them let out a startled gasp.

Ruth looked around gripping her blade, "Did you guys check all the levels?"

Stephen looked behind him, "Scoped them out. Something probably fell."

William gestured to Ruth, "Let's just keep watch. Ruth?"

Ruth nodded and went over to the illuminated bomb.

"So, the T-PEM remnants... I just wanna keep an eye out for them. They hung a few people before we ran them out of town," William said.

"Can't believe they escaped like... how many Lurkers?" Ken asked.

"Over a hundred," William replied.

"Absolutely crazy shit. They probably didn't make it through the night. It's too dangerous. I don't know anyone who can do that," Ken said.

Another metallic bang echoed through the building. Ruth shone her flashlight upward as she stood by the bomb.

William glanced back, "Do you see anything, Ruth?"

Ruth shook her head, "Nothing. I think it's just the building settling."

"Might be getting windy outside. Always is," Ken said.

"Maybe," William said.

They all drank for a while, going through two packages of bland soda.

Ken leaned back and gestured toward the trio with a soda in hand, "What are your plans for the future?"

Robert shrugged, "Live."

Ken chuckled softly, "Hell, ain't that why we brought the sodas? I say cheers to that. We're not dead."

They all raised their sodas and drank.

Ken continued speaking, "See, we had some plans. Maybe building a fancy fortress, figuring out how to grow food and collect water. Wish it'd rain more. Say, how'd you guys get all this water in the first place?"

William swallowed as the members of Ken's group stared at him, "Just luck. We've raided lots of grocery stores and have prioritized water. We just took a little too much in the past, so now we have plenty."

Robert leaned forward. His hands grabbed his plasma rifle discreetly.

Ken smiled beneath his visor, his voice rising slightly, "That's lucky. Every store we've been to has been ransacked by other people or the Lurkers. Getting these sodas was our luckiest find."

As Robert brought his gun up to rest on his lap, a voice came from the other end of the warehouse, "Can someone help me?" a young boy's voice said.

The entire group pointed their guns in the direction of the voice.

Andrew inched forward toward the voice, "We're over here! Are you okay?"

Ruth waved at Andrew and shushed him, "Shut up! It's not real!"

Andrew looked at her and tilted his head, "What do you mean?"

Robert snapped around as he saw a figure leap from above. He shot as it came from the air and landed on Ruth. It clawed at her, partially taking off her mask before shielding itself against the molten goo from Robert's rifle. The monster screamed and ran away in terror. The rest of the gun's stream flew over Ruth and hit the bomb. A sizzle sounded before a click, followed by a loud bang as the sides of the bomb opened.

Ruth gasped, shielded herself, and screamed, "Get down!!"

A flood of green gas streamed from the bomb and enveloped Ruth. The group scattered as the green tide spread through the air. Ken's group ran out of the building. Robert and William stumbled back as the gas bathed Ruth. It seemed to have no effect. It didn't corrode her clothes, burn her skin, or even make her cough. As everyone retreated, Lurkers came out from behind the shelves and levels above, fled the warehouse, and ran out into the city. Robert could hear the one he blasted stop screaming as the molten material solidified on its body and killed it.

"Ruth! Get out of the mist!" Robert shouted.

Ruth stood and ran out of the mist, brushing herself off as if she was covered in bugs, "Gah! I didn't even see that thing. It came out of nowhere!"

"Are you okay?" Robert asked.

Ruth grabbed her gas mask and secured it back on, inhaling loudly, "I'm fine, I'm fine. I don't think I breathed anything in."

"Do you feel anything?" William asked.

"Nothing," Ruth said.

Ken appeared in the doorway to the warehouse, "Hey! Move away from the gas! Come with us!"

They ran outside of the warehouse.

"Did you see how many Lurkers there were?" Ken asked.

"A dozen or so. They must've come in while we were talking," William said.

Ken gestured to Ruth, "I'm sorry about that. We made sure the building was clear. Is she okay?"

Ruth nodded, cupping the side of her mask with a hand, "I'm fine. Just got hit in the face pretty hard."

"What about the supplies?" Lisa asked.

"We'll have to wait for the gas to settle. Did anyone bring the sodas?" Ken asked.

# 27

# The Change

*9:54 AM, October 27, 2081*

\* \* \*

The infestation had taken hold. It was slow and creeping. First, it bonded with air and flowed through the lungs before entering the bloodstream. Once it broke into the heart, it circulated through the whole body. Then came damnation. Nothing could be done once the infestation took hold and was absorbed. It would start small. Cells would go haywire, multiplying or dying until small tumors formed. Then damage came to the structures of life. Organs were torn apart and moved as they grew uncontrollably. The mind was next. The infestation would manifest on the skin and create a visual abomination that caused onlookers to shy away. As the infestation conquered the flesh, hopelessness manifested. What could one do against such a wicked creation? How does one cope with the idea that they are the living dead, conscious of their impending mortality yet powerless to mend it?

\* \* \*

Ruth groaned and scratched her skin as Robert tried to keep her hands from the already irritated bumps covering her.

"You'll be okay, Ruth. Here, put this rag under your gas mask and on your forehead."

She clumsily grabbed the wet rag from his hands and stuffed it under her mask. She put it on her forehead and groaned more, "My skin! It's fucking crawling!"

"It's okay, Ruth! It's okay. I'll try to see if I can fix it."

She was boiling. Even with Ruth being half-nude and the temperature in the Tower being below freezing, she struggled to fight off a scorching fever. She said everything inside her body burned. Robert poured bottle after bottle of cold water on towels and put them on her skin. Her black, scarred skin rippled as if growing, and as Robert put the towels on it, he could feel lumps growing inside of her. They were everywhere, under the surface of her skin and on her bones. Robert grimaced. No matter what he said or did, she would keep scratching at her skin as if there were hundreds of bugs on her.

"William!" Robert shouted.

"Coming!"

William emerged from the door with a handful of pill bottles and knelt beside Ruth. Robert took one of the bottles, poured two pills, and helped Ruth sit up. William took off her mask as Robert gave her the pills and some water to swallow them. Ruth swallowed the pills and laid back, fussing with her hands until William helped her put her mask back on.

"I don't think the pills are helping," Robert said.

"They're not," Ruth whined, holding her head and slowly twisting back and forth.

"We need to get something stronger," Robert said.

William gripped the pill bottle tensely and looked up at Robert, "We don't have anything else. I've checked. I don't even know what to do with some of the stuff we have. The shit with needles? I don't know how much is too much."

"We traded away too much," Robert said.

"We have to get something. Do you think anywhere in the city might have anything?" William asked.

Ruth grabbed them both, "Don't go! Don't... don't."

"One of us has to go get something for you. Both of us won't leave," William said.

"I'll go. I think I know a place," Robert said.

"Where?" William said.

"Remember in the underground? West side of town, we hid a package before everything fell apart. Was for a doctor, a bunch of meds."

William shook his head, "You can't go into the underground. There's too many Lurkers and not enough room for you to turn tail. What if you get cornered?"

Robert gestured to Ruth, "What else can we do? Look at her."

William sighed, "All right, fine. It's crazy but fine. Go out there and do your crazy shit. I'll try my best with her. If you're gonna go, go before the sun sets."

"I'll leave now. Where's my gun?"

"Upstairs."

\* \* \*

Robert shivered as he walked down the street, watching his flanks and holding his gun nervously. Eyes were on him wherever he went. They were hungry, waiting, and just as nervous as he. Now and then, there'd be figures looming in windows. Often, simply pointing his gun scared them away into the ruins. He looked at his forearm occasionally as he followed the map along the old-world avenues and alleys. From time to time, the lights of his implant flickered. It was aging. The electrical connections that drew power from his muscles to control the device had begun to show wear.

Robert flicked his arm in frustration, "Come on..." he grumbled.

The biting wind blew through the city, howling and throwing trash around.

Out here, he was truly alone. No one could save him, and no one would find his body. He clung to all of his courage as he walked, pointing his gun everywhere he went and snapping in every direction. Eventually, the sound of wet, shoeless feet came close, plapping against the ground. They got closer at every turn as he moved. He snapped around and shot. The gun spewed molten material everywhere behind him, melting a trashcan and starting a small fire that ate up a pile of trash. Whatever had been following him retreated out of earshot.

"Little shits," Robert mumbled.

As he continued sneaking along, he listened for the return of the footsteps. He walked almost twenty minutes before reaching a gaping opening between the skyscrapers. Ahead was a massive shopping complex flanked by smaller ones and surrounded by a giant parking lot. The remains of a battlefield covered the lot—the frames of cars lay everywhere, surrounded by bodies and the occasional destroyed tank. A crashed plane stuck out of one of the complex' walls. One of its rotors gently rocked back and forth with the wind.

A few Lurkers piled around the bodies. Most of them gathered around skeletons, trying to break the bones for their marrow. He loathed the idea of crossing the lot since it was too open and visible. He crossed into the shadows of the skyscrapers along one side of the parking lot. Once in their shadows, he slinked along until he got to the other side.

Voices caused him to stop. He could not make out what they said but could hear that they came from the opposite side of the shopping complex. Robert hid behind a pile of rubble and observed. The voices came closer and closer, attracting the attention of the Lurkers. A small group went toward the voices before fleeing in the opposite direction. A squad of nine people emerged from a street and approached the complex. As he squinted, he recognized their outfits and masks—Ken's outfit.

As the group approached the store, a slam of metal came from one of the complex doors. Over two dozen people dressed with red T-PEM symbols marched out, waving to Ken's group. They walked out with weapons and supplies in hand. The two groups met peacefully, merged, and exchanged supplies. Robert was shocked. He squinted to see if Dan was among them. Unable to make anyone out, he turned and continued west.

* * *

Robert ensured that he had not been followed before approaching the subway entrance. A few metal railings blocked it off. He went over them and down the stairs to a pitch-black area below. Robert turned on his flashlight as he stepped down the stairs, jumped over some turnstiles, and entered a three-level metro station. On each of the three levels, railroads flanked both sides. The middle level had small stores, each of which had been ransacked and filled with trashed objects.

Robert occasionally paused to listen. Skeletons lay everywhere. All of them seemed to have died frantic, terrifying deaths. They looked as if they had been crawling away from a doom they could not escape. Robert didn't bother checking any of the bodies. He walked down to the lowest level of the station, looking left and right at the edge of the platform. Each tunnel curved in various directions. He hopped down to the tracks and began to walk along the tunnel.

Lurkers loved the darkness of the underground. They filled the sewers, stations, and plants like rats. William and Robert had already tried venturing into one of the old smuggling outposts, but twisted beasts had chased them off.

Memories of pre-war smuggling filled Robert's mind. He once cared since he had someone who mattered to him, and a world to contend against that was at least a little fair. Suppressed memories arose, sweet memories of Zilv. Was it his fault? Was it William's? He still blamed William for leading him to injure his foot, which had slowed them down. If he hadn't gotten hurt, he would've died with Zilv and been at peace.

It would have been better than this world. In the old world, the fiction of society existed. Robert could play with the rules and break them. He could go to work, buy whatever he could afford, watch movies, shower, and enjoy power. Thanks to Robert, the Tower did have power to some levels, but he had to manage Ignium generators daily instead of just paying a power bill. That was bittersweet. Everything in the Tower had to be monitored and taken care of, which was tedious. There was constant work against the universe in the Tower. They were never sure of anything. Who knew if the air wells would be swept away by the wind, if they could keep finding enough food, or if they would die while out and about? Nothing was certain.

Robert sometimes considered throwing himself from the top of the Tower. He wouldn't have to worry anymore or be lonely. The only thing that stopped him was the notion that he might regret the decision on the way down. Robert frowned. Maybe William and Ruth would miss him. Being with William and

Ruth was pleasant, but nobody would be like Zilv. No one would understand him like Zilv. No one made him happy like Zilv.

Squelching footsteps ran toward him from behind. He shut off his light and dropped to the ground. The footsteps approached and ran past, followed by three more pairs that growled and snarled. Robert felt the wind from one of the things that ran past as its feet came extremely close to hitting him. He waited for their footsteps to fade before standing up. He turned on the flashlight, observed the surrounding tunnel, then continued cautiously.

He climbed onto a platform on the side of the tunnel and found two doors. Both doors were painted red and were slightly ajar, locks broken. Robert went inside one and found one of the city's many water refineries and supply plants. They were large and collected from five major water storage facilities. Being inside was like being in a small factory building. Pipes snaked everywhere from giant closed-off water vats with vials and dials. Robert stood on the second floor and looked down at the bottom below. Forty-two garage-sized vats rose from the now-flooded first floor.

Dozens of Lurkers gathered around each staircase leading to the first floor, drinking from the murky waters. Robert gasped and ducked away, covering his flashlight with his hand. He was lost in the dark, though they had not noticed him. He followed the railings of the second-floor walkways until he was across. In the dark, he prayed not to stumble on anything. Robert moved his legs as slowly as possible, trying not to bang them into a pipe. He gasped as he walked straight into something solid. A growl sounded. Robert swung his gun. With a grunt, he slammed the thing into the railing, heaved it over, and threw it into the dark abyss. Shrill cries from Lurkers reverberated in the room as a splash echoed.

"Shit!"

Lurkers swarmed up from the first level toward him. Robert fired his gun. The mutants cowered away as the weapon spewed molten material toward them. He sprinted as they screeched in terror.

He disappeared down a few turns, crashed into a door he found, and ran out into a small concrete tunnel. He slammed the door behind him and followed the tunnel into a maze of tight tunnels. Each tunnel had a sign with a location code, a designation, a destination, and a company logo. Robert chose the one that led to a sewer system. He went down, came to a door, and went out onto a platform. This was the right place.

To his left was Benny, one of the many corpse markers left underground. By now, he was a skeleton. He still wore his mask, a down jacket, dirty jeans, and signature red shoes. His backpack was gone, though some trash was still left near the body. He had no time to take the mask and only whispered as he passed, "Hi, Benny."

He went to the edge and jumped into the murky sewage below. It had once been up to his knees. Now, it only went up to his ankles and felt more like mud than mucky water. He followed the central tunnel and looked down at each small branch that departed from it.

Soon enough, Robert found a small offshoot with a grate and lifted it. The package. The grocery bag contained various pharmacy pill bottles, small boxes, and a single large box the size of a Bible. Robert placed the bag on the edge of the grate and looked up.

A Lurker twice his size gazed down at him. Tumors covered its lopsided body, right shoulder, arm, and leg two times larger than the left. Lumps obscured the right side of its face, and three horrid eyes gazed down at him.

The monster ripped Robert straight off his feet and threw him across the tunnel into a wall. He collided shoulder first, screaming and falling to the ground. The beast swung toward him and let out a high-pitched cry as Robert rolled out of the way. The beast punched the wall, grabbing its fist in pain as Robert grabbed his gun. He fired a spray of molten material and coated the abomination's chest and eyes. A searing smell of flesh filled the air as the creature squealed in pain and stumbled away.

Robert grabbed the supplies and ducked as the beast swung at him. Missing, the blinded monster stumbled forth and searched the crevice for him. Robert was gone. It fumbled around, searching the tunnel. Carefully, Robert reached into the bag and tossed a box at a wall. The beast turned and crashed toward the wall, skull crunching as it collided with the concrete.

Robert ran. As soon as he found Benny, he got onto the platform and disappeared into a tunnel. After a few moments, he collapsed onto the ground, panting.

"Holy shit! Holy shit..." he mumbled.

His heart raced. Now came the journey back.

# 28

# Bloody Revenge

*1:16 PM, October 27, 2081*

\* \* \*

Robert stumbled over a pile of debris and continued walking. He ignored his aching body as he pushed on, harshly grasping the medicine with his left and firmly holding his rifle in his right. Nothing would stop him from getting to the Tower. Robert jogged down streets and alleys, trying to keep a decent pace without exhausting himself. As he ran, he called William.

"Robert! Are you okay?" William asked.

"I found it! I found it, William. Tell Ruth I got the stuff."

"I will! I will. Just hurry up! She's getting worse."

"Okay, I'm on my way!" Robert said.

They hung up.

No Lurkers leaped out from the shadows, and no humans stood in his way. The ruins seemed largely empty. The cityscape shifted slowly, the heights of skyscrapers rising and falling as he moved through the streets. This time he crossed below a highway, following the graffiti and looming ruins.

Everything seemed still as he ran in the desolation. The lines of ruined cars were like a surreal picture by themselves. Empty tanks, downed planes, destroyed drones, and torn-up skeletons sat at military checkpoints. So many skeletons. The city was a graveyard; it looked like someone had scattered bones around like a toddler littering toys. The sight of an intact skeleton was rare. Garbage heaps and trash covered the roads like autumn leaves. It all blew about in the wind, never decaying. As long as the city remained, so would the garbage, acting as permanent cancer from the old world.

Soon, the signs of the city shifted to different allegiances. The Tower itself stood in a once-contested part of the city. Robert followed the T-PEM graffiti, Militia graffiti, and military propaganda until he eventually caught sight of the Tower. It was so far away, yet so close. Robert could see its crown rising above the other skyscrapers from a distance. Smog obscured everything else but its stupendous figure, hiding their zip lines and the crater that held the air wells.

The sight of the Tower gave Robert more will to push on. He crossed into familiar streets and moved beneath buildings he recognized. As he crossed a road to enter an alley, he saw shapes to his right. His stomach dropped. There were dozens and dozens of people wearing a mix of clothes and holding various weapons. A majority of them wore red, covered with the marks of T-PEM. They headed the same way as him. He slinked into the doorway of a building, crouched in the shadows, and called William again.

"Robert, where are you?"

"Fisher Street, near the Tower. We got trouble, lots of trouble."

"What do you mean?"

"T-PEM's back. There's at least thirty people marching to the Tower right now. Like, right now."

"Get back here then!"

"I'm on my way!"

Robert bolted for the Tower, sprinting over cars and debris. Soon, he was in its shadow. He crashed through the only doors that weren't barricaded and slammed them behind him. Robert grabbed pieces of rebar and wove them through the door handles before pushing over brick-filled refrigerators on both sides of the doors. They landed with echoing crashes, blocking the doors from opening.

"William! William!"

"I'm here!" William shouted from above.

"Get the gun ready!"

"I'm on it!"

Robert went to a rope contraption on the bottom floor. He pressed a button and waited for the elevator to come down so he could get on. With a firm grip around the center rope, Robert pressed the button again and ascended. Once he got up to the plateau, Robert found William carrying ammunition belts to a machine-gun nest. Sandbags wrapped the entire floor, and Ignium wires went all over the floor to lights and machines.

William gestured to the gun and the lights.

"When they break in, we turn on the lights and gun them down."

"Shouldn't we at least wait for them to say something?"

"How many are there?"

"Over thirty."

"No way they are coming to just talk. Let them pile in and shoot."

"You're right. How's Ruth?"

William's jaw tightened as his gaze fell, "Terrible. Give me the medicine. She needs it. Call me when they're about to break in. Turn off the power to the elevators."

Robert took off his backpack, grabbed the medicine bag, and gave it to William. William disappeared upstairs. Robert watched him leave before he went to a panel and opened it, revealing twenty switches. He flipped three, turning off power to the gadgets powering the elevators.

He went to a large vibrating box near the panel and opened its side to reveal an Ignium power cell. It stood at his height. Its top was encased in plexiglass with machinery inside that spun around a blue orb. At the bottom, six holes were filled with giant, round Ignium batteries the size of water bottles. Most had been taken from power plants, backup generators, and the basements of apartment buildings. Each set of lights on their crowns showed how much power they had left. Robert checked their battery lives. Only one had low energy, leaving Robert confident they had enough power to last a siege.

Now came the calm. Robert trembled slightly. They had never had a human attack on the Tower. Hopefully, the machine gun would scare the small army off. Who was with the approaching army? Had Dan survived? Had Ken's group joined Dan? After Dan's group had discovered the Tower, they must've told other groups. Everyone must know.

The doors below rattled. They shook back and forth for ten seconds before being violently tugged against for another thirty. Voices faintly spoke outside. People bickered about how to break their way in. Robert went to the machine gun and aimed at the door.

A ringtone echoed in his head.

"Robert, where's Ruth?" William asked.

Robert furrowed his brow and looked behind him.

"What do you mean, where's Ruth? Is she not up there?"

"No, I've been looking all over."

"Did she go to the bathroom?"

"I checked. She's nowhere."

"She must be somewhere. We'll find her later. I need you down here. They've arrived."

"Have they gotten in?"

"No, I can hear them trying to figure out how to get in, though. Get down here before they do."

"I'm on my way."

William hung up.

Robert inhaled and exhaled. Banging came from various parts of the first floor. Outside, the invaders hacked and pulled at the fortifications. The glass broke first. A shout caused the other banging to stop as a chopping sound echoed. Slowly, they began cutting the large metal panels nailed to the window frames.

"I'm here," William whispered.

Robert moved a little as William lay beside him.

"They in yet?"

Robert pointed, "No, look down there."

A small crack of light beamed through one of the panels below, growing larger and larger as someone outside hacked it open. Gradually, a large hole was carved out of the wall, enough to fit a human.

Robert aimed the gun down toward the hole, finger hovering over the trigger.

William put his hand to Robert's shooting hand, "Wait, we need light. Give me a signal when they are in."

Robert nodded. William went to the power panel and waited.

A man crawled through the hole in the fortification, followed by a woman, then another woman, then another man. Slowly, the group came in, turned on their flashlights, and looked around. They spread out on the first floor and found the stairs demolished. As half the group gathered in Robert's line of sight, he waved at William. William turned on the lamps and ran over to the ammo belt. A bright light bathed the group below as they let out startled gasps. Robert steadied his aim. A rush of adrenaline coursed through him, and his mind became numb. He pulled the trigger.

People screamed as the machine gun unloaded into their bodies. It tore through their flesh quickly, spraying blood everywhere as people fell. Robert mowed down anything that moved. Those not caught in the gun's stream fled, escaping either out of the hole or out of sight. He blasted the bodies that still moved, stopping once thirteen people lay dead below him. He looked over the sandbags to see where the others went. A gunshot echoed from beneath. He ducked as a bullet hit the sandbag in front of him. Robert grabbed the gun and fired it at the hole in the wall below, putting bullet holes across the walls. He stopped shooting. This time, he was met with return fire as people below scurried to try and find a way up.

"Shoot the gunner!" a voice came from below.

"Mark! Shoot those things! Get the ropes!" came another voice.

People poured through the hole as Robert hid from the hail of bullets coming from beneath. Amid the gunfire, a whipping crack echoed. One of the elevators fell below.

"The elevator! Cut it!" William shouted.

Robert grabbed his plasma rifle, aimed at the elevator ropes, and fired. The gun spewed out burning material and melted through the ropes, causing the rest to cascade down. Another whipping crack reverberated in the room, followed by the second elevator falling.

He dropped as a spray of bullets narrowly missed him. A metal can landed beside them a second after.

"Move! Move!!" William shouted.

Robert stumbled after William and fell to the ground covering his head as William did. The can exploded and sent debris everywhere. The shockwave of the explosion went through Robert like a sledgehammer. It was like being hit by a tidal wave. The blast temporarily deafened him and caused his ears to ring. The machine-gun nest was gone. Near it, the rope of the second elevator moved back and forth, enduring the weight of people climbing.

"Come on, Robert!"

William stumbled up the stairs. Robert got up and tried to recompose himself. He grabbed his gun and staggered forward. The first invaders climbed up the rope and onto the platform as Robert ran up the stairs, chasing after him. He shot over a railing. The goo fell and melted their clothes, boiled the plastic of their gas masks, and cooked their skins. They screamed, flailing in agony before falling over dead.

The ones who didn't get hit shot back. Robert fell backward out of the way of the bullets and ran higher up. The invaders pursued.

"William!" Robert shouted.

No response. Robert went up and up, the invaders hunting him as he fled. Just as he was about to give up and turn to fight, he saw William in a doorway to one of the office spaces. He waved Robert over. Robert slinked inside the level and followed him. William had chosen a level full of hallways, corridors, and narrow rooms. The pair knew the maze well, which was confusing to anyone else. It was perfect. They hid, retreating to the rooms at the back of the floor.

"They went this way!" came a voice.

The invaders entered the floor. The pair went into a room at the corner of two hallways. Robert grabbed the scraps they had left on the office floor and stuffed everything he could into his rifle.

"You got ammo?" Robert asked.

"One clip in this pistol, you?"

"What? Speak up."

"One clip! We are hiding here!" William mouthed with exaggeration so Robert could see.

Robert nodded.

# 29

# Mors Omnibus

*2:43 PM, October 27, 2081*

\* \* \*

"There they are!"

Robert shot at the people down the hall, covering the surrounding walls and floor in steaming material. They shot back at him, bullets tearing up the wall Robert hid behind. Every time the invaders returned fire, William helped Robert reload. Both sides took turns shooting at each other.

"I'm out!" William said.

It was a tense stalemate. After some time, Robert had to replace the batteries in the gun, soon after which they ran out of material to shoot. He shot out one more time. The weapon only gave half of the stream it would usually spew.

"Shit!"

"What?" William asked.

"We need more material!"

"There is no more in here!"

"You're gonna have to go get some."

William blinked. His jaw dropped slightly, "What?"

Robert pointed out the hall, "Just go across the hall. There's more in the other rooms. Just toss it to me, and I'll reload. Go! Go now!"

William stood while Robert popped out with the gun and pulled the trigger. It only made a buzzing sound and shot nothing, yet it was enough to cause the invaders to duck for cover. William dove across and ran into another room. Robert hid as the invaders realized that he had run out of ammo.

He watched, hopelessly waiting for William to come back. His heart raced. William popped out from the hall and threw random objects into the room, which Robert grabbed and stuffed the gun. As people approached, he planted his back against the wall, hyperventilating in terror. Footsteps behind him cut his breath short. He listened as they reached the door frame. William ran toward Robert but stumbled back as a blob of molten goo hit the ground between the pair.

Like a lion, Robert jumped out and threw the butt of his gun into the visor of the first person. Dan. Robert's red face wrinkled in anger. As Dan hit the floor, his plasma pistol fell from his hands.

Robert dove for the ground as bullets whizzed past him. He turned the plasma rifle down the hall and spewed on many people. It covered three people, and its sheer chaos and surprise stunned the invaders. Robert kicked Dan and stumbled to his feet. He ran with William.

The invaders were lost in the maze as the pair ran out and up the stairs.

"We need to get to the ziplines!" William said.

"What about Ruth?"

"We don't have time! Let's go!"

They ran to a floor with a zipline, sprinting toward an open window with a line that went from the ceiling to a building across the street. William ran ahead and hopped on before sliding out into the open air.

The hum of a plasma gun sounded. Molten material flew past Robert's head, illuminating his body. Half went out the window, and the other half hit the zipline's anchor. The whole zipline collapsed with a metallic twang.

William cried out, "Robert!"

"William!" Robert screamed.

His heart stopped.

Robert was paralyzed. Tears rolled from his eyes as he looked out the window. William's screams stopped. He was gone. As Robert turned, his gaze fell on Dan. He dove out of the way as another molten stream escaped the pistol. Robert aimed his rifle and shot, but nothing came out. He screamed and threw the entire thing at Dan, diving toward him as Dan shielded himself.

The two locked together. In a flurry, they threw fists at one another until Robert gripped Dan's gas mask and started slamming his head into the ground. Dan's knee crashed into Robert's back, a fist knocking Robert's head up as Dan threw him off. Robert held the bottom of his gas mask and stumbled to his feet while Dan crawled away and stood. They stared at each other as Dan aimed the pistol. Before Robert could shield himself, Ruth tackled Dan. The pair crashed to the floor. Dan's gun flew from his hand as she smashed his head into the floor.

"Ruth!" Robert cried.

Her gas mask was gone. As Dan slowly stopped struggling, she bit into his neck and tore at the ligaments. Robert's whole body became stiff. She had become a Lurker —a savage, hungry, and deteriorating monster with uncontrollable aggression. Like a hungry dog, she tore Dan's body open, covering her body with crimson blood as she feasted.

Robert picked up Dan's plasma pistol.

"Ruth?" Robert called out.

Ruth turned to his voice and leaped toward him, clawing at the floor. He kicked her away with a scream, firing off the pistol at her. She screamed and flailed, clawing at her head. The molten material melted her flesh as she writhed. After a few seconds, she became still. Mercy.

Robert stared at her still body, mouth agape as tears flowed down his face. As he heard the voices coming from below, he began hyperventilating. He stumbled away from the two bodies and escaped to the stairwell.

The Tower was lost. Everything had been taken from him. Robert ran up the stairs to the roof and slammed the door behind him. At the top of the Tower, the windows roared and crashed with no resistance. He ran to the edge, where he grabbed one of three parachutes taken from a downed plane and tossed the other two over the edge. With hesitating, shuddering breaths, Robert put on the parachute and climbed to the edge. He could barely see the streets below. He hugged his backpack, fear rushing through him as he tried to summon the courage to jump.

The door slammed open behind him.

"There he is! Shoot his ass!"

Robert jumped. It was a rush as the cold wind blasted him, and the ground approached him like a speeding car. He pulled the parachute cord. The parachute unfolded and jerked him hard as it fought the polluted winds. Slowly, he maneuvered himself down to Earth. He flew behind the cover of a building and continued soaring above the streets. After two minutes, he landed. Like a clumsy baby elephant, he crashed into the ground. He landed on his feet and fell on his face, the parachute dragging him a little bit before he took it off. His whole body shook from the sensory shock.

He was now truly alone. Ruth was gone. William was gone. Zilv was gone. Everyone and everything important to him was gone. Robert was lost. There was nowhere to go, no one who would help him. There was only himself.

He had no idea what to do but walk. He didn't pick a set direction but wandered where the road took him, leaving the Tower behind. With nothing to lose, he had no fear. He walked in the center of the streets, moving aimlessly past the ruins and car shells. Robert passed the looming titans of the old world as hundreds of hungry eyes watched his every move. Alone, he was a prime target, though the daylight protected him from Lurkers too afraid to be seen. He didn't care.

Robert walked for hours. As he left the city's center, the buildings became smaller and farther apart. Slowly, the scenery shifted into apartment buildings, shopping complexes, and sandy spaces where trash piled. He came upon a highway and went on it, following miles of traffic jams. There were remains from the old world everywhere he went. Robert didn't pause for anything, ignoring his aching feet and body. His mind was blank. He struggled to recall anything, especially the events of the day. The only thing that lingered was the sensation of loss.

The idea of walking forever sounded pleasant. Robert wanted to walk. He wanted to leave everything behind and move until he fell dead. It was right. He would die, then be taken to Hell and tortured forever for his sins. Justice. He deserved eternal torment for everything he had and had not done.

The winds picked up as he left the city behind. The buildings and garbage became sparse. Finally, there were no cars on the highway. A destroyed military outpost sat at the end of it all. He went through it and continued. Eventually, the road became isolated, with no buildings to accompany it. After passing the checkpoint, he walked for an hour before collapsing on his knees. A vast and empty plain full of trash and sand surrounded him. Currents of wind followed dunes vacant of plants, animals, and even dead trees.

Silent, empty, and cruel. This was the nature of the wasteland.

# 30

# The Rebirth

*8:00 PM, October 27, 2081*

\* \* \*

The sun set on a dead world. The last forests had died, the monuments of men were ruined, and the only things that remained were either dead or too stubborn to die. Many of the survivors from the old world would perish. Those unwilling to do anything to survive, those with no will for the new world, or those who were just plain unlucky would not make it. Eventually, the cities would be emptied. Water and food would run out, and Lurkers would eat up the many desperate people who went out looking for more.

As the ruins of the old world decayed, a slight glimmer of hope would escape into the world. Genetically modified animals would escape from zoos and labs, creatures made to replace those that had gone extinct, creatures that could survive in the wasteland. Many would die, but those that survived would live alongside human mutants and become part of the new world's ecosystem.

The wasteland sands would eventually swallow up much of the garbage left in the world, while the rest would withstand the wear of time in cities until they became dust. It would take centuries for the Earth to recover. As the Earth did, so would humanity. For many decades, the wasteland would be still. The few survivors in it would fight tooth and nail to endure, establishing small settlements and hardy tribes. Many would choose to survive alone, too damaged from their pasts ever to trust again. This was common. Many from the old world carried scars that would never heal, damage from unimaginable horror and loss. Time would eventually wash away everything. Scars would be wiped clean by death, and the cancerous remains of old-world sins would be turned to dust by time's unending march.

# III

# Part Three

*"Then I saw a new heaven and a new earth,*
*for the first heaven,*
*and the first earth had passed away,*
*and the sea was no more."* – *Revelation 21:4*

# 31

# Tired Eyes

8:32 AM, January 1, 2100

\* \* \*

Murderer. Deceiver. Rat. Cannibal.

Nineteen years had passed since Robert lost everything. He was alone now. His tired eyes were sunken and bloodshot, irritated from the wasteland pollution. There was no energy in his expression. The living glow that people had was dim in him as if it struggled to carry on.

His forty-eight-year-old body was scarred and disfigured from years of wandering the wasteland. The old injury he had in his ankle had come back as a limp. A head injury had made his hands permanently tremble, and he had not been able to make fists in years. His skin tortured him as well. His whole body might as well have been a callus from pollution and fighting, and he was always dirty. Despite his gas mask, the times he had taken it off to eat or drink had worn his lungs. The wasteland air had corroded them, causing him to cough in response to a burning sensation in his chest and throat.

Slim from years of malnutrition, Robert had grown accustomed to the feelings of hunger, thirst, and exhaustion. Comfort and excess were figments of the past. He avoided sleep, too afraid to face the terrible nightmares of his traumatized mind.

Walking along the faded center line, Robert followed an old-world road covered in sand. The day was eerie and gloomy. The sun rose over the polluted horizon, lighting the sky in an array of somber colors.

He needed water. Dehydration had cracked his lips, and his tongue felt like sandpaper. His flask was dangerously low. It had been long since he had found a trader or a water-baron lording over a pump. Robert observed his surroundings, hoping to find buildings and cars to investigate for water.

Old power lines framed the road, some connected to ancient electrical systems and some to old Ignium systems. Time had destroyed most of them. Many were leaning, collapsed, or broken, their lines snapped and hanging downward. The winds blew currents of sand at him. He felt fortunate that the weather was calm this morning, though he was always on the lookout for what other survivors called "Doomstorms." Doomstorms weren't as common as years ago, but they were still a prevalent and deadly threat. They arose quickly, creating towering walls of sand that swept across the land in a tide of death. The Doomstorm winds could pick up a car, and the sands could shred paint off a house.

Robert walked along the road for an hour, examining everything he came across. Occasionally, there'd be a car left. Most were shells. The weather had shredded their paint, and their bodies were rusty. He passed them with a glance. They had nothing left for him.

Robert licked his cracked lips with his dried-out tongue, letting out a wheezing cough. His muscles cramped, and his eyes hurt. The skin under his dirty clothes felt itchy. As he pulled back his sleeve to scratch, he revealed a dark rash covering his forearm. He stared through his dirty visor, tracing his fingers over his old implant. The implant had run out of power at least a decade ago. Robert wished he could've called someone one more time. Anyone. It was "normal," and he deeply missed doing ordinary things and being normal. It was comforting and familiar, something the harsh new world did not have. What was "normal" out here? Nothing. Barely surviving, like Robert, was the norm in the wasteland.

After passing an old billboard, Robert spotted a group of cars in the distance. He could make out the scene when he got closer. The shells of a few dozen vehicles sat behind a roadblock, accompanied by a tipped-over semi-trailer and a rusty police drone. Robert approached the gridlock from behind and unholstered his plasma pistol. The weapon was now well-worn, having served Robert, Dan, and probably a soldier in its lifetime. Wear covered the body, its paint was gone, and its features were smoothed out by use. Many of its parts had been replaced by Robert over the years. Even so, it served him well, and he had gotten to know the weapon better than anyone else.

He searched the wreckage, suppressing his need to cough. He examined every car shell and dug in the remnants of cabins for leftovers such as Ignium wires and sensors. He found none.

Robert approached a farm truck in the middle of the traffic jam. The entire truck had been stripped of anything valuable and was full of sand. Unlike many old-world cars, manually driving trucks during agricultural and utility work was legal. Most cars had hidden steering wheels and would only come out in emergency mode. In contrast, trucks usually had the steering wheel out and hid it in self-driving mode.

Robert chose to pass on to the police drone. Stripped. Its rotors were gone. The police lights and gadgets had been taken, and parts of the cockpit had been sawed off. He stepped inside the cockpit, searching the compartment where officers put their weapons. It was gone, ripped out entirely of the drone. In its place was a hole full of sand.

He went toward a tipped-over semi-trailer. The entire semi-trailer was composed of a wheeled trailer with a small bay in front for optional human passengers. Robert turned on his flashlight when he approached the doors. The flashlight flickered to life, beaming into the trailer as he opened one of the doors with his pistol pointed inside.

A man sat opposite the doors, trying to open one of the crates in the trailer. He jumped and gasped as Robert shone his light on him, dropping his tools.

"Hands up!" Robert shouted before letting out a hacking cough.

The man raised his hands.

"Whoa, whoa! All right!"

"Come out here!"

The ragged man came to the edge of the trailer. He had a pipe rifle that hung from a strap on his back.

"The gun. Put it on the ground," Robert said.

The man nodded, took the gun off his back, and carefully put it on the ground.

"Now kick it away and step over there," Robert said.

The man did so reluctantly and went over to stand at the spot Robert pointed to.

Robert let out a wheezing cough as he watched the man, keeping his gun fixated as he hacked. His clothes were worn like Robert's, and his gas mask seemed to have been handmade with a flashlight attached to it. He also had a tool belt with a water flask on his hip.

"What is your name?" Robert asked once he stopped coughing.

"Sam."

Robert pointed toward the tipped-over trailer, "What's in there?"

The man shrugged, "I don't know. I've been trying to open them but can't get them open."

"I'm thirsty and hungry. Give me that water flask, or I'll shoot you," Robert said.

"It's empty."

"Shake it."

Sam grabbed the flask and shook it. It sloshed loudly, full of water. Reluctantly, the man gave the flask to Robert. Robert flipped his mask and haphazardly drank before putting the flask in a pocket.

"Why'd you lie? I bet you have food, too," Robert said.

"I don't have any food, but I bet we can work out a deal. I can get you more water."

Robert put his finger on the trigger, "No more funny business! Give me your shit, or I'll melt your ass!"

The sandy dirt behind Robert crunched as footsteps approached.

"Put the weapon down!"

Robert turned. A man stood behind a car, wearing an old smart suit with an animal hide coat over it and an old-world gas mask covering his face. In his hands was a Railshot Rifle, a powerful and deadly weapon that combined the power of a railgun and the lethality of a shotgun into a metal-spitting cannon.

Robert shot at the man. Goo flew from his pistol, causing the man to duck and dive behind a car. Robert shot as he found cover behind another car. Sam ran into the trailer.

The pistol fizzled and ran out of material. "Damn!" Robert whispered.

He grabbed what he could from his pockets, haphazardly stuffing material into the pistol. As Robert fumbled, a hum sounded behind him, along with a crackle of sparks. A hail of metal scrap spewed through the car Robert hid behind, a metal piece plunging into his side and knocking him slightly as it embedded itself.

Numb, Robert popped up and shot more molten goo at the man. He gripped his wound, turned, and retreated into the wasteland. The man did not chase him. Still, Robert didn't pause. He ran into the wasteland until his legs gave out, falling to his knees and gripping his side.

Blood covered the metal piece embedded in his side. The pain was piercing, as if the metal seared his flesh. Adrenaline rushed through his veins, and sweat covered him as his heart pounded. He sat there, inhaling and exhaling with as much control as he could, each breath feeling more and more like a chore. He had no medical supplies, and taking out the metal piece would kill him.

It was hopeless. There was nowhere to go and no one to help. Robert looked at the sky and stumbled to his feet, shuffling forward with determination. He wasn't ready to die. The survivor in him awakened like a bear, pushing him forward across the sand. Robert willed his way through weakness. Drenched in blood and sweat, his legs shook with every step. He found a road and followed it. The pain grew worse. It felt as if the world grew dimmer, and the sounds of the windy wasteland became distorted.

The silhouette of a convenience store appeared in the distance.

As he stumbled and shuffled closer, he fell to his knees and crawled. With the last of his strength, he cried out, "Help! Please!"

He collapsed onto his face. Time felt distorted. Someone rolled him over. He could vaguely make out the figure speaking to him. He blinked and then slipped away into unconsciousness.

# 32

# Healing Hands

9:54 PM, January 3, 2100

* * *

"We should leave him out in the wasteland!"

"We're not leaving him! I saved him. I can help him!"

"This is not a hospital! Throw him out! We barely have enough as it is!"

"What if he is part of a group, and they hunt us down? What if he can help us? If we need to, we can kick him out."

"You know what? If you're not gonna listen, fine! You do what you want. Once you waste all of our supplies, don't complain to me!"

* * *

Robert blinked and looked around. He was on a mattress inside an old convenience store filled with garbage and various objects. Old shelves full of supplies, TVs, and computers piled in one area. Automobile parts collected dust in another part while a line of old freezers filled with junk rested against one wall.

He vaguely recalled waking up a few times and hearing people talk, but that was it. Someone approached from a door leading to a back room. He couldn't make them out and could only see a gas mask and dirty wasteland clothes.

"Hey, hey. Don't move."

A woman knelt beside him, gently grasping at his smart suit. He slapped at her hands and jerked away.

"Hey! Calm down. I need to check your bandages."

Was this a trick? A ploy to gain his trust to betray him for personal gain? He was not tied up, but that did not mean that this woman did not plan to eat him. Why on Earth would she be kind to him and waste precious supplies on a stranger who could very well betray her?

Robert shook his head.

"How do you feel?" she asked.

The wound did burn now that she had brought his attention to it, and he felt thirsty. Even so, he only stared.

She stared back, then grabbed a water bottle and placed it beside him, "Look, you've been out for a while. I've cleaned your wound and patched it up. You don't need to talk but at least drink. Your lips are so cracked."

Robert looked at the bottle and slowly took it.

"Thank you," she said, stood up, and disappeared into the back room again.

Robert moved his mask and hectically downed the whole bottle. He threw it aside and flopped onto his hands and knees. The wound felt like it constricted him, searing in response to movement. Carefully, he got onto his feet.

He had been laid at the end of many mattresses. Most of his dirty, blackened clothes were carelessly tossed into a pile. His backpack, gun, knife, and other belongings rested against the heap. Robert grabbed his stuff, wrapping his other belongings in a bundle and snatching his weapon.

Robert fumbled across the trash-filled building to the front door. The whole thing was barricaded with wooden planks, stopping entry and exit. He grabbed one and tugged at it. Nothing budged, no matter how hard he pulled.

"What are you doing?"

Robert turned. Three people now stood in front of him, all of them fully dressed in masks. One seemed male, while the other two seemed female. Their clothes were dirty and stained, two wore animal furs, and all three had melee weapons hanging from their belts.

He waved his gun at them frantically, "Stay back!" Robert shouted and let out a hacking cough.

"Calm down! We're not here to hurt you!" the man said.

"Look, we don't have our weapons out!" said the woman who had greeted him earlier.

Robert pulled the trigger, aiming at the male. None of them reacted as they watched the gun do absolutely nothing. Robert gasped, looked at the gun, pulled the trigger again, then grabbed the barrel so he could bludgeon them with the butt, "What did you do to my gun?!"

The man raised his hands defensively, "Nothing! We just took the batteries and material out of it. We haven't stolen them and will give them back. But first, please calm down."

Robert looked between the three and coughed again before speaking, "I don't wanna stay here. I don't know what this is or who you people are. I have no business being here and no right to take from you. Let me leave."

"You haven't taken anything," the second woman said.

"What about the bandages? My wound?"

The first woman raised her hand slightly, "I put them on. They're given. If you want to go, you can. But I strongly suggest that you stay. It's windy outside, and you need rest."

"I want to go," Robert said.

They all looked at each other.

The man stepped forward, "All right, put your clothes on. I'll take you outside."

Robert looked as the two women left. The man waited for Robert as he put his clothes on. He dressed as quickly as the pain allowed. His clothes were damp, and dirt was smudged onto his fingers. None of it was remotely clean. Once he was dressed, he followed the man.

A set of ropes hung from a trap door in the ceiling. The man gestured for Robert to go first. Robert approached, looked up reluctantly, and tightly gripped the rope. With a grunt, he pulled himself an inch off the ground, then fell as searing pain went through him. Robert yelled after landing on his butt. He gripped his side and let out a painful, wheezing cough.

"Are you okay?"

The men knelt, trying to help Robert.

Robert pushed him back roughly, "I'm fine. I don't think I can leave."

The man stood and readjusted his clothes, "You can stay. Try to be grateful," the man snapped and left.

Robert gently cupped his side. All three of the people were younger. They were thin, though not as thin as he was. He considered taking advantage of their trust and killing them in their sleep. It would be easy. Just pull the trigger and spew molten material all over them. Then he'd have everything to himself. He could even eat them. He needed help and information; they probably knew the local area and who had shot him.

He got up and looked at his gloves which were blackened by dirt and blood. Robert looked down at himself, then stripped. The dirt wasn't good for his wound or his irritated skin. He set the clothes back in their original pile along with the rest of his belongings, keeping the relatively clean smart suit on. He approached the door to the back, where a hall led to bathrooms, a janitorial closet, and a storage room. He ignored the scribblings along the corridor when he heard voices from the storage room. He knocked on the door, and one of the women opened it.

"Oh, you okay?"

"Yes. I just wanted to talk."

\* \* \*

Robert sat in the blanket like a cocoon, keeping it tight around his head. He leaned against the wall, staring at a flickering Ignium light on a crate. The three sat near him. The women played chess while the man plucked his nails with a knife.

He gazed at Robert and flicked his head upward, "Ay, what is your name?"

"Does it matter?" Robert asked.

"I wouldn't ask if it didn't."

Robert paused. It had been a while since he had said his name or considered that he was a living person with a name, "Robert. What about you three?"

"David."

"Thea," said the first woman who had greeted Robert when he woke.

"Abby," the second said.

Robert felt weird. It had been a long time since he last socialized, and he had lost any love for humanity years ago. Being near anyone drained him. He didn't dare make friends or allies for fear of losing them, so he held back any social warmth.

David tilted his head, "Where are you from?"

"I don't remember. A city in ruins now," Robert replied.

"I see. I'm from California, was born there before everything fell apart. Thea here was born out in the wastes around here, and Abby's from somewhere in the Canadian wastes."

Abby smiled thinly, "Yeah, I grew up in a bone forest."

"Bone forest?" Robert asked.

"Yeah. All the trees and stuff died in the old world, so Canada and those places are just covered in dead trees. Fields and fields of stained trunks going out past the horizon. Winters were long and terrible, and you never knew when the trees would fall on you. My family left when I was, like... thirteen? I was the only one that made it down here."

After a period of silence, Thea spoke, "You're not the talkative type, are you?"

Robert shook his head. He looked around at all three of them, frowned, gazed down, and spoke, "I uh... I haven't spoken to anyone in a long time."

"Where have you been?" David asked.

"Walking," Robert said before coughing again.

David shook his head and raised his palms, "All alone?"

"I used to have people. I haven't for a very long time," Robert said and looked back up at them, "You're all young. I'm sure you've all seen things you shouldn't have in your lives, but the wasteland is your home. It is not mine. I don't need people. I don't want them, and I can't keep them. The wasteland takes everything anyway."

They looked at each other.

Robert sighed and lightly cupped his side, "Look, I'm sorry. I am grateful for what all of you did. I don't understand why you did it, but that was your choice. I'm just afraid."

Thea crossed her arms, "No one will hurt you here. I saw someone that needed help and helped. Like we said, you can leave whenever but we'd appreciate your help."

Robert thought about what she said and how she said it. He knew when people lied. They spoke differently and moved differently. It was shocking to hear such a genuine tone, and for a moment, he almost forgot caution. But he couldn't trust anyone. It was too dangerous.

# 33

# Stilted Watcher

*10:42 AM, January 18, 2100*

\* \* \*

"How do you feel?" Thea asked.

Robert cupped his side, "It stings, but I feel fine."

The wound had closed halfway and darkened as it scabbed, leaving a dull stinging sensation. They tried their best to clean it, though most pain came from unavoidable polluted air. Thea had told Robert that he was lucky that the shrapnel had only pierced his flesh, leaving his organs unharmed. Robert thought about the man who had shot him. He didn't feel the urge to get revenge but instead wanted to avoid him at all costs. It would keep him alive. Even so, if he had the chance, he would relish killing the man and taking his lethal weapon.

The wasteland was calm today. Stepping onto the roof of the old convenience store was always like a second awakening. The winds blew gently around them, currents of sand following the wind along the dunes and ruins. Robert was the second to get out onto the roof. Thea led, David was behind him, and Abby was last. Robert went to the edge of the building where the dry, cold, and sandy wasteland stretched beyond the horizon. Ancient trash stuck out of the ground, dotting the land infrequently like desert plants. They were scars, fading as time consumed them. One by one, the group went down another rope to the front of the store. Once they had gathered, David threw the tether onto a hook where it took two people to reach it.

"What are we doing?" Robert asked.

"Going on a search or, as you say, we're walking," David said.

Robert followed as David led the way. Occasionally, Robert would let out a wheezing cough or scratch his irritated skin. He preferred walking at the back of the group since that meant that none of them would look at him or think of something to say. Even after over a week, they still knew very little about Robert except that he ate and drank only now and then. They also knew that he barely slept and often screamed himself awake from nightmares.

Now that the wound had healed enough to move, he considered leaving every day but found that he didn't want to. He appreciated a break from being alone. They treated him kindly, and he could rest without being on edge. That didn't mean he trusted any of them; he had already planned to flee if issues arose. It was inevitable. Food didn't last forever.

Robert followed a sand-covered road. Distant ruins of farmhouses and barns appeared. Out here on the edge of the Great Plains were many farms and ranches, each a monument to ruined lives. Most were empty even before the great wars of the past. Their buildings had been turned over to the wasteland when crops stopped growing and cattle suffocated from polluted air.

"Hey, Robert?" Thea asked.

David and Abby had been talking for a few minutes, but it was all mumbling to Robert. He was sure he was losing his hearing but wasn't listening to them anyway. Abby and David didn't bother him, though Thea had taken it into her stead to make him talk to her.

"Yes?" he said after a pause.

"How did you get that wound?"

They only knew that he had been hit by shrapnel since they took it out but knew little beyond the suggestion he had been attacked.

"Well, I was out by a road wreck trying to get water from someone when someone with a Railshot rifle attacked us. You know, one of those shotgun rail guns that shoot shrapnel? I'm sure the other guy is dead, but I only survived because I was hiding behind a car. I imagine the car frame slowed down the metal piece."

"Trying to get water? By force or?"

Robert didn't answer.

"All right then, keep your secrets. You're just a strange man. All alone in the wasteland with absolutely no trust."

"There's plenty of lone survivors out here."

"A lot of them are alone because their groups fell apart or died. Mostly crazy people stay alone, but I don't think you're crazy."

"I'm not."

"I think your heart just hurts, and you're a little tired," Thea said.

Robert turned his gaze back to her. She was right, but he was surprised she even said anything, "Yeah," he mumbled before coughing.

David raised a hand and glanced back, "You gotta tell us something. Where you are from, maybe?"

"Uh... I used to live out east or so. One of the newer cities growing out of old cities with fancy stuff like big underground metro systems and that sort."

"Never been out east. Was it nice?" Abby said.

"No. Nowhere was nice. Most of the city was a slum before everything fell apart, but that was most of the United States."

"How old are you, Robert?" David asked.

Robert looked up at the sky, "I don't know. How long has it been?"

David shrugged, "No idea. Probably a decade or two. Last time I heard, it was eighteen years or so, but that was a long time ago. Probably twenty years by now."

"Well, I'm like forty-six, maybe forty-seven or forty-eight."

Thea raised a brow, "Wow, you were pretty old when everything fell apart. Didn't everything fall apart around 2079?"

"Mhm."

He let out a wet cough. Blood came up as he hacked. He lifted his mask, spat red onto the sand, and cleared his throat as he put it back down.

Thea turned around, her pace stuttering for a moment, "You okay?"

Robert nodded, though he felt concerned over the blood.

"I was probably six or so when everything fell apart. Can't imagine what it was like. I don't remember a lot," David said.

Robert fixated on the ground, "It was… I'll never outlive it. You young ones are lucky and unlucky. Lucky to either not have been around at the time or to not remember it and unlucky to live now. This is your world. It's all you know. Sorry, my generation left the world like this for you."

Abby shrugged, "Not your fault. How can we blame you?"

"Can blame all of us before you. Wasn't just me. It was everybody."

Thea pursed her lips, "What was the old world like?"

Robert thought about his response before speaking. At first, they were uncomfortable with his silent pauses but had grown used to them once they got to know him. He coughed again, then spoke, "Cold. It was always cold. Winters were especially cold. Everything froze over. I remember that even concrete seemed to ice over. Probably just polluted air settling and freezing. It was colder than it is now, which is fortunate. I think the world is warming up."

Abby furrowed her brow, "Ugh, it was colder? Don't know how you lived."

"Most people had smart suits that kept them warm. I miss them. So few left. The old world was also dirty. Everything was stained with grime and black residue: buildings, roads, signs, everything. Streets in my city were covered in trash. Mounds of it everywhere, like the sand dunes around us right now."

David's face wrinkled, "That's disgusting. Has the wasteland always been the same?"

"Yep. Most people, except those in small towns, moved into bigger cities at least a decade before everything fell apart. Everyone wanted to get out during the wars, though. I remember that so many people were homeless. They slept in the trash, and many died from sickness. Nobody noticed until they started stinking."

Thea shook her head, "Wow, was there anything nice back then?".

"Not really. Only power, filtered rooms, and grocery stores."

"Filtered rooms?" Abby repeated.

"Yeah. A lot of buildings had an entrance room where air would be sucked out and replaced by clean air, and the inside of buildings were sealed so that only clean air would be inside."

David uncrossed his arms and leaned forward, "That's weird. I'm sort of jealous."

"Yeah. I do miss taking my mask off comfortably."

They passed the ruin of an old church. Robert let out a wheezing cough again and cleared his throat once the coughing passed, "What's around here?"

David eyed the horizon, pointing as he spoke, "Well, there's a town around here that we've visited. Didn't get much out of it since most of the buildings are half-buried. Lots of hard work. We don't know if any of the buildings are safe, so we haven't decided to try and dig into any of the buildings. Of course, there are lots of farmhouses around here."

Abby pointed to their right, "There's a city in each direction, but I think the closest is east?"

Thea's head dropped, and her tone became lower, "We try to avoid cities."

Robert understood the notion. Cities had become hellscapes. They were concrete jungles that made up the first ecosystems in the new world. Composed of mutant animals and human mutants, cities were hazardous for survivors. They were filled with hungry predators, full of garbage and toxic material, such as broken Ignium machines and other appliances that leaked chemicals. Those who braved the cities alone were the most experienced and fearless. Groups who took up residence in old cities were often composed of tempered wasteland veterans.

After an hour or so of walking, they turned into the wasteland.

Robert glanced behind them, "Where are we going now? There's nothing out here."

David gestured ahead, "There might be. We've been tracking someone who's been walking out here. Same person every week. We always lose him, though."

Thea raised a finger, "There's probably water out here that he's getting."

"Water?" Robert mumbled, coughing lightly.

Water was hard to come by in the wasteland. It wasn't scarce since lakes, rivers, and creeks still endured, but pollution had made all bodies of water undrinkable. Most water came from water barons that controlled settlements where they usually pumped it from a lake or underground and filtered it. Some survivors, like Robert, knew how to get water from anywhere, including themselves. Robert killed for water. He would fight and claw to have some. He had left people lying out in the sand over a bottle of water many times. If it came to it, he'd also kill any of the people around him for water. He didn't do it out of malice but out of a deep and primitive need to survive.

Occasionally, Robert poked a visible hole in the sand as they walked, not wanting to get lost as they went out into the featureless landscape. Anxiety gripped him. He was unsure now if the trio was lying and bringing him out somewhere to do something horrible to him or if they were actually searching for some strange man and his water. His pistol was ready at his side. He was jumpy, and his heart beat faster as his hand lingered by the gun.

Abby pointed ahead and dropped, "Wait! Get down!"

They dropped. Robert grunted as he hit the dirt, his old joints popping.

"What is it?" David asked.

"Look over there," Abby whispered and pointed.

Robert squinted but could not make out anything. His eyesight had faded from age and pollution damage.

David cupped his hands over his visor, "I see them. What are they doing?"

Abby got onto her knees, "Just walking. Let's follow them."

As they crept forward, two figures came into his sight. At first, he could make out their silhouettes only. He saw more detail as they got closer. The pair had similar clothing and equipment to those he had met over a week ago.

The sight of a Railshot Rifle made him speak, "Wait, guys. Those two might be the ones who attacked me."

"What?" Thea said.

"One of them has a Railshot Rifle. I was shot by one of those," Robert said.

Abby looked at David, "Should we attack them?"

David shook his head, "No. Let's see where they're going first and set up an ambush later. We are not ready to fight."

They followed the pair from afar for ten minutes. They went over hills and dunes before finding a round hill. It was like a circle, only lowering in one spot. The pair ahead went through the dip and inside a basin, leaving the trio to scale the hill. They crawled to the edge and looked over. Robert made out a strange, towering structure. It was an old windmill sitting on stilts and covered in metal plates. Inside was a mess of pipes, gears, and other machinery leading to a pump and a spigot. At the end of the tap was a filter in the shape of a can. The windmill was tall and stood like a silent observer over the surrounding wasteland. The pair below poured filtered water into containers while conversing quietly.

Abby poked David and whispered, "They don't know we're here. We should attack now."

David shook his head, "No, we're not ready. Look at that one with the rifle. He could kill us all with one shot. We're going back now. We will set up an ambush soon."

Robert stared at the man with the Railshot Rifle. He didn't feel angry or spiteful but simply wanted to rip the gun from the man's hands and take it for himself. He also desperately wanted the water. After a few moments of bickering, David led them down the hill and took them back the way they had come.

# 34

# The Storm

\* \* \*

David set the pipe rifle in front of Robert and loaded his own rifle. The gun was constructed from junk and held together by zip ties and tape. Its condition and ability to shoot were questionable.

"What's this?" Robert asked.

"Pipe rifle," David said.

"Oh, I have a gun. I don't need this," Robert said.

"No, trust me. You need something a bit longer ranged than a plasma pistol."

"I understand that. I'm not really a good shot anymore."

"It'll be fine. Take both," David said.

Robert put his loyal plasma pistol away and held up the pipe rifle. The metal components of the gun had rusted, and the plastic was worn and rough in texture. He took a few magazines and loaded one into the gun before placing the rest in any pocket that would fit them. Abby carried a rifle, while Thea had a holstered pistol and something Robert thought was a blunderbuss at first. He blinked and realized it was a makeshift shotgun that could hold one shell only.

David rested against the wall and held the barrel of his gun, "Are you ready, guys?"

Abby patted herself down, checking all of her equipment, "Yep. Vests on, guns loaded, ammo on hand."

"Robert, do you have your vest?" Thea asked.

"No?"

"I'll get you one. Hold on," Thea said.

She left and returned with a vest made of metal scrap salvaged from all sorts of items, ranging from road signs to metal sheets for roofing. Robert had seen people wear metal armor, but none ever worked against his weapon. Metal armor made his enemies slow and helped cook the victims of his plasma pistol.

Robert frowned, "Does that work?"

David shrugged, "It doesn't make you bulletproof but might stop things like arrows and knives. We've found that it slows bullets down a little bit, which is better than nothing."

"Just don't lose your head," Abby said.

Robert took the vest from Thea. It was heavy and rough. He removed his backpack, placed the vest over his gear, and put the pack on again. The vest was uncomfortable and poked him in multiple places. Parts of it felt sharp and had welts pressed against his rib cage. He felt ridiculous and was sure the vest would tire him before it got used. Even so, he was willing to try it.

Everyone grabbed their guns and gear. They had tough jerky made from the flesh of mutants, water stolen from the windmill, and bandages made from torn clothes. Once gathered, they went out into the wasteland.

* * *

Robert followed David and Abby, with Thea walking beside him. Robert was unsure what to think about Thea. She had taken on the task of caring for him and constantly prodded him to eat, drink, and sleep. He tolerated it despite trying to convince her that he could take care of himself.

"You nervous, Robert?" Thea asked.

Robert let out a hacking, wet cough and shook his head, "No," he replied after clearing his throat.

"No?"

"I don't get nervous a lot anymore, especially when doing stuff like this."

Thea flicked her head, "I'm nervous. Hope it goes in our favor."

"I don't pay any mind to it. Best not to think of it."

"I have a feeling you're no stranger to pulling triggers."

"What gave you the impression otherwise?" Robert asked.

Thea glanced at him with wide eyes offering no response.

They diverted off the road. Like before, Robert made marks on the ground to find his way back. The winds picked up, and the sky shifted from calm to chaotic turmoil. Robert grimaced, jaw tightening. He watched the horizon's edge, though the distance was somewhat fuzzy. He kept an eye out for figures and shapes but saw nothing as they moved over dunes and hills. Eventually, they came upon the basin that contained the windmill and went around, avoiding the northern entrance where the valley dipped.

As they got to the hill's edge, David stopped them, "Is everyone ready? Guns loaded, masks on tight, everything?"

"Yep," Abby said.

"I'm good," Thea added.

Robert nodded.

"Good, let's go. Spread out along the hill. Robert, you want to take the first shot?"

Robert looked down at his pipe rifle and then at David, "I'm not really a good shot anymore. You sure?"

"It doesn't matter if you miss. You'll start the ambush."

"All right."

"Everyone up the hill," David ordered.

They all climbed and spread out flat on their stomachs as they got up to the edge and peeked over.

Robert's heart beat faster. The pair below filled up water and conversed. Robert aimed the pipe rifle downward and pointed it at the man with the Railshot Rifle. He breathed steadily, waiting patiently to line up his shot. With his old eyes, the man was a blur.

As he lined up the shot, the man turned and squinted at Robert. Robert shot, and the gunshot rang out into the wasteland. The recoil shocked him. The bullet hit the man, and he dropped backward. David, Abby, and Thea fired. The other man below dove toward the first one as the group opened fire. He grabbed him and dragged him to cover.

"Keep them pinned!" David ordered.

The four shot randomly, trying to hit the second man as he popped up on the right or left side and returned fire. Robert ducked and covered his head as a few bullets hit the sand below him, narrowly missing by a few inches. As the four fired, the first man below screamed. They kept shooting, the second man below ceasing his return fire abruptly.

Abby jumped up and ran down the hill, gun ready.

"They must be out of ammo! Let's go!"

David ran after her, "Abby! Wait!"

Robert and Thea looked at each other.

"Do we follow them?" Thea asked.

"Let's lay suppressing fire," Robert replied.

They kept shooting until David and Abby got around the windmill. Abby was tackled into view by the second man. The two struggled as they grappled with each other. David came around the other side, the first man kicking his hands.

"Fuck!" David screamed as he dropped his weapon and gripped his hand.

The weapon dropped as the man flopped forward and tackled David. The two fought and then kicked each other off.

"Robert! We need to help them!" Thea cried.

"Don't shoot! We might miss and hit David and Abby!" Robert shouted.

Abby drew a knife as she got on top of the second man and attempted to plunge it into his chest. David and the first man crawled to their guns before turning to shoot each other. Just as David turned, the first man fired. An arc of metal scrap flooded forth from the barrel of the Railshot Rifle. One moment, David aimed his gun. The next, he was dead. Metal shredded his body, annihilating any semblance of his head, chest, and arms and turning them into piles of gore and flesh. The rest of his body fell limp.

Thea screamed, "David!!"

The first man seemed just as shocked as they were and only recovered as the second man called for him, "Oliver! Oliver, help!"

"I—I'm coming!"

"Abby! Watch out!" Thea screamed.

The first man shuffled over and put the Railshot Rifle to Abby's head. Metal blasted through her head, killing her instantly. Her body fell to the ground, blood spewing from what had once been her neck.

Thea jumped up and ran down the hill. Robert followed, firing at the two men as they fled over the other side and into the wasteland. Thea and Robert climbed over the ridge and chased after the pair as they split and ran into the wastes in two different directions.

Thea pointed, "After that one!"

They chased after the second man over dunes and hills as they tried to get a good line of sight to shoot at him.

Robert stopped, "Thea!"

"What?

Robert stared in the opposite direction, "Those aren't mountains," he said, pointing in awe.

An impenetrable wall of sand reaching up into the sky thundered toward them. Howling winds and shredding sand signaled the arrival of a Doom-storm.

"It's a Doomstorm! Quick! Come with me!"

They ran over dunes toward a hill. Thea took off her backpack and pulled out a peculiar blanket. It was made out of rough material and felt hard to the touch. Rocks were woven inside its edges. They went over the hill. At the bottom, Thea dove to the ground and spread the blanket.

"Quick! Get under it! Go!" Thea said.

They crawled underneath the blanket and lay in the sand.

"Grab the edges and hold them down!"

Robert gripped one side and used his shoes to hold down the other. Thunderous howling came down upon them. The storm engulfed them, sweeping sand over the dunes like an unstoppable tsunami. The pair struggled to hold down the blanket. The hill in front of them absorbed the brunt of the storm's force, though the winds still tried to pick them up. Robert held tight. Time disappeared, swallowed into the belly of the beast as the Doomstorm crashed over them.

# 35

# First Outsiders

\* \* \*

Thea sat on her knees, sniffling over the two shallow graves. Robert stood at a distance. Sweat from digging stained his clothes, and his arms still hurt from work. The two graves in front of him were not grand, each adorned with a few rocks and marked by a single rusty pipe.

Robert felt no grief. He had not known David or Abby enough to care for them. Death was familiar. Their short time in his life was a blip, passing in a blink. Only Thea's grief bothered him since she cared about them. They meant something to her, and now that they were gone, she had to wrestle with the emptiness of having them taken. She cried quietly, rocking back and forth on her knees. It reminded him of Zilv. She wept like Zilv had. Zilv had always been quiet, expressing pain more through his body than his voice. Though the memories of Zilv hurt, Robert stayed beside Thea to comfort her.

\* \* \*

Robert followed Thea along an old-world road coated with sand and cracks. He was quiet. Since the death of David and Abby, he had let Thea lead their looting expeditions. She saw better than he could and knew the area better. Together, they explored many areas across the wasteland. They focused

257

on the windmill and avoided the direction the two men had fled. The pair dared not to fight the two men alone and only stole water when they thought they'd be safe. Even so, they had stolen gallons of clean, filtered water.

Robert felt young again. Having so much water reminded him of good times, which rarely happened. It was the feeling of prospering, the merchant's success he, William, and Ruth once had when trading water. So many years later, Robert could do it again with stolen water.

"Are you okay, Robert?"

"Yes, why?"

"Oh, just your breathing. We don't talk much, so I just listen to the pattern. Sometimes it changes."

Robert smiled thinly, "I'm fine. Old-man lungs."

Thea's brow wrinkled, "Old-man lungs?"

"Yeah. I've breathed in a fair share of polluted air in my time."

"That's not good. Are you okay?"

"I'm fine. I'm used to it. It shortens my lifespan, but at least I won't die from my own clumsiness or something stupid."

He wasn't as courageous as he sounded. Robert feared death and the pain that could come with it. He couldn't fail. The old and primal desperation to go on drove him, so Robert wandered.

"Don't talk like that. I've already lost enough people. I'm sure you know that too well."

"I have a feeling you're going to ask me about it?"

"Not if you don't want to talk about it."

"You're going to ask me eventually," Robert said.

Thea glanced back at him, her brow furrowed and her lips pursed.

He let out a wheezing cough and cleared his throat before speaking, "All right. Yeah, I've lost some people. Got kicked out when I was a kid. I had a friend named William who helped me survive the streets, even though hanging out with him was partly why I got kicked out. We were desperate, did drugs, sold illegal stuff, and worked with gangs. Like most people, we didn't have a place to stay since the streets and alleys were filled. Nice alleys, such as alleys with natural shelter, were guarded. You had to pay rent to someone to sleep there."

"You had to pay to sleep outside?"

"Yep. They'd typically beat you up if you didn't come with anything. So yeah, after William got arrested, I found a job, got a cheap education, and began working. William eventually got released. That was before the wars."

"Arrested for selling drugs?" Thea asked.

"Yeah, you couldn't do that in the old world."

"Weird."

"So, between the time William got arrested and when he got out, I met the love of my life while in school, Zilv. Zilv was... he was amazing. I don't remember where I met him. I just remember that he took a liking to me when I met him. I thought he was cute, so I gave him my social media contacts. He contacted me, then we went on a date, and then we fell into a relationship."

"He sounds cute," Thea said.

"He was. He supported me through everything. We both worked really hard together for a few years, got an apartment, and got off the streets. By the time we had the apartment, I had worked as an Ignium repairman while he worked as a freelance coder at home. He usually made dinner and that sort of thing and always asked me how my day was before I could ask how he was."

"I wish I could've met him. He sounded like a nice guy."

"I wish he was still here," Robert mumbled.

Robert's eyes watered. With a deep inhale, he carried on talking, "Then there was Ruth. I didn't actually know Ruth until after the old world collapsed. She was there with us in the early years. She uh... She was funny? She could climb everything and traversed cities from high above rather than on the streets. Oh, she was a mean fighter, too. She actually scared us when we first met her, but she turned out to be helpful. She wasn't super fond of people, so she refused to join us and live with us for a long time. Eventually, she did, but she always slept far away and preferred things like closets to sleep in. It was so weird that she could sleep upright."

"What the? That's weird. She just slept straight up? Like leaning on something?"

"Yeah. I never got an answer to why. I think Ruth liked to hide in closets. I don't know, it was strange."

"What about your tattoo?"

Robert blinked and looked down. He had forgotten about the tattoo on his neck, "Oh...I got that with William. We just wanted tattoos one day. Nothing special about the shape or whatever. We both just thought a snake looked cool. To us, it was pretty expensive, but we wanted to be manly and get it in ink instead of an implant like everyone else."

"Did it hurt?"

"Yeah, a lot. It was itchy and burned a lot afterward, but we thought it was cool. Showed all our friends and stuff."

Thea's trail of questions ended, "Hey, you see that building way down the road?"

Robert squinted. He could see a dark, squarish shape standing out fuzzily from the rest of the distance. He would not have noticed it if he had not been told.

"Kind of. Have you been here before?"

"No. Let's go check it out."

They walked closer until they found a warehouse. It was a huge metal building, something likely to have held farm equipment once. Its entirety was rusted and worn from enduring Doomstorms. Storms had destroyed all the windows, leaving gaping holes all over the structure. The entire building leaned slightly, though the fact that it was still standing demonstrated its strength against time and Doomstorms.

Outside was a tent and a few stacks of random materials, such as large pipes and bricks. Between all the piles was a group of eight people. The group was divided in half. The two halves opposed each other behind cover and pointed guns. They screamed and shouted, waving their weapons around.

The bickering intensified until everyone was silenced by the abrupt sound of a door slamming open. All of them looked over to the warehouse. A mutant stumbled out from a door. Its grotesque form seemed to have twisted like a rag. It stood on multiple legs with feet and joints facing different ways. Several arms stuck out from its body in every direction. Its head was the only thing facing a singular direction, though its features were distorted and fused with different parts.

After the mutant moved outside, another one stumbled out. It was an abomination of a different magnitude, crawling forth on three arms and two stunted legs. Then another mutant came out, followed by another one until a horde of thirteen had poured out.

Mutants were a part of the new world's ecosystem. Though many from the old world had died, their offspring had carried on under the wasteland's cruelty. Mutant children were as twisted and grotesque as their parents, frequently taking form in even more unique, horrid shapes.

The mutants screamed aggressively and flailed, running toward the two groups in fits of frenzied rage. The two groups battled the mutants, firing their guns and swinging melee weapons as the monsters tried to surround and flank them.

"Should we help them?" Thea asked.

"Why?"

"Could trade water with them."

Robert stretched his neck left and right, humming and grumbling before stepping forward. He shot his plasma pistol. Its molten venom spewed forth and covered three mutants. The creatures screamed in terror as they fell to the ground and clawed at themselves until they stopped moving. He continued shooting. The burning material sent the rest running, leaving the shocked and tired survivors behind.

"Who the hell are you people?" one of the survivors asked.

"Why do we care? Shoot them! They might be a part of an ambush!"

Robert reloaded the pistol with a bag of material and spoke loudly, "I would advise against shooting us. We just saved your hides!"

The people whispered among each other.

He coughed from speaking so loudly, lifted his mask, and spat out blood once he stopped.

"We know you're not gonna shoot us! If you wanted to shoot anybody today, you would've shot each other ten minutes ago. How about we relax, forget any thoughts about shooting, and just introduce ourselves? I am

Robert. This is Thea."

"I'm Tom," a tall man said.

"My name's Lisa!"

"Finnigan's my name!"

They all went around introducing themselves, relieving tension as they spoke.

"That's good. It's nice to meet all of you! What were all of you fighting for?" Robert asked.

Tom gestured to the warehouse, "This warehouse. We were fighting over who got to take it."

"This rusty tin shack? Why?" Robert asked.

"Good for Doomstorms! It's still standing, and it looks strong!" Tom responded.

Thea shook her head, "So, a big warehouse can't fit eight people?"

Tom exchanged glances with his comrades and stuttered, "Well, we... we're...."

Robert holstered his pistol, "We're fighting for no reason. Look, everyone can share the warehouse! You can even be on different sides. You don't know us, so we have a proposal!"

"And what's that?" Tom asked.

# 36

# Them Again

*11:03 AM, March 21, 2100*

\* \* \*

Robert pulled the cart behind him slowly, the jugs of water sloshing as the bumpy road rocked the cart. Thea walked beside him, eyeing the warehouse. The newly formed group of survivors had settled comfortably in it.

Everyone had worked to build a new community over the last month. They reinforced the building where it was weak, placed support beams where it leaned, barricaded windows, and strengthened doors. Inside, people had swept out the structure. They had cleared it from the sand, excrement, and rubbish from the destroyed mutant's nest.

The arrival of the pair had been welcomed. So far, Robert and Thea had not told anyone where they got water, which had granted them power. Thea was the pair's mouth since Robert barely spoke to anyone. She had talked their way into leading the fledgling community, paired with Tom and Lisa from the original two groups.

People ran to greet them as Thea smiled and waved at each person. Robert stepped aside, moving away to let people grab water jugs from the cart. He didn't talk and only nodded if someone bothered him with "hello" and "hi." Those who took the water thanked them and carried it inside the warehouse.

Robert crossed his arms as the people left, "Are we staying today?"

"Yes. Tom and Lisa wanted to talk with us," Thea said.

Robert didn't show his exhaustion with meetings and decision-making for a community. It wasn't him. He didn't see how a society could survive in the wasteland and thought it was a fruitless endeavor. He also didn't understand how four people were needed to make decisions. If something needs to be done, then it should just be done.

"Let's go and talk with them then," Robert said.

They went inside. When Robert had first entered the building, it had been a gloomy mess of waste and sand, bones scattered everywhere. The smell of sweat and must had faded, though it still resided in the walls. After sweeping out the sand and junk, the group revealed the warehouse's concrete floor, leaving space for tents. In the center was a large tent, left open with a table in the middle. Tom and Lisa were already conversing inside.

Lisa waved as they entered, "Oh, Robert and Thea! Did you guys deliver some more water?"

Thea nodded, "Yep. Lots of people are happy to see us."

Tom leaned on the table with both hands, gazing at the pair, "Well, your water has carried us through the last month and has helped us grow."

Robert crossed his arms, "Why are we here?"

Tom pursed his lips, "Well, we wanted to discuss the future of our community."

"We need to get more resources. Material, food, weapons, clothes, and even more water," Lisa said.

"Do you have any ideas?" Thea asked.

Tom shrugged, "Barely. We don't know the area very well, but I assume the years have cleaned everything out."

Lisa raised her hands, "We've thought about trading, but there are not a lot of other people in this part of the wasteland. Buildings are also far and in between. I've thought about having groups go to the closest city to try and scavenge there, but that's dangerous."

Robert groaned, "You're missing the obvious. Materials can be harvested from old buildings. We can make weapons from anything and clothes from wasteland animals. We have water handled. All you guys need is a weapon smith. And if worse comes to worst...."

"What then?" Lisa asked.

"We take," Robert stated.

"What do you mean, Robert?" Thea asked.

"I mean, we take. What are we, saints? I'm hungry. We're all hungry. Take it how you want. I mean, we take. We find it, and we take it. If it's in a building in the Wastes? We take. If we find it on someone, we take it."

Tom nodded, "Robert's right. We need full bellies to keep going on."

Thea frowned, crossing her arms, "It's bad karma to go marauding the wasteland. What if we make an enemy we can't take on?"

Robert shook his head dismissively, "There's no one out here. I will lead runs into the wasteland. I'm sure our chef would appreciate anything to cook with: old-world food, mutant meat, the occasional lost traveler."

Lisa nodded, "He's right."

* * *

Robert led the group of five as they left the warehouse. He eyed their surroundings, pipe rifle in hand. Robert had grown accustomed to the weapon. It was finicky, and the recoil was strange, but he appreciated its quirks and uses.

Even though Robert did not like communities, he knew deep down that it had helped him. He had gained weight from eating mutant flesh. It was tough, almost like beef, yet soft enough to remind him that they had once been human. Warmth had returned to his skin, his health had improved, and he felt less pain. The joy of power appealed to Robert. Being in control of the water had made his and Thea's lives easier, allowing them to manipulate the growing community to their benefit.

Robert was wary and vigilant for any shape in the distance. He wanted to come across one of the many growing herds of mutant animals subsisting on lichen and pioneer plants. It was a rare sight but always a welcome one for hungry survivors. He also watched out for those two men. He tried to recall what they had called one another but could only remember Oliver. He was unsure what had happened to them. Maybe the Doomstorm had taken them, or maybe they were still alive. They had not been seen in a month by anyone, but he felt that Oliver was similar to him: a tired man willing to carry on.

They scrounged through every dusty corner and sandy structure, raiding farmhouses that still stood along with barns and sheds. Eventually, the six of them filled their backpacks with junk such as old cans and jugs. Their luckiest find was a collection of rusty tools deserted in a sand-filled shed.

They continued searching, moving up onto another old road that was a two-lane highway.

A stocky man named Irwin spoke up, "Robert, do you see that?"

Robert squinted. In the distance, he saw smoke rising from the remains of an old building.

"Let's go! Guns ready. Let's check it out!

He broke into a jog as they approached the building and raised the pipe rifle. Robert could not determine what the building used to be since the remains consisted only of rubble and half-broken walls. A gunshot echoed through the air, and a bullet ricocheted off the ground in front of Robert.

"Take cover!"

The six survivors broke off from one another and sprinted to hide. Robert dove behind a car shell as another bullet whizzed past. They all hid behind a group of cars, listening as the opposing group in the building scramble to respond.

"Hold here! Don't let them get around us!" he shouted.

Both sides exchanged shots and missed as they were too afraid to pop up and aim. Gunshots echoed across the wasteland as bullets ricocheted off metal and made holes in the building's walls. It was a back-and-forth. None were brave enough to move forward, creating a stalemate.

"Robert!" Irwin shouted.

"What?"

"What do we do?"

Robert shrugged, "I don't know? Go around?"

Robert shook his head and waved, "No! We waste their ammo! Conserve yours!"

The exchange slowed as both sides popped off shots occasionally. Robert waited for a perfect moment.

"Get ready! You two, go around! Everyone else, suppress fire!" Robert commanded.

Footsteps crunched toward them. Robert looked toward the sound, eyes widening. Oliver and his friend came over a hill. Oliver's friend shot Irwin, who stood next to Robert. Robert ducked for cover as Oliver aimed his gun and brutally killed three more of Robert's followers, wounding a fourth.

A girl named Abigail shielded herself and fell beside Robert as metal pierced her arms and legs. Robert shot at the pair. They dropped to the ground, giving him time to escape. Abigail came with him, shuffling forward in pain. He left her behind to save himself, a gunshot echoing, followed by a thud.

Robert glanced back to see the woman dead. He gasped and sprinted, leaving the blood scene behind and escaping over the dunes. Eventually, he ran out of breath and looked back. No one had followed.

"Fuck!" he shouted.

Once again, he met failure and barely survived a run-in with Oliver. How did Oliver survive the Doomstorm? Where did they come from? Robert clenched his jaw. Now he would come back with a bag of junk and the death of five people weighing on his shoulders. He stood, inhaling and exhaling as he tried to calm down. Robert had to prepare for the emotional outcry of the failed run, and the anger people would have against him. It wasn't his fault, but no one would believe him.

# 37

# Rat King

\* \* \*

Robert sat outside in the dark and watched over the camp. He sat cross-legged, huddled around his pipe rifle as he observed the ongoings of the early morning.

The community had grown over the past month. It acted as a net in the wasteland, bringing in wanderers across the ancient roads with little to their names. Robert had allowed the community to see the location of their water, which enabled them to support everyone. Though hunters constantly searched for meat, mutant or otherwise, food was scarce. Tents had been built inside the warehouse, creating a small town. People had also begun setting up tents outside due to the lack of space inside, though they'd had to pull everything into the warehouse when Doomstorms came. People still blamed and hated Robert for the death of those five people. Even so, his words were respected and listened to.

New people often brought stories of being turned away from a bunker paradise called "Patria," a place where food and water were plenty. All Robert knew of the area was that it was ruled by a group of three leaders, one of whom was named Oliver. Robert assumed he was the same Oliver that had killed David and Abby. The two rising communities had been at war from birth. Whenever the two groups met, they skirmished. Patria often came out the victor. Robert loathed Oliver and his people and would be overjoyed to see them die. That day felt like it would never come as his community grew stronger.

Today was a different day. Those capable of defending themselves gathered in the camp below, taking up arms and preparing to move out. Under cover of darkness, they planned to go and take the ruins of an old town so they could loot it and hold it against Patria. Robert was to lead. Would they be ambushed? Would they meet mutants? Robert was prepared for anything but hoped this time wouldn't be a disaster.

Fourteen people gathered their weapons, supplies, and lights. It was a small army for the wasteland. One of them waved a torch at Robert to signal they were ready. He could not see the torch very well, though he could make out the light dancing back and forth in a pattern. He stood, gun in hand, and walked down to join the group.

"Hey, Robert, are you ready to move out?" James asked.

"Yes. I want everyone to make sure their weapons are loaded! Don't leave what you need behind! You all have a minute, then we are moving out!"

After a minute, Robert waved and led them into the wasteland.

They followed an old-world road covered with sand. Robert was quiet, walking with a focused intent and a firm grip on his gun. The people followed, quietly whispering as they walked and eyed their surroundings. Fifteen strong, Robert felt safe for once. No one would bother them, not even the Patrians with whom they shared the wasteland.

The town was a few miles away. Robert recalled stumbling upon it. They found it during a looting run in the middle of the day. Part of it had been half-buried by the wasteland. Other parts had intact buildings, while a few had entirely collapsed or fallen to ruin. They had not ventured within when they found it, but he did recall spotting a bar, a feed store, and a tractor supply store. He assumed everything had been emptied out.

After almost an hour, the silhouettes of the old-world buildings appeared on the horizon, faintly picked out from the early morning light. The sun had begun rising, dimly illuminating the dark, polluted sky. From a distance, the town was still. No mutants, no animals, no people.

They entered the first street. Robert paused at the threshold of the first two buildings, "Spread out into groups of five. Cover the whole town and meet back here. We have the whole day to pick this place clean. Understood?"

They all nodded and said, "Yes, sir."

Four people joined Robert as the group split into three packs and spread across town. Robert led his pack straight down the middle and through the town's central intersection. Beyond the winds howling and twisting through the ruins, it was surprisingly quiet.

He examined building after building, looking into gloomy, empty spaces. Many of the windows had been blasted in by Doomstorms or broken by survivors, leaving the fronts of many buildings filled with sand.

At the end of the town, they spotted another group ahead. Robert pointed his gun. The group ahead was split into seven and four people, pointing guns at one another.

"Take cover! Shoot off a flare!" Robert commanded.

His companions scrambled for cover, getting ready to ambush the group ahead. Robert could hear them talk from a distance. They seemed to have been hostile to one another initially but were working it out with words.

Robert waited. From behind, a flare shot out with a whistle, which rose into the sky and exploded into a bright orb that slowly fell back to Earth. The town became illuminated, and shouts were heard in the distance as the rest of Robert's group converged on the source of the flare. The group ahead looked up at the light and raised their guns as they realized they weren't alone.

"Fire!" Robert shouted.

They shot at the group. Robert killed one person. Another person fell a moment after as they scattered for cover. As the groups started shooting, the rest of Robert's small army came to reinforce them.

"Robert! What's going on?" James asked.

"We're not alone. We have a group split between those two buildings down there. Take cover, wait for my commands. If you can, shoot to kill. We need to eat tonight."

The man nodded. The army parted between two buildings, eyeing the street. He thought of flanking them or charging but considered either decision risky.

A deep, guttural groan came from one of the buildings between the two groups. High-pitched screams followed, along with a heaving breath. The shooting stopped. Hairs raised on the back of Robert's neck as everyone lowered their guns. Another groan echoed before the building wall in front of Robert collapsed as if hit by a wrecking ball.

A vast, heaping mass crashed from the building into the flare's light, revealing an abomination. It was at least two times taller than Robert and round in shape. Many torsos, heads, arms, legs, and entire bodies stuck out from the flailing and screaming mass. At the top were three bodies fused as one, their heads stuck together. The mass carried itself on eight arms and legs at its bottom, stumbling along. It was as if dozens of people had fused, screaming and crying in unified agony. A pack of mutants crawled out after the monster, sprinting on all fours as they spread out to attack either group.

Robert screamed, "Everyone, run!"

He took off as the monster crashed forward, grabbed one of Robert's people, and tore him apart. Arms and other grotesque limbs grabbed the man, ripped him limb from limb with relentless strength, and carried the flesh to dozens of gaping, fanged mouths across the giant's body.

Both groups split apart and ran around the town as the petite mutants pursued. They grabbed whoever they could and ate into them. Once they got their fill, they cried out, causing the voracious titan to stumble over, and rip apart still-flailing victims to feed its mouths.

Robert disappeared into an old restaurant and hid behind a counter. The shouting outside continued as people shot at the giant. Each bang caused it to blindly charge toward the sound and tear apart anything it grabbed. Eventually, it became quiet outside as people hid. Soon, only the heaving breaths of the behemoth and the various screams of the bodies fused into its mass sounded. The ground vibrated faintly as it walked. The whole thing stumbled and lurched itself forward to move. Robert took shuddering breaths, trying to still his hands as panic seeped through him.

He peeked over the counter and watched as the thing walked past his building. A shot echoed across the town, causing the beast to roar and crash in that direction.

Robert jumped over the counter and ran out into the street, searching for his group. The roads became dark again as the flare went out, leaving the torches and flashlights of the two groups. Robert couldn't make out who was who. He approached one of the lights to find two people huddled behind a sand-covered trash can. He didn't recognize them. They gasped, not recognizing him either. Before they could react, he shot both. As the gunshots echoed across the town, the monstrous roar of the mutant giant sounded, followed by its approach.

Robert went to find his group, leaving the monster to find nothing but the two bodies. He stumbled upon another group that recognized them.

"Robert! Over here!" James said.

"Where are the others?" Robert asked.

"We don't know. We lost them when that thing came out."

"Do you have any flares?" Robert asked.

"I have one. Why?"

"We need the light. Shoot it off. I'll shout to tell everyone who can hear me shoot that damn thing. We need it to bleed out. That's the only way we'll kill it."

James fumbled as he hastily grabbed a flare gun and shot it off, illuminating the whole town again.

"All right, spread out! You don't wanna be here," Robert said.

They nodded and ran off to different places.

"If anyone can hear me, shoot the beast! We need to bleed it out!" Robert shouted.

The monster cried out when it heard him, crashed from an alleyway, and charged at him. Robert shot at its top heads, hitting it twice before he turned and ran. He cut corners and went around buildings, his heart thundering. Robert cried out as it chased him. It was locked on him, moving where he went and ignoring everything else. People shot at the creature, filling it with bullet holes. Various bodies and heads squealed from pain, shielding themselves or swatting the air.

As Robert turned a corner, he slipped on the sand. A giant hand wrapped around him. The monster picked him up and threw him. He lost his pipe rifle as he flew through the air like a ragdoll before landing harshly in the rough sand. He coughed and crawled to his feet, seeing stars.

Dazed, he stumbled and fell but kept running as the monster chased him again. As Robert went between two buildings, people inside threw torches at the creature, causing it to stop and scream. Various hands and limbs swiped at the torches as two torches got stuck between folds of flesh and skin.

The fire stunned the monster as it spun around, screaming and squealing. Robert grabbed his plasma pistol and fired molten shots at the creature. The beast fell backward. The limbs facing Robert shielded the mass as hot molten liquid cooled on the beast, thrashing and swiping toward him. The rest of Robert's group shot the monstrosity to death. Eventually, it stopped struggling. The primary locomotion of the mass ceased as its bottom arms and legs stopped moving, and the top heads died. The rest of the bodies continued writhing and screaming, unable to move as the central mass died.

Robert approached it. Tumors, cysts, and a layer of sweat covered the monster. A few of the still-living bodies swung and screamed at him. Screaming came from bodies inside, their cries trapped in a prison of flesh. It was the most horrid abomination Robert had ever seen.

They let it bleed out, hoping that blood poisoning would kill the rest of the mass.

"Where's the other group?" Robert asked.

James stepped forth, "No idea, sir. I think they might have left."

They had lost three people to the monster, which had consumed their bodies.

"Spread out together. Look for the other group and for more mutants," Robert said.

# 38

# The War

\* \* \*

Three people walked into the camp. Each carried a bag of supplies from a recent raid on an encampment of survivors. The community had grown since they had taken control of local towns, holding out against the Patrians wandering the wasteland. Robert sat on a hill overseeing the camp from afar, leaning on his pipe rifle as he usually did. He was fond of doing this. He enjoyed watching the comings and goings of the encampment and the fact that no one bothered him.

The burden of war weighed on them. The fight against the Patrians had started as skirmishes for local supply spots and necessities—like water and food—but had escalated to complete warfare. People who survived Patria or were turned away came to Robert's community instead. They told stories of an underground bunker where the Patrians made their home. Unlike the camp, Patria had water from an underground reservoir and food from a greenhouse.

In the months prior, Robert had guided the community in preparation for an assault on Patria. Dozens of people were ready to fight. They had located the bunker and formed a battle plan. The assault they had planned was direct and swift, intended to hit like a hammer.

Today was the day. People gathered their guns and hugged their loved ones. Many were anxious, either pacing or sitting, twitching nervously. Few in the community were old enough to remember what war had been like in the ancient world. Most were younger survivors, born right before or after the fall of the old world. To them, the experience of actual fighting between two communities was new.

\* \* \*

Robert jumped as sand crunched behind him, "Hello, Thea."

"Oh, you greeted me first this time? Are you sick?" Thea asked with a chuckle.

Robert smiled, "Just hopeful today. It's been a long time since I've done anything like this war."

Thea frowned, "You know how I feel about this."

"It's necessary, Thea. This goes back months and won't stop unless there is a victor. Think about the reward... that bunker, safe from Doomstorms, and if the rumors are true, it has water and food."

"Look, me and you built this place together. Just be safe and don't die."

"I haven't died yet," Robert smiled.

"This is different. Just be careful."

"Where's your optimism today, Thea?"

"It's still there. I'm just nervous and concerned, all right?"

"I understand. You can come sit with me and watch if you want."

Thea nodded and sat a small distance away, looking over the warehouse. The camp below was full of busy people gathering supplies or huddling around fires while they warmed up dried meat.

Robert never trusted others and had only begun counting on Thea recently. Creating a community was stressful. The settlement came with maintenance and was always on the verge of disaster; food and water were constantly a primary concern. Starvation was the bane of wasteland communities.

"Thea?"

"Yes?"

"I'm not really a community type of guy, and I like to plan for the worst.

What would you do if this all fell apart?"

Thea glanced at him and pursed her lips, "Uh...I don't know. It's all so great. There are so many people you don't have to worry about mutants or rival survivors, just the basics. I might try again, make a new community."

"Would you give it a name? Like Patria?

"Maybe. Something like Uruk, like that one civilization way back in the day. Ever heard of it?"

Robert shook his head, "No. Where did you hear that?"

"I read it in a history book. It was supposedly an early city."

Robert's brow wrinkled, "So, you'd name a new place after Uruk?"

"Like New Uruk. Like New York, you know?"

"It's a weird name, but I can't judge. Not that I think this place will collapse any time soon. After today, maybe we should just call ourselves 'New Uruk' once we have the bunker."

Thea sighed, "It's so dangerous. Just use that stubborn head and survive."

"I always do."

\* \* \*

Robert and Thea walked down the hill to join the growing army, approaching a few dozen people. Some sat, others talked, and many nervously paced. All of them exuded the same air of anxious, fired-up nerves.

Robert raised his hand, "We'll be moving out in a few minutes! Gather what you need and load your guns! Medics, make sure you're supplied and ready to do your work!"

Lisa and Tom approached. Tom carried a blunderbuss-like gun made from pipes. Lisa stood beside Tom, unarmed.

Tom rested the butt of his gun on the ground, "How's it going, Robert? Are we ready to move out?"

"Almost. A few last preparations, and we'll begin," Robert said.

"You be careful out there, both of you," Thea said.

Lisa put her hands on her hips, "Remember, don't take risks. We need to conserve everyone we have. Take your time. Flush them out of that damn bunker."

Robert nodded, "I understand. We have a plan, and we'll stick to it. If we succeed, I'll send some people back to inform the community. If we fail, well, we'll be back."

Lisa gestured toward the warehouse, "If you do fail, retreat with as many as you can. Don't be crazy. If you lose too many, you need to retreat. Remember that we still have the warehouse."

A few of their soldiers, like Lisa and Thea, stayed behind to guard the warehouse, along with those who couldn't fight. Even so, they had an army ready to go.

Tom picked up his gun, "We'll be fine. Those bastard Patrians are gonna get what's coming to them."

"I think it's time to move out. I'll give the command," Robert said.

Robert approached their small army. A few were medics. Red-cross patches made from old-world red clothes marked their clothes. They all had different weapons, constructed from scrap or scavenged from around the wasteland. Some carried riot shields made from scrap metal that they would use to push into Patria.

"We're moving out! Follow me, don't bunch together, and watch our surroundings!"

Robert turned and led the army. Tom followed behind him. Robert waved at Thea as she watched them walk past those who stayed behind.

They marched over the dunes and across the sandy flats of the wasteland, kicking up a small dust cloud behind them. Robert followed the landmarks he had been shown. They turned at a faded stop sign, went straight at the sight of a tilted barn, and moved northward once they passed an old water tower.

Robert didn't get nervous often anymore, but this was an exception. Butterflies fluttered in his stomach.

"Over there!" someone shouted from the army behind Robert.

Two figures disappeared behind the dunes.

"After them!" another person shouted.

Robert snapped back, "No! They could lead us into a trap! We have our goal! Keep marching!"

Tom frowned, "But, Robert, what if they run back to Patria and tell them?"

Robert shook his head and waved at the army, "They'll never be ready in time for us. Hurry up the pace!"

The march turned into a jog as the army moved across the wasteland like a roving, unstoppable force. After thirty minutes, Robert noticed a hill with a dark shape at its edge in the distance. Guns and the tops of heads poked out of a tunnel, eyeing the horizon as the army approached.

"There's Patria! Let's get into formation! Split up onto either side! I want a squad in the front to distract their defense! Those in the front don't need to advance! Just keep the pressure and keep your heads down! Let's go!"

The army split into three large squads. One ran up onto the hill on the right flank of the tunnel entrance. Another part of the army ran left, taking longer to get around since they had less cover. The central part of the army went low as they moved forward since they had no shields at all. The battlefield was still as the army advanced. Robert crept forward, waiting to shout commands.

Screams sounded, breaking the windy silence. The field was booby-trapped. Soldiers fell into spiked pits, got their ankles crushed by spiked rollers hidden in the sand, and stepped on bullet traps that shot through their feet and legs. An explosion rang across the sands as a person stepped on a small mine, screaming as he was flung away.

"Medic! Over here!"

"Medic!"

Medics tried to help impaled people as they screamed in cruel traps. The rest of the army marched onward, though Robert could see many were fearful of where to step. The sentries at the front entrance of Patria opened fire all around them.

Robert ducked, "Fire back! Shoot them!"

A hail of bullets, arrows, stones, and molten plasma came from all around the tunnel entrance and killed a few Patrians. The rest ran as a pipe bomb fell in front of them. The bomb blew their cover into shreds, leaving nothing when the sand and smoke settled.

"First wave!" Robert shouted.

A group of soldiers ran into the tunnel. The army gathered around the entrance behind a shield wall when gunshots echoed from the tunnel. The humming sound of a Railshot Rifle silenced all of them as metal ricocheted in the tunnel.

Oliver!

"Second wave! Shields forward!" Robert growled.

Men and women marched into the tunnel with their shields up. Another dozen people with guns and bows backed them. Robert followed with Tom at his side, the last of his army trailing the pair. Patrians shot at the shield wall, and soldiers fell dead as Oliver's lethal weapon spewed metal everywhere. Robert aimed and tried to shoot him. Oliver dropped for cover as a hail of bullets and arrows killed the people around him, causing Robert to miss and kill another Patrian instead. Oliver popped up again and shot before diving back down for cover. A few men with shields dropped to the floor as they fell dead, though others picked up their shields and continued. The wall moved forward while Oliver retreated to the next set of barricades. Robert's army captured the first quarter of the tunnel.

"Keep advancing! We're pushing them back!" Robert shouted.

An explosion knocked Robert off his feet. Bombs detonated underneath and around the army's front line. Smoke filled the tunnel. Dozens died. Robert regained consciousness after a few seconds, a ringing sound singing in his ears.

Survivors retreated from the tunnel, leaving the injured behind. Bloody corpses sat all around Robert, some still moving and writhing. They couldn't be saved. Patrians moved forward to take their tunnel back. Robert crawled to escape. He couldn't get back to his feet and contemplated giving up. As he lay down, two hands grabbed him.

"What are you doing? Get up, Robert!"

Tom ripped Robert to his feet and ran with him, dragging him out of the tunnel and into the wasteland.

The battle was catastrophic.

# 39

# The Ambush

*4:56 PM, August 7, 2100*

\* \* \*

The news of the Patrians coming to the town was a surprise. People ran across the ruined town, rushing into buildings and hiding in corners.

"Let's go! I want guns in that building! You four, behind there!" Robert commanded.

People ran to the spots he directed them to. Only thirty people were with him, but it was enough.

Maybe Patria thought they had weakened from their devastating loss a month ago. Maybe they thought the town was abandoned, or perhaps they were desperate. Robert was unsure. He walked among the ruined buildings nodding to the men and women hidden in the windows. They were nervous. Many were veterans from the last month of fighting against Patria. Those who had survived the assault on Patria and still followed Robert were the most bloodthirsty, filled with hate over their fallen comrades.

Robert approached one of the tallest buildings in the town. A sniper named Liam sat at the top, entirely concealed and still.

"See anything!" Robert shouted up to Liam.

"Nothing so far, sir! I will tell you if I see anything!" Liam shouted back.

Robert chewed his lip and paced. He had no idea whether the Patrians knew that they were here. The minutes crawled on as Robert walked through the street. His fingers squeezed his pipe rifle anxiously while he waited for the sniper's call.

"Robert! I see something on the horizon!" the sniper shouted.

"What is it?" Robert shouted.

"Dust! I see people! I think they're Patrians!"

Robert turned to the rest of the town, "They're coming! Everyone, get ready and hide! You know what to do!"

He sprinted across the street and jumped behind a window with some of his men. Robert dropped to a knee, peeking out. The wind seemed to still as voices became audible, followed by footsteps. The Patrians were here. They marched into the town, two dozen spreading out across the town while unaware of the awaiting danger.

Robert pointed his gun as his men prepared to fire. He locked onto a Patrian, inhaled, and shouted, "Fire!"

Gunshots filled the air. A crossfire of bullets slaughtered the Patrians in the main street. The remaining Patrians ran, scattering for cover and blindly firing back into the buildings.

"Go around!" Robert shouted.

A few of Robert's soldiers jumped out of the buildings and sprinted around them to flank the escaping Patrians.

A Patrian shouted, "Pull back!"

Another cried out, "They're flanking!"

More of Robert's soldiers popped out to press the advantage. The Patrians retreated in a single direction, trying to regroup. Soon, both sides fell into a two-way battle as the Patrians retreated into buildings and behind corners. Robert's men pushed from the opposite side. A few men and women tried to wrap around on either side to enclose the Patrians completely.

Robert dove for cover as a spray of metal shrapnel erupted through his men. Oliver. He had been caught in the trap. Robert grinned. Panicked shouting came from the Patrians as his soldiers kept firing.

Oliver shouted, "We need to retreat back to Patria!"

A Patrian shouted in response, "We need these supplies!"

"We've lost too many people already! We've lost!"

More Patrians fell to Robert's men, dying from bullets and arrows as they were surrounded.

Oliver cried out again, "We're retreating now!"

"Yes, sir! Come on, let's go!"

The Patrians escaped in the only direction they could, piercing through the few soldiers who had flanked behind them. They ran out into the wasteland. Robert's soldiers were held back by Oliver. He shot over and over, metal shrapnel spraying everywhere and killing anyone it hit. After a dozen shots, he ran out of ammo. His gun fizzled as it only surged with energy and nothing to fire.

Robert shouted, "Push forward!"

Oliver retreated as Robert's soldiers rushed him. A shout came from one of the men, silenced as Oliver swung his gun into the man's face, breaking his gas mask. Before the man could get up, Oliver smashed his face with his boot and took flight into the wasteland.

The Patrians who had retreated shot at them, keeping them at bay and allowing Oliver to escape before anyone could catch and shoot him. Robert didn't have his men chase the Patrians despite their advantage and his desire to kill Oliver.

"Halt! Let them go!" Robert shouted.

Sarah protested, "But we have them on the run!"

"Who knows if more are out there! We have our victory, and if they get back to Patria, they'll help demoralize the rest of them."

# 40

# The Blitz

*12:23 PM, September 8, 2100*

\* \* \*

People waved as Robert entered the camp.

Tents were everywhere around the main warehouse, composing homes and stands. People traded; some worked; some walked around guarding the camp. Everyone was out and about during the peacetime between fighting.

The settlers felt that the Patrians had weakened, and the surety of wasteland control was on everyone's mind. Though he thought the war was soon ending, Robert felt skeptical and wary. Despite the community's losses throughout the war, more and more people joined them daily. Often, they were survivors of Patrian attacks or rejects from Patria.

He crossed the camp and entered the warehouse. His eyes adjusted to the gloom revealing a maze of tents filling the building with little streets sprawling throughout. Like outside, people were everywhere inside the warehouse—guards, merchants, workers–all out and about moving the community forward.

The people who lived in the warehouse had been some of the first to start the community. Many didn't like him. Out of the four leaders, he was the most disliked yet the most listened to. Robert didn't care. He didn't need approval; he just needed the community to keep going so he could get food and water. He didn't even have a tent and often chose to sleep in a corner away from everyone else. Corners felt safe since danger could come from fewer directions. It was an old but good habit, though some considered him a little weird.

"Thea?" he called out.

"Over here!"

He went around a few tents and found Thea cleaning her gun outside her tent.

"Hey, Robert! What's up?"

"I'm about to call a meeting with Tom and Lisa. We were gonna discuss the plan for our second attack on Patria."

Thea put her gun down and frowned, "Do you really think now is the right time to strike?"

"We've been talking about it for a while. We haven't lost to them in a while, and they seem to be weakened. I haven't seen a Patrian in two weeks. It's like they've all disappeared into their bunker and left the wasteland for us."

"You're probably right. People around the camp have gotten impatient anyway."

Thea stood, sighed, and joined Robert in his walk to the main tent.

Robert let out a hacking cough, clearing his throat from blood, "Are you okay, Thea?"

"Just sad, that's all. All this fighting is tough, and I miss David and Abby. I wonder what they'd say if they were here."

"Well... if I miss somebody I've lost, I just try to keep going for them. There's lots of people from the old world that I miss, like Zilv. I imagine he'd tell me to keep going and keep pushing if he was still with me."

"That's... kinda comforting."

"I'm old and grumpy. That's the best I have to say."

"Well, you may be old and grumpy, but at least you're willing to try. I appreciate that."

They found Tom and Lisa in the largest tent in the warehouse. They were already discussing plans to deal with the Patrians, brooding over a table covered with random objects meant to represent people and landmarks.

"Robert, Thea, how are you guys?" Tom asked.

"I'm fine," Thea said.

"Tired," Robert said.

"Do you ever sleep, Robert?" Lisa asked.

"Never. Let's get down to business. What is our plan?"

Lisa leaned on the table, "So far, we have a few ideas, but we've been thinking about one in particular."

Tom crossed his arms, "We were thinking of getting a weapon in everyone's hands that can fight, splitting into two armies, and hitting Patria from two sides. We were thinking of luring them out, maybe somehow getting their army out."

Thea tilted her head, "Any ideas on how to get their army out?"

"So far, not really," Lisa replied.

Robert raised his hand slightly, "I have an idea. We take a small group of our best shooters and pick off their patrols around the bunker. They have a bunch. If we kill enough of them, they'll send out a response. Then we close in and attack. With their main offense gone, we invade the tunnel. They won't expect it, especially if they go out to respond to our small group. We just need to figure out where all their traps are."

Tom shook his head, "How do you know they'll respond? And what happens if they find our best shooters? We can't lose them."

Robert raised two fingers, "If we have two armies, we can have them on opposite sides. One is behind our shooters, so they can retreat and get supported if attacked. When the Patrians push into our first army, they'll retreat right into our other army," he coughed and wheezed before shrugging, "Do you guys have any better plans? It won't be as disastrous as you think. I have not seen any Patrians in a while. They have lost each confrontation with us since our last invasion of Patria, and they are getting demoralized. We are winning, and it's time to end it."

Thea stood beside Robert, "I think Robert's plan will work. I am willing to volunteer to lead the second army. I'm tired of this war, and I'm tired of staying here and waiting for all of you to come back bloody. We need to finish this."

Tom frowned, "All right, if you want to. I think we should do this plan."

"Me too," Lisa said.

"When are we attacking?" Thea asked.

"Today. Let's do it when it starts getting late," Robert said.

\* \* \*

Shouts came from all over the camp.

"Let's move! Let's move!"

"Grab your guns! We're moving out!"

Over three-quarters of the community was rounded up to go fight. The small army gathered outside the settlement.

"You know where to go?" Robert asked.

"I know where the town is, and I think I know where Patria is," Thea said.

Robert nodded, "When we move out to attack, we'll send someone out to alert you, so you know when and where to go. We have some people left who survived Patria."

Thea looked down at the ground. Her jaw tightened before her gaze lifted toward Robert, "Are we really ending this, Robert?"

"I think so. Maybe there'll finally be some peace after all these months. The wasteland to ourselves, a bunker, enough for everybody, and so many people that no one can challenge us."

"You remember when you first met me?"

"Not really. I wasn't really awake for the first part."

"Yeah. You were face down in the sand when we first met."

Robert chuckled, "Yeah."

"I remember when you first came to us. Bleeding, starving, thirsty. You've come a long way. I don't see your ribs through your clothes anymore, your lips aren't cracked, and I think you've been sleeping more."

"Yeah, it's all thanks to the community. And you. I still get nightmares but being bullied into going to bed has been surprisingly helpful."

"I don't bully you!"

"Oh yeah? Robert! Go to bed! Robert! Bed, now! Or I'll cover you with sand!" Robert said in a mocking voice.

Thea laughed, "Okay, okay, I do. You need to sleep, though!"

"You're right, you're right. At least I can safely sleep here."

Thea gestured to the horizon, "Just imagine in that bunker. You won't even hear the wind."

"That'll be nice."

A group of almost twenty men and women stood ready.

"Ma'am, sir, we're ready," Shane said.

Thea's smile faded, "Well, I guess it's time for us to go. Good luck, Robert. See you later tonight?"

"Maybe. We'll see how everything goes. You be safe," Robert replied.

"You, too. All right, everyone! Let's get moving! On me!" Thea commanded.

Thea led the small army into the wasteland, disappearing over the dunes.

Robert turned back into the camp. The rest of the army prepared for the evening while Thea's group moved out into the wasteland to march around Patria. Robert went about in the camp, spreading commands and ensuring people did what they were supposed to do.

Butterflies fluttered in Robert's stomach. He felt satisfied, as if he had already achieved a goal he had chased for a long time. They weren't there yet, but they were so close.

He walked among the tents, checking in on people. Those who remained behind helped those who would participate in the invasion. Many people took the time to say goodbye to their loved ones before they went to battle. Robert paced. He went back and forth, going in and out of the warehouse multiple times.

Eventually, Tom came and found him, his pipe shotgun in his hands, "Robert! There you are."

"What's up?"

"Just checking in on you. Is everyone getting ready?"

"Yeah, I handled everything. You excited?"

Tom grinned and raised his gun, "Certainly! Get to use this again."

"Yeah. I'm glad—"

An explosion echoed in the distance. Both spun to see a plume of dust rising into the sky. Thunderous warbling echoed across the dunes. Squinting, Robert could make out machines driving toward them in the distance.

A scream came.

"Robert?" Tom asked.

Robert's eyes widened as he stumbled back, "Oh my god, the Patrians are attacking. The Patrians are attacking! Go! Go! Get a defense together! Gather everyone!"

Tom ran off to gather soldiers while Robert went to the edge of the camp, shouting.

"The Patrians are attacking! On me! On me! Let's go! Those who are not fighting hide in the warehouse! Let's go!"

Men and women rushed to his side, following him to the edge of camp.

"Form a line! Guns ready! Let's go!" Robert commanded.

They lined up on one side of the camp. Some people hid next to tents while others lay in the dirt.

"Fire on my mark!" Robert shouted.

The machines approached. An Ignium motorcycle erupted from the army toward the camp, followed by a mass of soldiers. Two men rode the bike, the driver resting a Railshot Rifle on the front. Oliver.

"On my mark! Ready! Fire!" Robert shouted.

Bullets and arrows flew out from the line, missing the motorcycle rider and hitting a few distant soldiers. The motorcycle flew toward the line like a bullet. A spray of metal came toward them. Metal shredded four men and women. The motorcycle blasted through that part of the line, disappearing among the tents.

"Fuck! Defend the camp!" Robert shouted.

He pointed at a woman who carried two hatchets and a crossbow made from various materials, "You! Kill the motorcycle rider! I want him dead!"

"Yes, sir!"

"You!" Robert pointed at another man, "Run! Go to Thea and tell her what happened! Go! Now!"

Running, the woman followed the motorcycle into the camp while the man disappeared through the settlement and into the wasteland. The bike's warbling Ignium engine echoed through the encampment. People screamed when metal shot everywhere. Robert turned back toward the wasteland as the machines sped toward them. It was unlike anything he had seen, reminding him of old-world cars. One of them exploded, sending a shockwave through the camp. Between the screaming Patrian foot soldiers and thundering machines, the defenders broke. People ran. Only a few brave soldiers stood with Robert as the horde reached them.

Arrows and bullets pierced the defenders, killing those who fought back. It was futile. Robert ran when his line fell, sprinting while Patrian soldiers flooded the camp. People screamed as Patrians killed mercilessly and tossed firebombs around the warehouse and the tents. The bombs sparked intense flames that filled the air with smoke and ate up everything in their path.

Robert ran through the camp, trying to help people escape and narrowly avoiding getting run over by Patrian war machines. The Patrians had already broken into the warehouse. They looted and slaughtered while the building burned. Robert shot and killed every Partrian in his path. He hit one in the back and another one in the head. He charged into the last, putting two bullets in her chest.

He got to the main tent, where he found Tom, Lisa, and a man who had chosen to stay and defend them.

"Tom! Lisa! Are you okay?" Robert asked.

"We're fine! We need to leave!" Lisa said.

The camp burnt. The warehouse slowly began collapsing as the fires consumed the pillars that supported it. It was a cataclysm. Everything they had worked for was burned or looted. Those who had trusted them and helped build the community lay dead in the sand. Any fight Robert had left in him died with the camp. Thirteen Patrians arrived, pointing their guns and shouting. Robert dropped his pipe rifle and raised his hands. His mind went blank as they grabbed him. Sounds became a mumble, and the world blurred. Lisa, Tom, and the soldier screamed and resisted as they were all dragged out.

Oliver shouted over the flames and chaos, "Patrians! Take their supplies and burn the rest! For Patria!"

"For Patria! For Patria!" his soldiers responded in a chant.

Robert didn't resist as they were taken outside the burning camp. The Patrians cheered and looted, brutalizing those they captured.

"Outsider scum!" one of their captors said.

"What should we do with them?" another one asked.

"Hold on! Line them up," Oliver commanded as he followed the group.

They were each put on their knees, held entirely still with faces pointed upward. Tom, Lisa, and the soldier resisted, while Robert accepted without resistance.

"Who are these Outsiders?" Oliver asked as he approached the line.

"We took them from a big tent, sir. There were plans and maps in there. We think it was where they planned attacks on us. One of these four could be the leader."

Oliver examined them from afar, "Which one of you is the leader?"

None of them responded. Oliver's face became red under his mask before he struck Tom with the butt of his gun, "Who is your leader? Who is it!"

Oliver prepared to strike Lisa.

"Me!" Robert called out.

Oliver's head snapped toward Robert before he pointed to the ground, "Lay him on the ground."

Robert's heart pounded as he struggled, "W—what are you doing?"

Oliver approached Robert, readying his gun.

"You won't get away with this, bastard tyrant!"

Oliver put the gun to Robert's head. Robert exhaled, closing his eyes. After so many years of struggling, pushing, and being alone, it was over. He would finally see William and Ruth again. He would finally see Zilv. In his last moment, Robert thought of Zilv's face, delicate cheeks, and innocent eyes.

Oliver flexed his finger. The gun spewed out its sadistic, iron venom.

# 41

## Mortem Obire

*4:00 PM, September 8, 2100*

* * *

And so, the sun loomed over a changed wasteland. Another fragment of the old world had died, soon to be buried by the ever-shifting sands. Robert had finally found peace.

Thea's army waited for thirty minutes before news arrived from a tired, sweaty man. The war was over. They had lost. Faced with losing everything and everyone they loved, most of the army was overcome with grief and hatred. The Patrians had taken everything: their community, families, and hopes. Thea didn't shed a single tear. Instead, innocence broke in her. It would never heal. In a rage, Thea led her army back to the community to exact vengeance. Instead, they only found the ash and rubble from what the Patrians had left behind. That which had not been taken back to Patria had been burned, broken, and tossed in the wasteland sand. They dug through the rubble for hours, finding nothing but bodies. Robert's body lay amongst the ruin.

Most did not want to chase the Patrians. Thea wanted blood but realized that the survivors needed her help. The army discussed what they should do and decided to flee with Thea as their sole leader. She accepted and led them east, away from the newly risen dominion of Patria and the tyranny it would soon have over the wasteland. They walked until they came upon the ruins of a city, braved the rubble, and established a new community.

This new society rose from the ashes of the old world, built on agriculture and industry. In honor of Robert, she named the fledgling city "New Uruk," the cradle of the new world. Despite holding her people first and sacrificing anything for them, darkness loomed in Thea's heart. She swore vengeance and led New Uruk toward her only goal: *death to Patria and death to Oliver.*

-= THE END =-

# Thank You!

**A BLOODY CIVIL WAR · A RAPIDLY COLLAPSING ECONOMY · A GLOBAL DEADLY PLAGUE**

–

Please accept my sincere gratitude for your support of my second book. I hope you enjoy reading it as much as I enjoyed writing it!

If you like this book, you'll love what we have coming next. Join the VIP list to stay updated on news and the latest releases! – https://etgunnarsson.com/news/

To support me further, please leave a review and constructive feedback on the following websites or equivalent. Positive reviews will help other readers find *Abandon Us* and *Forgive Us* and help me develop the Odemark series further.

- Amazon: https://www.amazon.com/E-T-Gunnarsson/e/B08R3FRGLQ
- Barnes & Noble: https://www.barnesandnoble.com/s/%22E.T.%20Gunnarsson%22
- GoodReads: https://www.goodreads.com/author/show/20991531.E_T_Gunnarsson
- BookBub: https://www.bookbub.com/authors/e-t-gunnarsson

# About the Author

TRANSLATING IMAGINATION INTO WORDS

E.T. Gunnarsson translates imagination into words. His debut book, *Forgive Us*, was awarded Best Sci-Fi at the 2021 San Francisco Book Festival and Best Post-Apocalyptic Book at the 2021 Fiction Awards. *Abandon Us*, the prequel to Forgive Us, is now available at major book resellers.

Born and raised in the Rocky Mountains (9,000 feet altitude!), E.T. now resides in southern Colorado with his dwarfed Cane Corso and his lifelong interest in Norse myth and culture. A storyteller from an early age, Mr. Gunnarsson spent his formative years developing his writing skills on international role-play sites.

Outside of writing, E.T. is a well-versed individual. He trained with two different Olympic squads, is an expert in Norse mythology, an experimental cook, a woodcarver, an avid action role-play gamer, a Judo brown belt, and a Brazilian Jiu-Jitsu purple belt.

It's easy to find E.T. on Facebook and Instagram: just search for his name. His legendary interviews can be found on YouTube and other websites. Or, visit etgunnarsson.com to reach his publisher.

**You can connect with me on:**

- https://etgunnarsson.com
- https://twitter.com/etgunnarsson
- https://www.facebook.com/etgunnarsson
- https://www.instagram.com/etgunnarsson
- https://www.youtube.com/@etgunnarsson

**Subscribe to my newsletter:**

- https://etgunnarsson.com/news

# Also by E.T. Gunnarsson

**Awards**

Winner, Post-Apocalyptic – 2021 American Fiction Awards

Winner, Science Fiction – 2021 San Francisco Book Festival

Finalist, Science Fiction – 2021 Best Book Awards

Honorable Mention, Science Fiction – 2021 Hollywood Book Festival

Honorable Mention, Science Fiction – 2021 New York Book Festival

Runner Up, Science Fiction/Horror – 2022 New York Book Festival

Honorable Mention, Science Fiction – 2022 San Francisco Book Festival

**Forgive Us: A Post-Apocalyptic Survival Thriller**
**SILENT, EMPTY, AND CRUEL. THIS WAS THE NA-TURE OF THE WASTELAND.**

*Ignium, a new form of energy, poisoned the earth. Generation after generation, survivors fight on to endure the ruins of civilization.*

In 2153, fledgling nations clash over land and resources. London, a wasteland veteran, struggles to protect his adopted daughter Rose as the world decays around them. Little does he know that both he and Rose will soon find themselves drawn into war.

*Just how far is London willing to go to protect Rose from a world full of violence, hate, and apathy?*

Fans of *The Gunslinger* and *Mad Max* will love E.T. Gunnarsson's multi-award-winning book *Forgive Us*, a story readers call *"thrilling, brutal, awesome, and completely unique."*